THE
DEAD ROAD

Also by Seth Patrick

The Reviver
The Returned
Lost Souls

SETH PATRICK

THE
DEAD ROAD

Thomas Dunne Books
St. Martin's Press
New York

This is a work of fiction. All of the characters, organizations, and events portrayed in this novel are either products of the author's imagination or are used fictitiously.

THOMAS DUNNE BOOKS.
An imprint of St. Martin's Press.

www.thomasdunnebooks.com
www.stmartins.com

Library of Congress Cataloging-in-Publication Data

Names: Patrick, Seth, author.
Title: The dead road / Seth Patrick.
Description: First U.S. edition. | New York : Thomas Dunne Books /
   St. Martin's Press, 2018.
Identifiers: LCCN 2017041046 | ISBN 9781250021748 (hardcover) |
   ISBN 9781250021731 (ebook)
Subjects: | GSAFD: Occult fiction. | Horror fiction.
Classification: LCC PR6116.A8455 D43 2018 | DDC 823'.92—dc23
LC record available at https://lccn.loc.gov/2017041046

Our books may be purchased in bulk for promotional, educational, or business use. Please contact your local bookseller or the Macmillan Corporate and Premium Sales Department at 1-800-221-7945, extension 5442, or by email at MacmillanSpecialMarkets@macmillan.com.

First published in Great Britain by Pan Books, an imprint of Pan Macmillan

First U.S. Edition: February 2018

10 9 8 7 6 5 4 3 2 1

THE
DEAD ROAD

1

The house was old, and it looked it.

The man Kendrick was going to see had lived there for almost five decades now, isolated in a valley in the north of Arkansas. He owned most of the valley, too. All that wealth was inherited – the kind of sums that tended to push people one way or the other, either in an obsessive quest to enlarge that fortune, or towards the indulgences and eccentricities that only the rich could afford.

Virgil Drayton had gone the latter route. At seventy-two, the man had the visual appeal of a walking corpse, the product of decades spent avoiding leaving his house. Drayton's eccentricity of choice was paranoia, and it had taken its toll.

Kendrick parked up on what had once been an opulent gravel driveway, a ludicrous fountain in the middle that hadn't seen the flow of water in years. Within the fountain was an elaborate raised pool now clogged with weeds. Above the ornate centrepiece, an ugly rusting sculpture was barely holding together. It stood as a reminder of where all that wasted money had come from: steel.

Drayton had explained it to him the first time Kendrick had been here – the sculpture was inspired by the steel skeleton of the vast buildings that had contributed so much to the company his grandfather had created. The artist had intended it to embody the notion of *potential*, the optimism of the times. Now, red and decayed, it looked more like a jumble of used hypodermic needles, or nails loaded with tetanus spores.

The gravel of the driveway was a patchwork of invading vegetation. The once-lush landscaped gardens had long abandoned any pretence at obedience, and gave the impression of a green army laying siege to the building they'd once been ordered to guard.

The building was vast, three floors and eighty rooms, but hardly any of it was used now. Kendrick had been shown perhaps a dozen of them by Drayton and his sole companion, a butler. All the rooms had appeared well-kempt but with plenty of visible wear and tear.

There was an unmistakably musty smell to the place. The one time he'd managed to look around a little more when his hosts had been distracted, he'd found room after room of mouldering junk, the infrastructure of the place almost rotting before his eyes. He'd been cautious about where he'd placed his feet, in case the rot had spread to the floor.

Drayton, childless and (paid help aside) friendless, seemed to have been content for the house to keep pace with his own physical deterioration. His death would be unnoticed and unmourned; the house would die with him.

Kendrick wondered if Drayton's butler was implicated in this. Surely some of Drayton's fortune would make its way to him in the end, so why let his master waste large portions of it trying to salvage the old homestead? Assuming, of course, that there was much of the fortune left. Drayton's paranoid fantasies hadn't simply kept him from venturing out into the real world for the last three decades. He'd been far more hands-on than that, actively (if remotely) seeking out those he considered experts in the areas that most interested him, and funding them through various indirect means. Drayton claimed to have the most complete library in the world on hidden conspiracies and fringe theories. He didn't denote the subject matter as that, of course – he called it *suppressed truth*, and referred to his library as The Grail.

It didn't seem to matter to Drayton when theories clashed, or made no sense at all. He believed every word, however outlandish it seemed, and his obsession was precisely the reason Kendrick had sought him out. The man had money and contacts, and Kendrick needed both. At first, Drayton had denied all knowledge of his involvement. The money and paper trails connecting him to his carefully chosen experts had been very well disguised. The idea that he'd been found out terrified him, but Kendrick had won him round. Kendrick's own history and his extensive knowledge of the underbelly of democracy managed to pique his interest.

That was when Kendrick had laid it out.

'Winnerden Flats,' he'd said. 'What do you know about it?'

Drayton looked at him with greedy interest, an unnerving wheezing audible with every breath. 'The revival research facility the Afterlifers supposedly destroyed?'

Kendrick nodded. They had been sitting in Drayton's study, and even though it was only his first time here Kendrick had the feeling the man kept this room exclusively for guests. Somehow, it didn't seem *inhabited*. Old photos of dead ancestors stared out defiantly from frames on every table and shelf. Drayton was wearing an ill-fitting black suit, which Kendrick presumed was *also* just for the benefit of guests. The man seemed almost dead as it was; with the suit, the corpse-in-a-coffin look was complete.

Drayton shrugged. 'The official story is this. They took all the best revivers to a research lab out in the desert, everyone got excited and hoped we'd find out what revival actually *is*, and boom! Sabotaged by a group of Afterlifers. The place is blown to hell and back, but the only things the public sees of the destruction are some satellite images.'

'And did your "grapevine" give you any alternative theories?'

'I heard some things,' said Drayton. 'The first one is that they faked the deaths so they would have the revivers to themselves.'

'"They" being . . . ?' said Kendrick.

'The Elite! Whatever you want to call them. It's a dumb theory, since most of the best revivers were always working privately anyway. The Elite don't need elaborate shit if they can just buy what they want. Anyway, a more likely theory claims it was nothing to do with the reviver research. Their presence was just incidental. Michael Andreas, the guy who ran the facility, was obsessed with beating death at its own game. He was developing a virus to stop the aging process. It got out and turned lethal, killing everybody in the building, so the military torched the place with a bomb about ten times bigger than a standard MOAB.' He gave Kendrick a testing look. 'A MOAB is almost as powerful as a mini nuke but without the radiation.'

'I'm aware,' said Kendrick, with a sly smile. 'The bomb actually used was called a MOLEK. Only the US military has anything that powerful, but they'd never admit it.'

Drayton's face lit up. It was exactly that kind of detail which had convinced him Kendrick was on the level.

'So, what do *you* believe?' said Kendrick.

'Well, I also heard that the Elite intentionally *doctored* the virus because they already had their own version and didn't want us poor bastards to get a hold of something similar. Now *that* sounds about right to me!'

The irony of Drayton including himself in the category of 'poor' was almost enough to make Kendrick laugh, but he controlled himself. He leaned forward. 'Let me tell you what really happened,' he said, as Drayton looked at him eagerly.

Kendrick had explained it: an ancient evil had used the revivers to break through into our world, aiming to destroy or subjugate everyone on the planet. To achieve this, the evil needed a human host, a vessel to channel its power into.

It had been defeated, and the vessel killed, but it had been a close call. Those people who had already succumbed to its influence had carried dark shadows with them – shards of the evil entity, parasitic and controlling. Some of those shadow-infested followers had perished when the vessel had died, but most had simply vanished.

Presumably, they were still out there, and they would be seeking another way to complete their goal – to find another vessel and bring their master back.

It was a story so insane that even Drayton struggled to believe it.

It also happened to be the truth.

*

That first meeting with Drayton had been sixteen months ago. Now, Kendrick walked to the front porch. There was a grand old bell-pull by the door, but he'd learned the first time he'd come here that it didn't work. Instead, there was an intercom box hidden in a recess, the plastic faded from age.

He pressed the button. 'Mr Wellborough,' he announced. It was the false name he'd been using for his meetings with Drayton. After a minute the door was opened by the butler, Ferris. The man had the nimble posture of someone who rarely sat still, and while he was only a decade younger than Drayton, it may as well have been a century.

'Ah, Mr Wellborough,' said Ferris, inviting him in. 'Mr Drayton will be with you in a few minutes. Please make yourself at home. Drink?'

'Bourbon, neat.'

Ferris led him to the study. 'Can I take your bag?' He held out his hand, ready to take the satchel Kendrick carried over his shoulder.

'No,' said Kendrick. 'I have things Mr Drayton should see.'

Ferris still had his hand out. 'I must insist on looking,' he said. 'Security.'

Kendrick nodded, but rather than pass the bag over he opened the top wide and let Ferris rummage around in the folders of paperwork.

Soon enough, Ferris seemed satisfied. He poured Kendrick his drink. 'I'll go and see if Mr Drayton is ready for you,' he said, and left the room.

Kendrick toyed with his bourbon as he wandered around the study, all the dead ancestors glaring out at him. This was where he'd always met Drayton – four times so far. He'd spotted the locations of the two hidden cameras within minutes of the first meeting. As casually as he could, he turned to hide his actions from the cameras and slipped a package out from the hidden pocket at the base of his bag. It was heavy, which was why he'd been so careful not to let Ferris handle his bag directly – the weight of it would have given away the fact that something was amiss.

A little more wandering, and Kendrick was in place to slip the package behind the sideboard, again out of view of the cameras.

*

For months, Kendrick had almost believed there was some kind of God on his side; that the Beast they'd faced had truly died. Every single person they had known to be carrying one of those parasites had either died or vanished; Kendrick had pressed the reviver Jonah Miller into service for six months afterwards, looking for indications of survivors. Miller was the only one who could actually see those *things*, those dark *shadows*, on the shoulders of their hosts – parasites, living off willing victims, steering them to allow the power they served to ascend to a level of global control.

They found none. They started to think it was over.

If only it had been that easy.

An attempt on Jonah's life brought their complacency to an end. He'd been run off the road, the attacker pulling a gun but fleeing after it jammed. Inept as the attempt had been, it had scared Jonah badly, and had made him far more reluctant to help in Kendrick's operations.

Kendrick thought about Jonah. He'd liked the young man. Admirable, in many ways. Courage like that was often punished. He wondered if Jonah's eventual fate had been inevitable . . .

And so Kendrick's tentative hope had been crushed. There were still followers. They were still out there. They needed another *vessel*, and their goal might be attainable again. Kendrick's new hobby had formed at once: locate these people and kill them, whenever they popped up. He didn't have Jonah Miller any more to determine whether they were actually hosts to the evil or just fanatics, but even if the latter was the case, it didn't mean they wouldn't stumble onto a means of achieving their dream.

Drayton's network of researchers had been set the task of keeping an eye out for suspicious activity, and they'd found it more than once. Each time, Kendrick had taken care of it.

Those he had dealt with so far had varied hugely in their sophistication. Some had been dabbling in the kind of magical tosh more suited to a teenage party; others had found their own low-level revivers and were attempting more sinister things.

He'd killed them, either way. He wasn't going to take risks. Fiery deaths were his preferred method, just in case they did carry shadows with them. Those *things* could try and make anyone a host, if they needed to. Kendrick had personal experience of that, and he was damned if he'd let it happen again. None of the kills were close-quarter, certainly.

Ferris returned to the study.

'Mr Wellborough? Mr Drayton requests that you join him downstairs.'

'Downstairs?' said Kendrick. 'You mean The Grail?'

Ferris gave a sly smile. 'Mr Drayton mentioned it?'

'Many times,' said Kendrick. 'I wasn't sure I'd ever have the honour.'

'Then today's your lucky day,' said Ferris. He led Kendrick down the hall to a small stairwell. 'Go on below,' said Ferris. 'I'll buzz you in.' He reached into his pocket and took out a remote handset that had the same aging-plastic look as the intercom on the door.

Kendrick went down the short flight of stairs and glanced back; Ferris pressed a button and the door lock disengaged.

'Mr Drayton is sorting through some papers, I believe,' said Ferris. 'Just go on until you see him.'

Kendrick went through the door and found himself in a small plain-concrete storage room, cardboard boxes of cleaning fluid and cans of food stacked around the wall. There was a strong stench of artificial pine. The room seemed *off* to him – too new, for a start – but he immediately understood what it was. 'When does the hidden door open?' he said.

From far behind him, Ferris answered. 'Pull the outer door closed first,' he said.

It made sense that Drayton would have put in some effort to hide his Grail. Kendrick did as Ferris said, and heard a click from his right. Part of the wall moved, and he pushed at it to reveal the inner entrance.

Within was a corridor, which looked like the original stonework of the building foundations. It was dimly lit by a solitary light-fitting just above him. There was a single door thirty feet away. The stench of the cleaning fluid was just as strong in here, he realized.

Kendrick clenched his fist a few times, uneasy, and started to walk to the other door.

When he was halfway, a rattle of metal behind him made him spin round, just in time to see a frame of bars come down to block his way out. Kendrick ran back to them and kicked the bars to test their quality. They were disappointingly solid.

'I'm afraid Mr Drayton insisted,' came the voice of Ferris, over tinny intercom speakers. 'You know how he can be.'

Kendrick said nothing. He gave the bars a derisory glance and headed to the other door again. Yes, he *did* know how Virgil Drayton could be. It didn't make him feel any more comfortable about allowing himself to be trapped like this.

He reached inside his bag, to the second hidden pocket – a padded one, where he'd put his gun. He took it out, and felt a little better. Then he opened the door, and everything got so much worse.

'Fuck,' he said. The room ahead was perhaps forty feet across. Archive boxes were piled high by the walls, and there was another doorway at the far side. This was Drayton's Grail, certainly – a conspiracy theory nut could spend a lifetime revelling in the lunacy here.

The most notable feature, though, was the chair in the middle of the room, and the man who was tied to it, his mouth duct-taped.

Virgil Drayton.

Drayton was looking at him with terror. Kendrick stepped

forwards and carefully peeled the tape from his mouth, dragging a cry of pain from the old man. He stepped away again and let Drayton get his breath back, his ragged wheezing worse than ever.

'They . . . they brought it here,' said Drayton.

There was a terrible stench in the room, fighting with the overwhelming artificial pine he'd already smelt – Drayton had soiled himself, certainly, but there was more.

'When?' said Kendrick. 'How long have you been down here?'

'Two days,' said Drayton, desperate. 'I'm sorry . . . They must have drugged me. I woke up like this.'

Kendrick frowned. 'You keep saying "they". Be *specific*.'

'Ferris is part of it, that's all I know. I have no idea for how long.' Drayton stared at him, eyes wide. 'I wasn't sure, you know? When you told me about the shadows. I didn't . . .' He shook his head, tears falling from his eyes. Then he turned suddenly, looking at his own shoulder as if it frightened him. '*It's on me . . .*' he said, and Kendrick felt his guts twist. 'I can feel it burrowing in.'

'Jesus Christ,' said Kendrick. He took another step away from Drayton.

'I'm fighting it, but it'll get me in the end! Oh God, kill me.' He nodded to Kendrick's gun. '*Kill me.* I'm an old man. I can't hold out. This will take my *soul*.'

Kendrick shook his head. 'If I kill you, it'll try and get *me*.'

Drayton crumbled, sobbing. 'But . . . but I *told* you,' he said. He met Kendrick's gaze, and there was absolute horror in his eyes. '*They brought it here.*'

A chill crept into Kendrick's mind. 'They brought the thing on your shoulder,' he said, hoping that was what the man meant.

Drayton shook his head. 'No. They brought the thing it *came from*.' The old man turned his head to the door in the far wall. 'It's through there. I hear it breathing sometimes.'

There was ice in Kendrick's blood now. 'They found their vessel,' he said, and Drayton nodded.

The intercom crackled. 'I'm afraid your efforts to stop us have been in vain,' said Ferris.

'You've worked for Drayton for two decades,' growled Kendrick. 'How come you turned on him so easily?'

'Oh please,' said Ferris. 'How can you know how easy it was? It's only a matter of time before a man accepts his fate . . .'

Kendrick took a long breath. 'You carry one,' he said. 'You carry a shadow.'

Ferris laughed. 'Of course. When the vessel perished, not many shadows survived. They hid. When they found out about Mr Drayton's new interest, it made sense to get an insider's point of view. *My* point of view.'

Drayton couldn't bear to listen. 'You son of a bitch!' he yelled. The effort left him coughing.

'We know who can be tempted,' said Ferris. 'And we know who can't. Mr Drayton was the latter. Bringing him into the fold will be long and difficult. I was more *willing*. Mr Drayton will be useful if he survives. You'll prove to be more of a challenge, I imagine, but we have plenty of time for you to get acquainted.'

Kendrick reached into his bag one last time. In the padded pocket was a small device, something he'd never considered he would have to use so early; he took the device and put it in his pocket. When he'd been in the study before, the package he'd positioned had been placed in a carefully chosen spot, because the wall it now rested against would allow the fire to spread within the wood-slatted cavity. It had been placed as an insurance policy, just in case Drayton had become a liability. He had another package, still in the hidden compartment in his bag, which he'd hoped to place elsewhere in the house before leaving.

Change of plan.

'You'll be glad to know your efforts to stop us were irritating,' said Ferris. 'A new vessel has been harder to find than we ever thought possible, especially when you kept interrupting the work. But we did it at last. A blank slate, that was the trick. A tabula rasa. Uncorrupted by something as mundane as morals. Free of a sense of humanity.' A buzzing came from the far door, and it opened fractionally. 'Perhaps it's time for you to meet your new god.'

Kendrick started to walk towards the door.

'Don't,' warned Drayton. 'You don't want to see it. Just kill us both, and end it.'

Kendrick ignored the old man. He wasn't ready to give up, not yet.

As he neared the door, the smell he'd not quite identified got stronger. He placed it now: the stench of rotting meat. He looked back at Drayton and imagined the dark bloated creature that pulsated on his shoulder, forcing its way into his mind. Kendrick wouldn't let that happen.

He could hear something now – something heavy, a slow shuffling step coming nearer. He reached out for the door, ready to throw everything he had at the slim chance of survival.

But whatever happened, he'd keep one bullet for himself.

2

The name on his FRS security pass said 'Robert Geary', but everyone called him 'Never'. He'd had the nickname even before the Forensic Revival Service existed, when he'd emigrated from his native Belfast for a dream job at the FBI lab in Quantico. Forensic data recovery had been his specialty back then; he'd been twenty-five years old and eager to impress.

In a way, he still worked in data recovery. Instead of pulling information out of damaged hard disks and flash memory drives, the job of the FRS was to pull information out of another kind of damaged object.

The *dead* kind.

*

Revival had been around for five years when he was at Quantico, and nobody understood what it was. They still didn't, not really, but in those early years everyone thought its mysteries would reveal deep truths about the nature of consciousness, or yield a scientific basis for some kind of *soul*: a means, however vague, for the patterns of thought and personality to survive death.

The research project that attempted to shed light on these mysteries was known as Baseline, and for years the researchers involved struggled to make headway.

But no light was shed.

All anyone knew was that a tiny percentage of people had a newfound ability to bring back the recently deceased. When the dead came back, it was only for minutes, and it wasn't with any meaningful *life*. Just a few crude functions, at best – breathing and speech. No blood flowed in their dead hearts. No neurons fired in their dead brains. The phenomenon was impossible. It was baffling.

It was also undeniable.

The impact that revival had on criminal investigation came when studies showed that the people who performed revival – the revivers themselves – had a profound insight into the emotional state of their subject. Crucially, the reviver would always know if a subject was telling the truth. The dead could be questioned, and their statements believed with certainty, or identified as outright lies.

There was a long, hard battle to allow testimony gathered from a revival to be admissible in court, but the battle was won in the end. In Quantico, a small unit of revivers was set up as a pilot scheme, and Never Geary had made damn sure he was involved in what he thought was the most important development in forensics since fingerprinting. As the most tech-savvy member of the team, he'd been the one to devise the technical underpinnings of how revival was recorded for court use.

When that small pilot scheme grew and became the Forensic Revival Service, Never went with them to their first office in Richmond, Virginia, and there he'd stayed.

That first office became just one of twelve across the country, but he resisted any attempt to promote him out of what he'd quickly come to think of as his home.

He was the Senior Revival Technician in what was now the Central East Coast office of the FRS, managing the other Techs on staff. The duties of a Tech amounted to ensuring that a revival was successfully recorded following the very guidelines he himself had been instrumental in codifying, and not throwing up when confronted with some of the more severely mangled corpses which came their way regularly enough – corpses that his seniority tended to guarantee would wind up in his inbox.

A big part of the reason he'd stayed was his best friend, Jonah Miller – the youngest reviver the FRS had had on their books when it started, and also one of the most capable. Nineteen at the time, Jonah had been fragile and vulnerable, and over the years that hadn't changed much. He and Never had hit it off from the start, and Never had found himself enjoying his role as protective older brother.

Then everything changed.

Revival opened a door, and something had come through. Jonah and Never, together with Annabel Harker, the daughter of a murdered journalist, had witnessed the rebirth of an ancient evil and had barely escaped with their lives. The events at an isolated laboratory in a place called Winnerden Flats had seen the death of many of the best revivers in the world. It had also seen the death of one of Jonah's oldest friends, and it had changed him.

When it happened, twenty months ago, Jonah had sunk into a long depression – something that had worried the hell out of Never, even though he'd had his own problems to deal with.

*

Those events, and everything that had happened since, weighed heavily on him as he arrived early at work that Friday morning. He swiped his pass and thought of himself ten years younger, as the FRS first came into being. It felt like a lifetime ago.

His desk was in the open-plan office on the second floor, and when he reached it, things were quiet enough. The handful of staff dealing with overnight problems hadn't had much to do except log revival requests from the various agencies who could seek one. Urgent requests were typically for on-site revivals in automobile incidents, where clearing the debris was time-sensitive but shifting a body would reduce revival chances significantly.

The FRS had been forced to limit the circumstances when they would agree to such cases, though. Too many good revivers had been lost at Winnerden Flats, in what the rest of the world thought had been a terrorist attack. Many of those revivers had been working for private revival firms, of course, where the pay was better and the working conditions far superior – at the FRS, there was little respite from grim brutality, nothing like the peaceful family-attended private revivals that many individuals paid a hefty price for. Those were mainly about emotional healing and closure – saying goodbye to a loved one.

Forensic revivals rarely had much time left for that kind of thing, after all the questions had been asked. And in private cases, of course, the subject of the revival was *expecting* to be brought back, and had *wanted* to be. Many times, Never had been present at FRS cases where the subject was extremely hostile or traumatized. They weren't exactly comfortable experiences.

He sat at his desk and got on with things, writing a report on the overnight requests and starting on equipment checks to prepare for the day ahead. Work seemed more stressful than ever, these days, but part of that was the reduction in success rates for revivals and an accompanying dip in office morale. They'd lost their three best revivers, Jonah included, a year and a half ago. The other two had died at Winnerden Flats. Replacing them had been impossible, and the private companies had started to lure away the second-tier revivers as well. It meant that cases the FRS used to take at the drop of a hat were now subject to extreme scrutiny before being accepted. There was little point in getting a reviver to attempt a case if they were very likely to fail, especially since they would be out of commission for a day or more as a result of the attempt.

He skipped lunch. At 3 p.m., his boss Hugo Adler arrived, having been in DC for a few days attending FRS committee hearings. The hearings had focused on what was seen as a crisis in the recruitment process – Never was pleased to see him, as he was taking the rest of the day off but could only leave when Hugo showed up.

'How's it been?' asked Hugo.

'We've had a few interesting cases,' said Never. 'Some fuckwit driver tried to kill a jogger, ended up ploughing into a tree and going through the windshield.'

'*Tried* to kill?' said Hugo. 'Really?'

'Really,' said Never. He allowed himself a smile. Morbid

humour was a reflex at the FRS, something that helped you survive the day-to-day unpleasantness. There was little better than an idiot killed by their own stupidity. 'Lex was the reviver. When the subject was brought back, he acted like it was accidental, but Lex got him to spill the beans quickly enough. Turned out the jogger's husband had given him two grand to do it.'

'Good result,' said Hugo. 'How's Lex getting on?'

Lex was one of the few decent revivers they'd recruited recently, and she'd made her mark in the three months she'd been there.

'She's doing well,' said Never. 'Considering how new she is to it, her success rates are way above average and her questions are canny.'

'Glad to hear it,' said Hugo. 'What else has come in?'

'Suicide lottery,' said Never. 'Genuine, so enough said.' One of the earliest policies the FRS had brought in was to randomly choose from cases that were deemed to be un-suspicious suicides, just to check that nothing untoward had happened. These 'suicide lottery' cases had revealed an un-nerving number of well-disguised homicides – about one in fifteen had at least some degree of foul play involved, ran-ging from full-on murder to mind-games played by those with a vested interest in seeing the victim take their own life.

In genuine cases, of course, the subjects were less than happy about being brought back, typically because of an intense regret for what they'd done and the pain their family would be facing. Among revivers, these cases were disliked more than just about anything else.

'And a drowning victim who hadn't *actually* died,' con-tinued Never. 'A mix-up led to us getting the call, and nobody thought to let us know there'd been a mistake before a three-hour drive. Funny part was a relative saw our team arrive and overheard them mention the victim's name. Cue unbounded confusion, plenty of shouting, tears. Did I say funny? I meant *awful.*' He thought it probably *had* been funny, in the end – that was usually how people reacted if the outcome was a good one, the desperate relief coming through in smiles and laughter.

'What's our fail rate been?' asked Hugo.

'Not *so* bad,' said Never. 'Four cases. None was thought to be particularly challenging, but no luck. How did the recruitment meetings go?'

Hugo frowned. 'Nobody's really talking about it publicly, but the numbers have fallen every quarter for the past year. Fewer people are coming forward as possible revivers, and while it may be due to less willingness to take on that kind of career, it really does seem like less people are developing the ability.'

'Ouch,' said Never. 'Any extrapolations?'

'If it keeps falling the way it is now, in another year there'll be almost no new revivers coming into the FRS, at least at the skill level we insist on currently. The private companies will mop them all up.'

'And they'll poach more and more of our existing staff,' said Never. 'Wonderful.' They'd already cut back on support staff, and Never had been forced to let two of the revival technicians go, people who'd been with them for a long time.

'You off somewhere nice?' said Hugo. He nodded to Never's desk, where a bunch of flowers and a bottle of whiskey sat.

'I'm meeting Sam,' said Never. Sam Deering was the man

who had been responsible for the formation of the FRS – he had been the one who first understood the potential for the forensic use of revival, and had then guided the research that would lead to its acceptance in law. And just as Never had taken on an elder-brother role with Jonah, Sam had been a surrogate father. Jonah's own dad had died when he was ten years old, and he'd hated his stepfather.

Sam had retired almost three years ago, but he'd kept in touch with Jonah and Never.

'What's the occasion?' said Hugo.

'It's been a year since the funeral,' said Never.

'Oh shit,' said Hugo. 'I'm sorry.'

'Yeah,' said Never. 'Sam wanted to visit the grave, so . . . Yeah. Hence the whiskey.' Hugo almost looked in pain. 'Hugo, don't beat yourself up. I'll see you Monday, OK?'

Hugo nodded and went to his office. With a wince, Never stood. His injury was making itself felt today; he downed a couple of painkillers, grabbed his flowers and his whiskey, and headed off to the cemetery.

*

When he got to the grave, Sam was already there, and Annabel Harker was with him. They had their backs to him as he approached; Annabel noticed him first. He gave her a wave and she nodded back. She looked about as comfortable as Never felt.

'Sam,' he said, as he joined them. Sam shook his hand for far too long, his eyes wet and red.

Never noticed the bouquets that Sam and Annabel had already set down on the grave, and added his own sorry-looking bunch of flowers. As he stood, he winced.

'How's your . . .' said Sam, gesturing vaguely to Never's chest.

'Good and bad,' said Never. The injury was from Winnerden Flats; Sam had no idea that Annabel, Jonah and Never had had any involvement. *Nobody* did, except Kendrick and Sly, two government spooks who'd gone rogue in an attempt to stop the catastrophe as it unfolded. Never didn't like to go into detail with others about his wounds. It was, in every sense of the word, a sore point. The story he'd had to tell everyone was about as bland and, well, as *stupid* as they came.

The truth was as far from bland as it could be: a man possessed by an entity that was close to *satanic* had torn out one of Never's ribs, while he was conscious, partly as a demonstration of power, and partly because the fucker had a sick sense of humour.

When Never was recovering in hospital, he'd tried to come up with a plausible excuse for the scarring the assault would leave him with. Frankly, he'd wanted to choose something that *sounded* good – something that would paint him in a decent light. Something, perhaps, that he'd be *proud* of.

Sadly, the choice wasn't his. He'd discovered this when, still confined to bed, he'd raised the topic with Kendrick.

'You fell from a ladder while helping to paint a friend's barn,' Kendrick told him. 'You landed on the rusted edge of a sheet of metal, shattered your rib and suffered from an infection as a result.'

'That's the official line?' said Never, hopeful that he could tweak the story to include some aspect of, say, *courage*.

Kendrick had passed him the notes hanging from the

end of his bed, to show him it was official. 'Now and forever,' he'd said.

So, there it was. His chest hurt like hell, pretty often, and it certainly *looked* like shit, but the story he would have to tell would always put him in the role of clumsy dickhead rather than brave defender of civilization.

Great.

He looked at Sam, who was just watching the grave. Their short conversation had, it seemed, ended. He wondered if he should try and say something else, but his ability to pick an opening gambit was notoriously bad. If he opened his mouth, there was a good chance that what came out would be, 'Been to any nice funerals lately?'

Or possibly worse.

The three of them stood in silence, for what felt like decades.

Eventually, Sam spoke again. 'I don't think it'll ever feel real, do you?'

Annabel and Never shook their heads.

'He's gone,' said Sam. 'Nothing can change that, but every day I think there's been a mistake. You know what I mean?'

This time, Annabel and Never nodded, and Never felt an almost overwhelming urge to say *something*. He resisted.

'Thanks for meeting me here,' said Sam. 'I know it's hard for both of you, too, but it's meant so much to me to visit him. One year on.'

After a few more minutes of silence, Sam nodded and shook Never's hand. He turned and hugged Annabel. 'He deserved better than this,' Sam told her. 'You both did.'

They watched him go, walking as if the weight of the

world was on him. When he was out of sight, Never felt a tangible relief. He heaved a sigh, and caught a glance from Annabel. She clearly felt just as relieved.

'You coming?' she said.

'I got left off by taxi,' said Never. 'I came prepared.' He nodded to the bottle of whiskey, which was in a bag but still obvious in shape. 'So, yeah.'

'I noticed,' said Annabel, pointedly. She led them to her car. 'Well, that was horrible,' she said, once they were inside and the doors were closed.

'It's been a bad year all round,' said Never. She started the car and drove, and Never found himself thinking of the grave, and the name carved on the headstone: *Jonah Miller*.

He wondered, as he often did, whose body *actually* lay in the coffin. Because it sure as hell wasn't Jonah's.

3

Jonah sat and stared at the television, even though it was switched off. The last year had been difficult, staying inside this goddamn house – or compound, which is what Annabel often called it. The name didn't matter.

It was a prison, and he'd been the one responsible for locking himself in here.

Annabel had gone to meet Sam and Never on the anniversary of Jonah's faked funeral. He was miserable at the thought of what this was doing to Sam, but it had seemed like the only way. After Winnerden Flats, Kendrick had asked for his help. Jonah had been the only one who could see the shadows, the parasitic creatures who, somehow, were all part of the same entity.

Jonah had seen that entity in dreams and visions; a vast Beast, dark and corrosive, striding across the lands of the world, reaching down to consume the flesh and souls of whatever it could grasp. Since Winnerden Flats, his dreams had intensified, and grown ever more vivid. Now, he saw the same shadows that he'd seen clinging to the shoulders of those human hosts – saw them scurrying around the feet of the huge Beast that strode over cities, burning everything it touched.

After the victory at Winnerden Flats, the vessel for that dark Beast had been destroyed in the most thorough way Kendrick could devise. There was no coming back, not this time.

Jonah had lost friends, though. Two of the revivers he'd long worked with were among those killed, but there was someone else: an old flame, called Tess Neil. She'd been the key to their victory, but she'd lost her life as a result.

And the last thing she had said to Jonah was this: *The Beast is coming. Be ready.*

Had he let himself think, even for a second, that their victory had been complete? That it wasn't just the human vessel who had died, but the Beast as well? Simply, *yes*: he had. Tess's words brought an immediate end to such naive hope. The kind of power that the creature seemed to possess wasn't the kind that could be defeated so easily. After all, whatever ancient battle had led to it being imprisoned in the first place hadn't ended in its destruction. Instead, it had been *contained*, in a prison constructed from souls.

Perhaps it couldn't be destroyed. Like energy itself, maybe it could only be converted from one form to another.

So, Kendrick had asked for his help to see if the shadow creatures and their human hosts still held positions of power. Many of those who'd been suspected had simply vanished after Winnerden Flats; months of careful observation revealed no shadows wherever they looked. Then Jonah had been attacked: run off the road, then a gun had been put to his head. A gun that jammed. His attacker had fled on foot, his vehicle too damaged for him to drive.

After that, Kendrick and Sly had traced the would-be assassin and discovered ominous connections. Whether or not the shadows were still around, there were definitely *humans* who wanted them to be, and wanted to ensure their rise to power. Those people had identified Jonah as a threat. They weren't subtle, and they weren't restrained. The only time they would leave Jonah alone – and by extension his friends, and everyone he loved – was when Jonah Miller was dead.

He'd pleaded with Kendrick to make it happen, and Kendrick had reluctantly obliged. Annabel had bought a new property in the Radio Quiet Zone in Virginia. It had been turned into a low-profile fortress in the eighties, and it ticked all the boxes on Jonah's list. Remote, secure, self-sufficient, and large enough to stop him going mad.

Kendrick had made it all happen pretty damn quickly. Almost before Jonah knew it, he was dead and buried, and free to focus on answering the most important question of his life.

What had Tess meant by '*be ready*'?

How the hell could anyone be ready to face off with the devil?

*

Jonah was at the door waiting when they arrived.

'There he is,' said Never. 'Here.' He handed over a bottle of whiskey. 'For a dead guy, you still drink too much.'

Jonah took the bottle, avoiding looking at Annabel. In truth, he *did* drink too much these days. He'd kept Tess's last words to himself, all this time, and it had eaten away at him. The hope that Winnerden Flats had truly been a final victory was still holding on – just about – in Never and Annabel. They seemed to be swayed by the notion that it was *people*, ordinary and untouched by shadows, who were the only remaining problem. Kendrick and Sly, he knew, didn't operate that way, but Never and Annabel thought of what they did as 'playing safe' and 'covering all bases'.

Keeping something so important from his best friend and his lover wasn't easy. Doing so while trapped in the same damn house for a year had almost sent him over the edge. Overconsumption of alcohol wasn't helping.

Right now, though . . . right now, he was going to get drunk with them both and try his best to put the end of the world out of his thoughts.

He gave Never a hug, and then gave Annabel one too.

'Should I ask how it went?' he said.

'As well as you'd expect,' said Annabel.

They went down a floor to the upper basement, which Jonah thought of as his lair and had turned into a games room. Chock-full of diversions, from pool table to massive TV, it was entirely free of the things that had truly consumed him while living here – the *dark* things that haunted his dreams. For that, Jonah had a stack of notebooks hidden away where Annabel wouldn't find them: notes, supposedly, on how to save humanity from extinction. So far, those note-books contained essentially nothing of use.

Jonah opened up the refrigerator and passed Never a can of beer. 'I'm guessing you don't want to hit the hard stuff right away?' he said.

'Best not,' said Never. 'What are we eating?' He looked at Annabel as he said this, and Annabel glared at him.

'Any reason why you think I'm the one to ask?' she said.

He went a bit pale, but recovered quickly. 'Yeah, fair cop,' he said. 'But let's be honest, you actually cook decent food. Jonah can reheat, and that's about it.' He shook his head. 'You'd think you could actually do something useful with your time, mate. There's a whole *world* of delicious recipes out there, just begging for you to cook them for me.'

Jonah cracked open a beer and shrugged. 'We have a ton of pizza,' he said. 'But if you want to make some stroganoff or risotto, feel free. I'll stay here and drink.'

'Pizza . . .' said Never. 'Sounds perfect.'

*

'One rule,' said Jonah, as they all flopped onto the couches that faced the massive television. 'We don't talk about the things we don't talk about. Funeral, Winnerden, Andreas. None of that. Deal?'

'Deal,' said Annabel. 'As long as you stick to a rule of *my* choosing.'

'Name it,' said Jonah.

'Relax and enjoy yourself.'

'I'll try,' he mumbled, ignoring the eyes-to-the-ceiling response from Never and Annabel.

The TV came to life, Never fiddling with the remote. 'Time for mindless junk,' he said. 'It's been a *long* day already.' He noted Annabel's look of warning. 'Yeah, yeah, for reasons not to be mentioned. But I want to have a movie, preferably with a ridiculous level of action, and then eat pizza while being trounced at pool by the shark over there.' He nodded to Annabel, who had honed her pool skills with her dad since she was twelve. 'So let's pick something!'

Jonah sat forward. The TV had come on to a rolling

news channel, with the sound down. 'Put the volume up.' There was footage of a ship, with what looked like a small submarine on the deck. The footage was interspersed with shots of dour heads-of-state looking terribly serious.

'I heard about this earlier,' said Never as he complied and raised the television volume. 'They found a submersible drone attached to one of the main transatlantic comms cables. Russia and North Korea are blaming each other, but there's a theory that some investment company spotted a pattern in share prices the last time there was a big Internet outage in Asia, and wanted to create something similar.'

'The drone was capable of severing the cable?' said Annabel.

'Yeah,' said Never, but he shrugged. 'It's not as big a deal as you'd think. Accidental cuts happen all the time. Anchors get snagged, old debris gets tangled up. There are thirty ships that spend all their time maintaining these things, and they fix cuts every week. One cable going down makes no difference, but now and again, a clusterfuck of accidents sparks panic because it actually slows down network traffic. People can't watch Netflix in high definition! Riots on the streets! To really knacker the system you'd have to cut every cable in multiple places at the same time, and even then it'd be up and running within days.'

'So why's it such a big deal?' said Jonah.

'It's not, really,' said Never. He glugged his beer down and went to get another. 'This is all symbolic reaction. When there's a little spate of accidents that'd normally go un-reported, adding one more on purpose – and knowing it'll happen – lets someone stir up shit. North Korea can embar-rass the West, say, or Russia can distract from some dodgy crap they're pulling. Or a global company can make a killing on stocks. Whichever. Just keep your fingers crossed that the submersible doesn't have a "made in the USA" stamp on it.' He grinned, returning with his second can and flopping back down into his seat.

Jonah was watching the news, looking utterly morose.

'For fuck's sake, put the frown away!' said Never. 'We're less than a minute in, and you're already breaking the rules!'

Jonah shook his head. 'Every time I look, the world feels like it's turning to shit.'

'The world *always* feels like it's turning to shit,' said Annabel, smiling. 'Humans are primed to think they're living in the worst time ever, because they're primed to think everyone else has it better than them. Even the people in the *past* had it better, hence the world must be getting worse.'

'Meanwhile, they have a crisis if their broadband goes down for more than a minute,' said Never. He flicked away from the news and brought up the available movie rentals. He highlighted one. 'I've heard good things about that, any objections?'

'Oh look,' said Annabel. 'An action movie featuring a surprisingly tough yet attractive woman!' She looked to Jonah, and managed to get a smile from him.

'Are we *allowed* to mention Sly?' Jonah said.

'Yes,' said Annabel, grinning. 'Since it makes Never blush.'

'Quit it,' said Never. 'Let's pick our movie and sink into a relaxed stupor.'

'Truth or dare!' barked Annabel.

'Truth!' said Jonah. 'How are you getting on with Sly, Never?'

'That's *not* how the game works,' said Never. 'Can't we just focus on picking?'

'Shut up and answer,' said Annabel.

'OK,' said Never, sagging somewhat. 'I like Sly. We get on very well. She's made it very clear I'm not her type. I've *met* her type, actually. We went out with a few of her friends.'

'Sly let you meet her friends?' said Annabel.

'Oh God yes,' said Never, almost with a shiver. 'Let's just say it wasn't the most comfortable night of my life. Thank Christ they were interested in the FRS – well, the gruesome parts. If I'd talked about the stuff I spend most of my time doing, they'd probably have beaten me to death out of boredom. It gave me an insight into why I'm not her type, though. She prefers guys who can crush rocks with their eyelids. I suspect she enjoys my company because she finds it quaint.'

'You are quaint,' said Annabel.

'Cheers.'

'And do you still . . .' She batted her eyes. 'Harbour feelings?'

'It's the *When Harry Met Sally* thing, right?' said Never. 'A man and woman can't just be friends, unless the man knows the woman would literally garrotte him if he ever came on to her.'

Annabel narrowed her eyes. 'I don't recall that part,' she said. 'You must have watched the Director's Cut.'

'So,' said Jonah. 'When did you two last meet up?'

'Three weeks back,' said Never.

Jonah nodded. 'And did she have anything to . . . you know. To report?'

'First off,' said Never, 'I would've already told you if she had. Second, we're not talking about any of that shit. But no, she didn't have news. Which is always good. We had lunch, and a laugh, and I had my little heart broken all over again.' He pouted extravagantly. 'Now pick a fucking movie.'

*

After the film, Jonah went to put the pizzas in the oven while Never volunteered to get some wine.

'Just get something red,' said Annabel. 'Don't agonize.'

'You know me,' said Never. 'It'll be fine.'

He'd volunteered because he loved the house Annabel had bought, and he wanted the excuse to explore the place.

At its core was a building erected in 1893, above the workings of a failed copper mine – the owner had been a man who paid through the nose for mineral rights after locating what he'd thought to be a rich seam of copper ore in a region that supposedly had almost no copper deposits. A year of drilling and a hundred tons of ore later, and the seam had gone. What was left amounted to about three hundred feet of tunnels and two caverns. The core building felt like something Edgar Allan Poe would have written about, bare stone walls that had the feel of a medieval castle to them, and, in 1978, a new survivalist-leaning owner had decided to extend outwards and down using the blandest forms of construction known to humanity – poured concrete and cinder blocks. The result was bizarre. That was why Never liked it so much.

It was situated in the Radio Quiet Zone, a hundred-mile-square area near a major radio astronomy site, which strictly limited radio emissions to avoid interference with the observatory. The region had long been a draw for those with slightly *quirky* ideas on how badly radio waves could affect people, although as cellphones were essentially banned in the area, people came to live there for the sheer freedom from constant communication. Given the way the new owner had altered the house, Never reckoned he was definitely more of the tinfoil-hat variety.

The house even had its own nuclear shelter, in the lower of the two caverns, and while the shelter was an unsophisticated metal box with basic air filtration, the simple fact of its existence seemed unbearably cool to Never. Sure, it smelled a bit like old socks inside, but the only thing he could think of that might beat it was owning a Second World War submarine.

The wine cellar was part of the old mine tunnels, just inside the tunnel entrance in the lower basement, one level down from the games room. In the wall of a short spur, thirty-two large holes had been drilled. When she bought the house, filling them had been one of Annabel's first actions. She'd asked Never how much he knew about wine, and Never had laughed.

'As far as I'm concerned there are two types of wine,' he'd told her. 'The stuff I like, and the stuff I'll drink anyway.' He hadn't been kidding.

When she'd told him not to agonize over choosing one to go with the pizza, she had almost certainly been taking the piss.

He went downstairs and through the lower basement, with a home gym in one corner where he knew Jonah spent much of his time now. His friend had bulked up a little, weights and exercise probably the thing that had been keeping him from going under in this last year. Certainly, after

Winnerden Flats, he'd seemed to blame himself for not being fitter and stronger, as if an extra few pounds of muscle would have made any difference at all to what they'd been through. And even though he was exercising, Jonah still looked like shit – pale, hair cropped with clippers, and dark rings around his eyes. He claimed he was sleeping well, but Never doubted it.

The rest of the lower basement was used for storage, and Never tried to ignore what was there – a shitload of bottled water, canned food, box after box of equipment. Torches, medicines, and Christ knew what else. The previous owner was a survivalist, yes, but none of this stuff had been *left* here. It was all new, and every time Never came down here he'd noticed more of it.

He opened the door to the tunnels. It was a thick metal door, lockable from the other side, and going through it felt like entering some kind of mountain fortress. Yes, he got a kick from that, but it worried him how Jonah thought of it.

He switched on the tunnel lighting and pulled two bottles at random from the drilled wine holes. Both were Italian reds; he took it as a sign and set them on the ground, then took his chance to explore a little further.

He allowed himself five minutes to head down to the lower of the two caverns. It was mostly a natural water-eroded void, Jonah had told him, but it had long been dry. The nuclear shelter seemed like overkill down here – the rock itself was its own shelter, really. The air filtration was all that the cavern lacked, just too many ventilation sources around that would have funnelled radioactive fallout into the space, if the worst came to the worst.

Well, one *form* of the worst. There were other kinds of Apocalypse, after all.

He got to the shelter and opened it up, popping inside for a little fix of ten-year-old kid adventure. He wondered, as always, if anyone else would be quite as transparently juvenile as he was, coming into this thing.

He hoped so.

He swung the door shut with a huge grin on his face. He'd been in here a few times before; Jonah had seemed a little reluctant to show him the ropes, maybe because Annabel had grown to hate the thing, but Never had insisted. He flipped up the light switch. The shelter had a stack of old lead-acid batteries to power it, charged by a gasoline-driven generator, but for as long as Jonah had lived here it had run off the mains electricity supply instead. The generator had broken down the first time Jonah tried it out, and had become something of a running jibe that Never teased Jonah with constantly – when Never had suggested that Jonah buy a new one on the grounds that there was no way Jonah would ever have the mechanical ability to fix it, Jonah had bristled and sworn that he would. One day soon, Never knew, Jonah would back down and accept his help.

One of the fluorescent tubes kept flickering, but really it just added to the atmosphere. He readied himself to hoist up to the higher of the two bunks that were bolted to one wall.

Then he slipped on something wet and fell over. The floor, naturally enough, was *hard*. He followed the water back to its source, and saw that it was a mundane slow drip from the air filtration system. He hand-tightened a nut and the drip stopped. Just before he stood, he noticed something under the lower bunk, so he reached under and pulled out what was there.

Notebooks.

He sat on the bunk and – with a single guilty glance to the window in the entryway – opened the top book.

The first thing he saw was a sketch of a landscape, tall buildings in the distance. Overlooking it was a dark shape, drawn in thick chaotic pencil strokes. It resembled a winged demon, he reckoned, but there was very little detail to it.

He sighed. Jonah had described this stuff to him before – the things that haunted his dreams. And while he'd spoken very little about it since Winnerden Flats, it wasn't like Never had expected it to just stop.

Seeing it like this still made his heart sink, though.

He flicked through the pages. More cityscapes, more creatures.

Then there was one that chilled him: the face of Michael Andreas, the man who'd been the creature's vessel. The sketch looked like him, too, and Never hadn't known that Jonah possessed such a level of artistic talent. The myriad little *mouths* that covered the skin of the face were well-observed and gave him a shiver of recognition, remembering how Andreas had seemed to be struggling to maintain his human shape. He shivered, remembering when that leering face had come so close to his own, as the creature cut out his rib . . .

He groaned, nausea sweeping over him for an instant. He turned the page.

Next was a series of sketches, focusing on people's *shoulders*. Their faces weren't drawn, the key part of the image being the shadows they bore, those parasitic parts of the

38

creature that latched on to human hosts. Again, Jonah had told him repeatedly about the nature of the things, but this was the first time Never had seen what Jonah had seen.

In his sketches, Jonah had captured a distinctly repellent quality. A sheen, a *glistening*, covering the bulbous and sickening mass. Long dark tendrils, like ancient fingers, stretched down and vanished into the flesh of the host. He realized that the sketches were a series showing the same creature over time, pulsating horribly.

On the next page was another portrait, but the feeling Never got from this one wasn't horror. It was sorrow.

The portrait was of Tess Neil. Jonah had known her when he was in his teens. She was older than him, and he'd developed a punishing crush on her – something which, Never suspected, he'd not got over.

Tess had died in Winnerden Flats. Jonah had carried her body out, and had insisted she had a proper burial, something Kendrick had arranged.

Her face had been drawn with a delicacy that showed how much he'd cared for her.

Underneath the portrait were the words: *The Beast is coming. Be ready.*

He flicked through more pages, then opened up another of the notebooks.

There was more of the same, and on one page Jonah had written 'be ready?' again and again, in increasingly desperate scrawls.

He was startled by a knocking sound, and looked up.

Jonah's face was at the window in the door.

'Having fun there?' said Jonah, his voice muffled but still

audible. Jonah opened the door and came in, his expression grim; Never wondered just how long he'd been watching.

'Shit,' said Never. 'I'd rather you'd caught me with porn.'

This, at least, drew a reluctant smile. 'Speak for yourself.'

'I'm sorry, mate,' said Never. He closed the notebooks. 'I didn't mean to pry.'

Jonah sat next to him. 'The pizzas won't be long,' he said. He had a slightly pained look to him.

'I lost track of time.'

'Don't mention any of this to Annabel, OK?' said Jonah. He put his hand on the pages of the top notebook. 'I've kept these here because Annabel doesn't come into the shelter. It creeps her out.'

'You're tormenting yourself,' said Never. 'Maybe Kendrick can get hold of someone who can help. It's post-traumatic stress. You need to talk it through, with a professional. Even when something's over, you need help to process everything that—'

Jonah shook his head. 'It's not over.'

'Right,' said Never. 'I know, there are still people out there who want to kick it all off again, but—'

'No,' said Jonah, firmly. 'It's not *over*. There's something I didn't tell you.' He pointed at the words on the open page: *The Beast is coming. Be ready.* 'This wasn't me. This was *Tess.* Her last words. She knew, Never. She knew more than anyone that it would return. She knew it would be down to *me* to stop it.'

Never could feel something inside him dissolving, a nugget of hope he'd been holding onto for a very long time. He'd be lying if he said it was a shock, though – sometimes you can know a hope is naive, and still get comfort from it.

'You should have told us,' he said. 'This isn't something you can deal with alone.'

'Maybe not,' said Jonah. 'But I wanted to give you both a chance – a chance to really think it was finished.'

'Did you tell Kendrick and Sly?'

'I told Kendrick. Whether he told Sly, I don't know.'

'Does he believe Tess was right?'

Jonah shrugged. 'He has to assume she was, and so do I.' He took a long breath and let it out slowly. 'Don't tell Annabel,' he said again. 'Not yet. Not until I get some kind of handle on it.'

'If you say so. But you should think about telling her sooner rather than later. It's eating away at you. Even I can tell, and I have the empathetic capacity of a melon.'

'I'll think about it,' said Jonah. 'Tell me something, though. After Winnerden, did you believe it was over, deep down? And don't just tell me what you think I need to hear. Tell me the truth.'

'Ah,' said Never. 'The truth . . .' He gave himself a few seconds of thinking time, but it looked like honesty was going to have to suffice. 'Of course I didn't believe it was over,' he said. 'I just hoped it had been kicked so far into the long grass that it'd be decades before anything happened. Or better yet, *centuries*. I mean, whoever it was that imprisoned that thing the first time, that's all they were doing. A temporary respite. A *very long* temporary respite, admittedly.' He shook his head, thinking about something that had crossed his mind many times. 'How did *they* know what to do? I wonder about that. Did they work it out, or did they get help?'

'It wiped out their world,' said Jonah. 'If they got help, they got it too late.'

'Well,' said Never, standing up. 'This relaxing fun-spree isn't going to plan, is it?'

Jonah put his notebooks back under the bunk. He sighed. 'I feel like I'm just killing time until it all kicks off again, and then it'll be *my* fault when everything turns to shit.'

'Fuck that,' said Never. 'Let's eat pizza and drink wine. Because right now, we're in that respite part, and there's no point wasting it.'

4

The hangover was mighty.

Maybe the boil had been lanced, but whatever the reason, after their brief chat in the shelter Jonah seemed to relax. Pizzas were eaten, wine was drunk, and then a mammoth session of pool ensued.

Annabel beat them both, naturally. When she finally shepherded Jonah off to bed, Never stayed up for a while longer, finally crashing on one of the couches. He didn't wake until early afternoon, but he made some breakfast. Annabel and Jonah emerged, but Never was the only one who could stomach eating.

When he left, Jonah gave him a big hug. It was good to see Jonah still with a smile on his lips. Annabel gave Never a ride home.

'Any plans for the rest of the day?' she asked.

'Sleep,' said Never, and that pretty much covered him.

*

When Never rolled into work on Monday morning, he was feeling buoyant. He'd spent Sunday gaming, and the stress that had been building in the run-up to the visit to Jonah's grave had gone. Seeing Sam always brought out a strong feeling of guilt. When Kendrick had arranged Jonah's 'death', he'd made clear how important it was not to reveal the truth to those they were trying to protect, however strong the temptation. The whole purpose of the lie would be compromised. Indeed, Kendrick had tried to convince Jonah that even Annabel and Never should be left ignorant of the truth; Jonah had considered that one step too far.

But knowing that it made them all safer – Sam included – didn't mean much when Never could see the pain in the man's eyes, as he stood by the grave.

The discovery of Jonah's notebooks hadn't hit Never as hard as he might have expected, though. When Jonah was 'killed off', the immediate dangers had subsided. The normality that came with it was such a relief that, on the whole, he'd been able to push out the fears. Nightmares of Michael Andreas aside, he'd made a huge effort to convince himself that whatever might happen in the future, his own involvement with that whole subject was over.

His effort had paid off, and he put that success down to his grandmother – his dad's mum. She'd lived in her native Aberdeen, and the family had visited her every year. She'd hated sea travel and didn't trust aircraft, so it was the only time they got to see her. She'd been on her own, his grandad having died before Never was born, but she was a fiercely intelligent woman who always spoke to Never like he was an adult.

He'd loved his grandmother. She spoiled him, for a start. Whenever they were out shopping, anything that caught his eye tended to find its way into her shopping trolley, and that was certainly welcome for a ten-year-old. But the reason for his devotion was much deeper, and it hadn't been until after her death that he'd really understood the root of it.

'You were two peas in a pod,' his dad said to him once, a few years after she'd gone, and that hit the nail on the head. When it came down to it, he wasn't all that *like* his mum or dad – his dad had no trace of a Scottish burr, for one thing, while Never still hadn't lost his Belfast accent. His gran understood him better than anyone because their person-alities were so similar. She would come out with things that were as hilarious as they were inappropriate, leaving him in fits of laughter while his parents looked on in vague horror. Sometimes he would be the one to say it, and get a severe glance from his mum.

During one visit, Never had fallen ill with a chesty cough, and his parents had left him with his gran while they went out for the day. He had decided to ask her about something his dad had said. Her house was on Church Road, but his father sometimes called it something else: the Dead Road.

When she came up to the bedroom to see if he was hungry, he asked her why his father called it that.

'Did you ask your dad?' she said, sitting on the side of the bed.

'I did. He said people called it that because everyone who lives here is so old.'

She grinned and burst into laughter. Never frowned. 'What's wrong?' she said.

'It doesn't make sense! Dad grew up here, so when he was young *you* weren't old.'

'That's true,' she said. 'But your dad was right. *Half* right, anyway. When your dad was a child, the road was full of craggy old dodderers like I am now. There was a handful of young families, but mostly it was wrinkles and white hair.'

'What do you mean he was *half* right?'

'What's at the top of the hill, Rob?' She always called him Rob, the same as his friends did, even though his parents insisted on calling him Robert.

'A church.'

'You know the funny gateway to the church? It's a lych gate. Do you know what that is?'

He shook his head.

'It's a side entrance to the church grounds, where bodies are brought for funerals. Every funeral used to bring the body up along this road, and carry it in through that gate. Somebody gave the road a nickname, because sooner or later *everybody* comes up this way. Everybody dies, and wherever a funeral procession started, it'd get here in the end. Eventually, we all travel along the Dead Road.'

'Ah,' he said. 'OK.' He started to cough. She handed him a tissue.

'I suppose old people living here is funny in a way,' she said. 'Less distance to travel!' She gave him a big grin, but the talk of death hadn't exactly left him feeling cheery.

She reached out and tenderly pushed his hair from his forehead. 'You know, when your grandfather died, I was determined not to go the way so many of my friends have gone – once one went, the other was close behind. They gave up and were just waiting. Mind you, they're not the worst. I've known people all my life who just had no hope within them, none at all. They were already walking along the Dead Road, because nothing seemed to matter.' She shook her head. 'We all die, Rob. But for some people that's all they see ahead of them.'

'At school they said the sun would die, too. In, well, billions of years.'

She smiled. 'And does that worry you?'

He smiled back and shook his head. 'Don't be daft.' He started to cough again, and this time he hawked up some thick green sputum. He spat it into his tissue and grinned.

She took the tissue with a grimace. 'Nice. If you *are* going to die today, at least wait until your parents get back or you'll get me into trouble.'

'I'll try,' he said, still grinning.

'Good. I'll go and get some soup.' She stood, and at the side of his bed she paused. 'A life lived without hope . . .' she said, wistful. 'Some people start travelling on the Dead Road a *long* time before they're in a coffin, Rob. Don't you ever do that.' She raised an eyebrow. 'Promise me.'

He'd made her that promise, and he'd always tried to stick to it. Even now.

*

The office was quiet that morning, although one of the comms links to an offsite storage location had gone down. The video and audio evidence collected at revivals was backed up to other FRS offices, as well as to three sites the FBI still shared with them. With just one down it was hardly a crisis, but it was a good policy to get these things back up and running as soon as possible. They'd had occasional problems with the comms hardware at their end, and it was easy to check and straightforward to fix, so Never got stuck in.

By noon he'd resolved the issue, but the day was about to get much busier.

At 12.23, Hugo Adler got the call. He came to Never first. 'Something's come in from Durham, North Carolina,' he said. 'Probably a murder-suicide, could be something more.'

While a suicide was only revived if the lottery came up, murder-suicide was a different matter entirely. 'More?'

'They want to rule out foul play by a third party,' said Hugo. 'I'd like you to be on site.'

Durham was a two-hour drive away. Two there, two back. At least three hours at the site. It'd be a long day. 'Really?'

'Better to have a senior staff member on it,' said Hugo. 'Who's our highest rated available reviver?'

'I'll take a look.' He checked. 'Lex. Have you estimated?'

Hugo nodded. 'Husband and wife, no kids. Wife was shot in the head, single bullet. Small calibre. She's our subject. Estimate came out at fifty per cent for a J5 rating. Lex is what, a K4?'

'Yep. Should be eighty per cent or better for her. Well worth the trip. How come the husband's not the subject?'

'I've put the pictures from the site on the system,' said Hugo, and Never brought them up.

'Ouch,' he said. The first images were inside a garage, which had been all but destroyed by fire. In the middle of the floor was a shape that Never immediately knew was the husband, pretty much incinerated.

'Not even the best of the best would have a chance with that,' said Hugo. 'If it's suicide, the guy obviously didn't want to be questioned.'

'No shit,' said Never. Hugo had paused for a fraction of a second before he'd said 'the best of the best', and Never wondered if he'd been about to say 'Jonah'. There was no question of attempting to revive the man, certainly.

It had always fascinated Never how suicide rates had measurably reduced in countries that performed revivals of suicides. The rates hadn't plummeted to zero, by any means, but just the idea that your actions would be questioned *even if* you died seemed to put some people off. The fact that it weighed on the minds of those considering suicide was borne out by the figures. Large-calibre ammunition and fragmenting bullets were one of the options people took to make sure they couldn't be revived, but so was fire. Some did both, but the key thing was that the extra steps needed – and the extra thought that had to be put into it – was an effective deterrent. Most suicides were spur-of-the-moment acts of desperation, and it had long been known that any kind of additional barrier made it less likely for a person to go ahead with it – keeping a gun unloaded with the ammunition kept separately slashed the risk of suicide.

Having to buy ammunition specifically for the job, or having to set a fire too, had an even greater effect.

He saw Lex enter the office, carrying a coffee. She was smiling, but she wouldn't be for much longer. He looked at Hugo. 'Do you want to tell her, or shall I?'

*

The house in Durham was single-storey, in the suburbs of West Hills. When they got there, it had been taped off, a dozen neighbours hanging around with their arms folded, watching with concern.

The air was full of the stench of gasoline, burnt plastic and broiling meat.

As she got out of the car and got a nose-full, Lex closed her eyes. 'No way,' she said. 'Are we going to have to *work* in that stench?'

'You'll stop noticing in five minutes,' said Never. 'I guarantee. Besides . . .' He pointed at the bulk of the house, which was almost untouched by the fire. The husband had kept the garage door closed and the fire hadn't spread. 'The wife was shot in the bedroom, far end of the place.'

He went to the back of the FRS car and took out a forensic coverall, putting it on quickly as Lex got her own and did the same. Then he unloaded two of the equipment cases. 'Grab those other two,' he said to Lex, and she did.

'This is the first one of these I've had since I joined the FRS,' said Lex. 'A head-shot, I mean.'

'They're not much different to others,' said Never. 'From what I've heard.'

She gave him a look. 'I've had the training, Never. Actually *doing* it is a different matter.'

A white screen had been erected to shield the contents of the garage from onlookers, and as they walked past it, Never had a peek around the side. The husband's remains were still there. 'Yikes,' he said. 'The report said he didn't shoot himself, you know. Most people who take that route light the fire with one hand and have a gun in the other, to make it quick.'

'What the hell makes somebody do something like that?' said Lex.

'Time to find out,' he said, and they went inside.

*

The woman's name was Patti Trent, thirty-one. She was lying on top of her bed, fully clothed, legs straight, arms by her sides. The detectives in charge of the case described her as looking posed, and Never thought so too – neatened up, after she'd been shot in the head. The bullet had entered her left temple, but it hadn't emerged. The gun, it transpired, was her own. The working hypothesis was that her husband John had shot her, then had taken his own life in the garage.

'What do you reckon?' asked Never.

Lex frowned. 'It doesn't look *too* bad,' she said. 'Depends if the bullet hit the back of the skull and bounced back a bit. Fingers crossed it didn't.' She took a small meds box out of her pocket and opened it, taking her revival meds out. She dry-swallowed them. 'Call me when you're ready and we can get started. I don't want to get back to Richmond too late, if I can help it.'

She left Never to get on with the equipment set-up.

There was a dining room close to the bedroom, which he decided was ideal for observation – he would sit in there with the two detectives and monitor the camera feeds, while Lex got on with the revival without distractions. Once he'd set up a workstation, he took the cameras through and placed the three tripods. Recording protocol required three viewpoints: one wide-angle, taking in the full room; one that captured the whole body and the reviver; and one close-up.

It didn't take long to prepare and hook everything together. Most of the time was spent on testing the config- uration. Problems during a revival were rare, but incredibly distracting.

When he was done, he fetched the detectives and Lex. She went into the bedroom, wary and silent as most revivers tended to be, while Never took the detectives into the dining room.

He'd put a small folding chair next to the bed for Lex to use. She sat in it and took the woman's hand, while Never watched closely. There wasn't much to see, of course, but he needed to be ready in case she needed help. If it turned out to be harder than expected, it was entirely possible for her to lose consciousness and slip from the chair.

She was fast, though – twenty minutes in, and Never saw a telltale tremor in Patti Trent's cheek.

'She's coming,' said Lex.

'Good work,' said Never.

The dead woman took a long breath. Time for questions.

'Patti? My name is Lex Turner. Do you know what happened to you?'

Patti was silent, but after ten seconds or so Lex raised her left hand and did a thumbs-up. A reviver could sense a huge amount about their subject, even when there was no speech – she must have thought Patti understood the situation, and it wasn't going to be a problem. That was one of the key failure-points in a revival, if the subject failed to come to terms with their own death.

Patti finally spoke. 'John shot me,' she said. 'He killed me.'

'Case closed,' said one of the detectives, and when Never looked at him he shrugged. 'Well, it is. With no third party involved, this is just a coroner's case. No police investigation needed.'

'Fine,' said Never, keeping the irritation he felt out of his voice. 'But let her do her job, please. Keep it down and sit still.' He switched on the audio feed to Lex. 'Lex? The police are happy for you to lead the questioning as you see fit.'

Lex looked at the camera and raised a sarcastic eyebrow. She knew exactly what that meant.

'Yeah,' said Never. 'I know.'

She turned back to Patti. 'I'm a reviver with the Forensic Revival Service. I'd like to ask you some questions about what happened. Do you know why John did it?'

'He was under stress, I think. He'd been acting strange for months.'

'In what way?' asked Lex.

'Is he . . . did John shoot himself?'

Lex winced. She looked to Never again. Telling her the truth might make Patti fall silent and halt the revival, but lying to her could easily breed mistrust, and again that could bring things to a stop.

'Your call,' said Never. 'Sorry.'

Lex shook her head with frustration. 'John took his own life, yes. How had he been acting strange?'

A good compromise. She didn't have to tell her he *burnt* to death, and getting another question in right away was a smart tactic.

Patti took another slow breath. 'Distracted. Angry. He'd been drinking.'

'He'd started to drink?' said Lex. 'Is that why he'd changed?'

'No. He'd been drinking today. He was more like his old self when he drank.'

Lex looked to camera and wrinkled her nose. *Huh?*

'A new one to me, too,' said Never.

'Schizophrenic, maybe?' said one detective. 'Some self-medicate. Helps their symptoms.'

'I thought that was nicotine,' said his colleague. 'Not alcohol.'

With a hand wave, Never signalled for them to be quiet.

'Did John say anything to you, Patti?' asked Lex.

'He said he didn't want me to be around for the silence. He said he wanted to spare me that.'

'What did he mean, Patti?'

Another breath. 'I don't know. He said he was sorry. Before he took out the gun and shot me. He was sorry.'

There was very little else that came. Patti hadn't been afraid, as such – she'd been concerned that he was having an affair, and certainly wasn't worried for her life. Lex let her say what she needed to say, and then she let Patti Trent go.

'What the fuck was that?' she asked Never as he started to pack away the equipment.

'Don't let it get to you,' said Never. 'The Coroner's Office will sort it out. When they talk to his work colleagues, and see if he'd been to a doctor. As of now, it's none of our business. Old case, been and done. There'll be plenty of them.'

'Don't you ever follow up old cases?' she said.

He thought about Daniel Harker, Annabel's dad. *That* had been an old case, and he and Jonah had certainly followed that one up. 'It's a bad habit to get into,' he said. 'Let's leave it at that.'

5

Jonah's Monday morning started with Annabel heading off to work.

Before she'd met Jonah, Annabel had been forging ahead with a career in journalism. She'd inherited wealth from her father that meant she didn't need to work; it was her father's death that had led to her meeting Jonah in the first place, and she'd dropped everything to investigate the background to his death. That investigation had led to Michael Andreas, the man who had inadvertently freed the entity they'd faced at Winnerden Flats.

Andreas had owned a hugely successful biotech company, but it had been his own fascination with cryogenics that had been his pathway to catastrophe. Now, he was dead. Andreas Biotech had been quietly broken up and the pieces sold off to other firms. Continuing to investigate in the aftermath of what had happened at Winnerden Flats was deeply risky, she knew, and Kendrick had made it absolutely clear to her – she had to keep away from it to stay safe.

She had also decided that she needed to keep herself busy, so she'd taken on a range of stories that were as far from Andreas and his followers as she could get. After some soul-searching, she'd wanted to do something useful with her time, and had settled on political and business corruption, posting articles through several news sites under aliases. Some old contacts gave her leads that would take more time and money than they could justify spending, and Annabel dug around, occasionally finding something that had meat on it. Her work consisted of a vast amount of drudgery, and there was a hell of a lot of lunches in DC, forging friendships and connections.

Jonah was entirely happy about it, though. It was hard and satisfying work, and the kinds of scandals she'd been uncovering had been very much in the mould of good old-fashioned investigative reporting – where those caught out hung their heads in shame, rather than attempting to assassinate those who'd caught them.

Once she'd left the house – for yet another lunch in DC, with yet another contact – Jonah tidied up the breakfast dishes and had a second coffee. The weather was warm, so he decided to get some sun, thinking of how Never had made more than one pointed reference on Friday night to how pale he looked. He was the first to admit Never was right, though. He'd spent the first six months terrified of being outside, even though the property had a large proportion of its grounds walled off with a garden that verged on overgrown. It had taken one of Kendrick's rare visits for him to be convinced that there were no drones flying over them, spying on the house. Kendrick, usually one to hedge his bets, had been entirely confident that Jonah's supposed death had done precisely as intended. Andreas's followers didn't regard Annabel as a person of interest beyond her relationship with Jonah, but the danger of them targeting her to get to Jonah was very real. Once Jonah was 'dead', that danger passed.

Iced Coke in hand, Jonah wandered around the garden, starting to think that he should spend some of the time he had keeping the place under control. They certainly weren't about to get gardeners in, so it really fell to him to do something about it before it got out of hand.

Not today, though. Today, he would top up on vitamin D and try not to think about his notebooks, still hidden down in the shelter.

He failed entirely on the latter. He'd started writing in those notebooks with a vague notion of *planning*, but all he'd managed was to catalogue the images that stalked him while he slept. When he was being the most rational, he told himself that Tess had known no more than he did about what was coming. With her final words, she was just being open about it – the powers that had been unleashed weren't going to be stopped forever. Sooner or later, the Beast he dreamed of would try and *rise*, ready to destroy, ready to consume. The creature had *told* him what it was – the souls of a thousand worlds, corrupted and twisted, drawn together into a being that despised those who still had life. It wanted them to *join* with it, because that was the only thing it understood. At its heart, Jonah believed, the creature was mindless hatred.

Be ready, Tess had said. Perhaps she simply meant be ready to *survive* it. The last world the Beast had taken had managed to imprison it for untold millennia, so it definitely had vulnerabilities. Maybe the best Jonah could do was stay alive until those vulnerabilities led to its downfall again.

But perhaps Tess had known more.

Those who had imprisoned the Beast had used their own souls to create the prison, and it was those souls that Andreas had stumbled on. Lost in the dark for countless eons, they'd forgotten who they were, or what purpose they served. Andreas had expected these ancient beings to reveal truths that would transform human knowledge. He discovered a way to bond each of these lost souls to a human host, but in doing so he dismantled the Beast's prison.

There was no way Andreas could have known. When the last of the souls was freed and the prison was breached, the Beast took Andreas as its vessel, and sought to use his body as a conduit to draw out the unimaginable power that it had once possessed.

The secret to defeating the Beast was surely known to those souls who had trapped it before, but most of them had perished along with the humans they had been bonded to. The only survivor was Tess, yet the soul she carried with her was traumatized to the point of madness. Instead of answers, all Tess got were nightmares that threatened her own sanity, horrifying visions that plagued her constantly.

So, perhaps she *had* known more – glimpses of knowledge just out of reach, enough for her to think that Jonah could fight the creature when it came back.

Tess had been tormented by the possibility that the secret to defeating the Beast was within her grasp, if she could just have the wisdom to see it.

Lying in the sun, Jonah felt the same torment.

*

After a while, he dozed.

He was roused when he heard a car on the road and

thought he recognized the sound of Annabel's vehicle. It was early afternoon, but that morning she'd said she might not be out that long. He sat up, pleased that he'd not be alone all day after all.

Then he heard brakes squeal, and locked tyres grind through dirt. Their house was in a valley with half a dozen other scattered properties, and the road was raised in places above steep gullies. In his mind he saw Annabel crash down into one. He was up in an instant and running to the front gate. He hesitated, realizing he'd not been past that threshold for a year, but the thought of Annabel in trouble propelled him out, pounding down the private lane until he reached the road.

There was a huge cloud of dust in the air further down, obscuring everything. When he was close enough to see the car, skewed across the band of stony dirt that ran alongside the asphalt, he saw that it wasn't Annabel's after all.

'Shit,' he muttered.

Someone was slumped over in the driver's seat; nobody else was in the vehicle. Either he had to help them or leave. He looked around, but there was no other sign of activity; there were no other cars coming.

What choice did he have?

He went to the driver's door and opened it. Inside was an older woman, perhaps late sixties. She was breathing, her eyes closed, a look of distress on her face.

'Ma'am?' said Jonah. 'Can you hear me?'

The woman's eyes flickered open. 'Steven?' she said, visibly struggling to focus.

'No,' said Jonah. He thought for a second. 'I'm . . . Rob. I live nearby.'

She gathered herself and sat up, then rubbed at her face. She noticed the entrance to the driveway up ahead. 'Are you staying with Annabel?' she said. Jonah felt his eyes widen. 'I live further on,' she said. 'Annabel introduced herself a while back but I don't get to see much of her. She didn't mention anyone else.' She smiled at him, with a little mischief. 'I'm Cathy,' she said, and Jonah knew she was about to offer him her hand to shake. He was adept at avoiding that. He'd already moved away from the door and was pretending to check the car for damage. Contact between revivers and non-revivers was typically accompanied by something called *chill*, which was a sensation that ranged from a sense of cold – people often compared it to someone walking over their graves – to a feeling of extreme fear and a taint of death. With Jonah, it was always at the severe end of the scale. And although it didn't happen with everyone – Annabel and Never being two examples – it was the norm.

Hence the reason he needed to avoid shaking Cathy's hand.

'Your car seems OK,' he said, and he went to the other side of it rather than return to the open door. The moment would pass, he hoped, but if he went back now Cathy might still hold out her hand. Then he'd have to pull out some feigned illness and decline. *I'd rather not give you this flu*, perhaps. An old favourite, that one.

'I'll be fine,' said Cathy. 'I get light-headed when I panic. I've had it for years. I should've known better and taken a minute before I left the house.'

'Panic?' said Jonah. 'Is something wrong?'

She nodded. 'My grandson's five. I just got a call from my son-in-law that he was injured in an accident. He's at

Loudon Children's Hospital, so I'm on my way there.' She gave him another smile, but now Jonah could see the panic in her eyes. She still looked pretty foggy.

'You sure you're OK to drive, Cathy?' he said.

Cathy nodded, but Jonah could see that she wasn't up to it. He made a decision. He looked up and down the road again, hoping that someone – preferably Annabel – would show up. Being seen outside on his own road was one thing, but going further afield . . .

'Look,' he said. 'Just let me drive you there, OK?'

'Really?' she said, obvious relief flooding her.

'Sure. Someone would be able to give you a ride home, right?' Cathy nodded. 'Come on, then. You shift over, I'll move your car outside our drive. OK?'

She agreed. Once he'd parked up, he ran to the house and hunted for keys to the four-by-four. He wasn't certain where they were, not having used either of the two cars since they had come here, but Annabel had hung a set up in the kitchen. He grabbed them, got to the car, and drove out to where Cathy was waiting.

'I really don't want to be any trouble, Rob,' said Cathy. For a brief moment Jonah had to wonder why she'd called him 'Rob'.

'No trouble at all,' said Jonah. 'What are neighbours for?'

The drive to the hospital took an hour, and Cathy stayed close to panic the whole way. At times, she started doing breathing exercises to calm down. Other times, she tried conversation. Jonah preferred the exercises.

'So are you and Annabel an item?' she asked.

'Yeah, we've been together a while now.'

'You're living together?'

'Sometimes.' He was making sure to keep it all short and simple. And *vague*.

'She's a journalist, right?'

'Yes.'

'What do you do? If you don't mind me asking?'

'Computers,' said Jonah, not missing a beat.

'Me too,' said Cathy, and Jonah's heart sank. He wasn't sure how much supposed expertise he could fake.

'What kind of . . . stuff?' he managed.

'I used to work at Green Bank,' she said. 'The Radio Telescope?'

Jonah couldn't help but smile. Living in the Radio Quiet Zone, if you didn't know about Green Bank you'd *really* not been paying attention. 'Wow,' he said. 'Are you an astronomer?'

'Used to be,' said Cathy. 'Been retired for a decade. I was always hands-on with the hardware. I was the one who'd pull out circuit boards and get stuck in rather than wait for replacements to get to us.'

'I have a friend who'd *love* you for that. So you stayed in the area?'

'I met my husband there, we bought our place and didn't ever want to leave.' She paused. 'He died three years back.'

'I'm sorry.'

'I miss him, that I do. He was more of a mathematician than I was, but he always wanted to understand the tech side better.' She smiled. 'He was hopeless at it. Our daughter's out in Gainesville, with little Grady and his sister.' Her hand went to her mouth. 'I hope to God Grady's OK.'

When they pulled in outside the entrance to the ER, Cathy heaved a sigh. She looked worn down.

'Are you sure you'll be all right?' said Jonah.

'I'm sure,' she said. 'And thanks.' As she spoke, she reached out and put a hand on Jonah's arm. He was wearing a long-sleeved shirt, but the material was thin – he felt an unmistakeable chill as she touched him. He could see a flicker of puzzlement on Cathy's face, but she said nothing, just got out of the car and gave him a grateful wave as she went into the building.

*

When he got back home, he winced as he saw Annabel's car parked in the drive. The moment he shut off the engine, the front door opened. She was standing there, arms folded, face like thunder.

He got out and walked over.

'Where the hell have you been?' she said.

He explained, although he made sure not to mention the chill. Angry as she seemed, there wasn't much for her to complain about.

'I'm sorry,' said Jonah. 'I didn't see what else I could do.'

'Get in here,' she scolded, but she gave him a long hug. 'You just don't have the capacity to be a selfish bastard, I guess, which isn't a bad thing. So, your name's Rob, then, huh?'

'It is.'

'And you work in computers?'

'I do.'

'Great. So now we have *two* Nevers, do we? And I thought one was plenty.'

'Cathy mentioned you'd already met,' he said.

'I figured it would happen one way or another, better to

get it out of the way early. Still, Cathy seems nice enough. Although when I spoke to her, she didn't mention the astronomy. She just said she was a proud grandmother.'

'We tech-savvy folk hide our lights under a bushel, don't we?'

Annabel grinned. 'Jonah, you've hidden yours *incredibly* well.'

*

She remained a little unsettled into the evening, so Jonah tried to help her relax by making dinner (well, *reheating* dinner) and asking her about her day. The nitty-gritty of journalism held about as much interest for Jonah as office gossip, mainly because it was hard to follow unless you were heavily invested in the subject matter. The bits and pieces of information dripping through were rarely in the *All the President's Men* category, and most of what Annabel found out about were things she'd promised not to divulge.

As evening wore on, she headed off to run a bath. Jonah was tidying away the dishes when the doorbell rang.

He checked the security camera.

It was Cathy. She looked impossibly weary.

Jonah took a deep breath and went to the door. 'Cathy?' he said as he opened it. 'What's wrong?'

'I know who you are,' she said. 'And I need your help.'

6

Jonah felt his stomach lurch.

From behind him came Annabel's angry voice. 'What the hell do you want?' she said. Jonah turned to her – she'd got out of the bath and thrown on her clothes, her hair still wet.

'Calm down,' he told her.

'Why?' said Annabel. 'She comes here and threatens you . . .'

Cathy shook her head, distressed. 'I'm sorry. I didn't mean it to sound like a threat. Believe me, I didn't want to do this. But I googled revivers, and I saw your picture in an old news story. It said you were dead, but I kept looking at the picture and I thought about that weird feeling I'd had when I touched your arm, and . . .' She closed her eyes. 'I wish I didn't know, Jonah,' she said. 'But I do, and I need your help.'

Annabel came down the stairs, raging. Jonah held up his hand for her to wait.

'Grady,' said Jonah. 'He didn't make it.'

Cathy's tears flowed. 'He'd stepped in front of a car,' she said. 'He had chest injuries. They thought he was doing well, but his *heart* gave out. His heart. He was five years old.'

'Her grandson,' he said to Annabel.

Annabel looked to the ceiling, half in sympathy, half in anger. Jonah saw her face set firm; she was steeling herself. 'You can't do this, Cathy,' she said. 'You can't come into my home and *do* this.'

'They couldn't afford the insurance,' said Cathy, distraught. 'Do you know how much the policies are these days? *Crippling.* And to hire a reviver outright, they charge the equivalent of decades of payments, and even then you don't get the best people. A fifty-fifty chance they'll succeed, and you pay the same either way, whether you get to say goodbye or not.'

Annabel shook her head. 'Don't you get it? Do you think Jonah's gone to all this trouble just for *privacy*? If people know he's not dead, it puts his *life* at risk. You can't ask him to do that. You *can't.*'

'I know,' said Cathy. 'I know you must have your reasons. I shouldn't have come. It's all been . . . it's been . . .' She shook her head, lost; then she turned and walked out.

Jonah was torn. He'd always had the same problem – he wanted to help, even if it was a bad idea. Saying no to someone in that kind of pain didn't sit well with him. He looked at Annabel. She shook her head, but it was a resigned shake.

'If you're going to do this,' she said, 'then you need to be careful. You do it exactly the way I tell you to, agreed?'

He thought about letting Cathy just leave. Even though he hardly knew her, he didn't think she was the kind of person who would abuse what she'd found out. He could refuse her request, if he chose to.

Like hell he could. He knew what it meant for that one

last chance to say goodbye to those you loved. He knew how important it was.

'Agreed,' he said.

*

He went after Cathy and told her what he'd decided. She was grateful, but it was with a degree of shame that she accepted his offer.

'I don't know what you'll think of me after this, Jonah,' she said. 'But I'll always hate myself a little for having asked.'

Jonah shook his head. 'Don't,' he said. 'You did the only thing you could.'

Annabel's conditions were simple enough: when the body was released to the parents, it would be brought to Cathy's home. Jonah's face couldn't be seen. The story had to be agreed up front, and Cathy would have to stick to it: that she had cashed in every favour she was owed, and had managed to get a private reviver to volunteer. No questions were to be asked about who or how. No recording would be made.

Jonah added further conditions. The parents would only be allowed into the room after the revival was successful, and would leave before he released the boy. Given that he didn't know the full extent of the injuries, he wasn't prepared to have it any other way. He would try for a vocal revival, that being one where the lungs and vocal cords are intact enough to allow speech. Revival was usually mishandled in movies, since live actors were necessarily playing the role of the corpse. In reality, the only controlled movement present in the body came from the chest, throat and voice box. Any other muscle activity was essentially random

– twitching, usually of smaller muscles such as the eyelids or cheek. The eyes rarely moved at all. The dead couldn't see, and they could only hear what the reviver said, nothing else.

Vocal revivals were the most compelling kind of evidence for court, and for private revivals they were also the preferred option, but in cases where the damage to the body was too great, either through injury or because of the time elapsed since death, then a non-vocal procedure was the only option. Only the reviver would hear the words of the subject, and would repeat them aloud, or use a one-handed stenography system to relay the words to those watching.

All Jonah knew about the boy's injuries was that he'd suffered damage to the chest. A vocal revival could still be possible, but the accompanying sounds might prove too distressing – liquid, muscle, bone, a creaking and gurgling that nobody would want to hear from the body of a loved one.

By keeping the parents out for the beginning, he could make sure that those kinds of things wouldn't be an issue.

*

The release of the boy's body required that no post-mortem was necessary and, further, that there was no pending request for a *forensic* revival. Both were officially ruled out by the next afternoon, and by early evening the body of Grady Reed was in the guest bedroom of his grandmother's house.

There was one other thing Jonah needed, though, and for that he'd had to ask Never to come round after work.

Annabel answered the door just before 7 p.m., and Never came in with a look of baffled irritation.

'Can I ask what the fuck?' said Never. 'Just, what the fuck?'

'Did you bring it?' said Annabel. Jonah was coming through from the kitchen and gave Never a sheepish wave.

'Of course I brought it,' said Never. 'Also: what the fuck?'

'Hand it over, then,' said Jonah.

'Here,' grumped Never. 'Standard field med pack.' He passed Jonah a small plastic box with medication. Revivers were prone to a variety of problems, ranging from nausea to a form of PTSD. Performing revivals on a regular basis took its toll. Jonah, with one of the shortest recovery times in the FRS, had been particularly at risk as he'd be able to perform more revivals in a given period. The medication they took in advance of a revival was proven to reduce the problems they were exposed to, but the dosage of each drug was controlled precisely. The med packs contained a wide range of doses of each medication that, in combination, allowed their own prescription to be adequately approximated.

Jonah snapped the protective tab on the med pack and looked at the various blister packs. 'I was on six hundred and thirty-seven micrograms of BPV,' he said. 'Can you make sure I add this up right, Never?'

'Yeah, yeah, give it here,' said Never, starting to pop out the pills Jonah would need. 'Five hundred. One twenty-five. Ten. Two. Easy.'

'The BPV was always the tricky one,' said Jonah. 'My anti-nausea is a standard dose.' He took the pills and headed to the kitchen for a drink to take them with, along with a couple of aspirin from the cupboard.

When he came back, Never was standing with his arms

folded. 'She won't tell me what's happening,' he said, nodding to Annabel. 'So out with it.'

Jonah explained.

'You are *such* a fucking boy scout, Jonah Miller,' said Never.

'Tell me about it,' said Annabel. 'But I wouldn't have him any other way, I guess.'

'Conceded,' said Never. 'Sorry to cut and run, but I'll let you two handle this one yourselves. Dead kids are not my idea of time off.' He turned to leave, but paused. 'Oh, I'm working the weekend, off Thursday and Friday. If you want a repeat of last time?'

'Maybe not quite a *repeat*,' said Annabel. 'You two overdid it by some margin.'

'*You* weren't exactly teetotal either, as I recall,' said Never.

'I reckon I'll need it,' said Jonah. 'But like she says, we'll try and cut it back, huh?'

'Hah!' said Never. 'Amateurs!' He put his hand on Jonah's shoulder, and his expression grew serious. 'Be careful,' he said, and off he went.

*

Jonah rang Cathy's landline to let her know he was coming soon. He'd typed up instructions for her – Annabel wasn't coming, either. Cathy would sit in the room with him and bring the parents inside. She would also have to abide by the lie Annabel had suggested. It wouldn't be an easy thing, lying to her own daughter on such a day of family torment, but she agreed without hesitation.

It was already dark when Jonah drove up and parked at

the entrance to Cathy's drive. He wore sunglasses and a hoodie, with the hood up. Cathy brought him in. Jonah saw a doorway ahead, open a crack, silent faces barely visible: Grady's parents, Sara and Armel. They had a daughter, too, a little older than Grady, but she was staying with friends. They'd not thought she was strong enough to deal with the revival.

Cathy brought Jonah to the room where Grady's body lay, and shut the door. Jonah took off his sunglasses, lowered his hood, and looked at the boy. The undertakers they'd used had been familiar with revivals, of course. They'd prepared his body with a minimum of disruption. He was laid out on a mid-level transportation trolley that was well-padded and large enough to seem like a small bed, once the sides were folded down. His little face was clean, with the slightest hint of make-up disguising some abrasions. His body was dressed in vaguely formal clothing, the kind of thing a kid would be made to wear to church – their finger constantly tugging at the collar, complaining of its tightness.

But these clothes were a facade, a one-piece that opened at the back and could be laid on top of the body without it being moved significantly, something that was crucial for revival. It was then tucked under the legs and arms and tightened to appear like shirt and jacket and trousers, creating an effective illusion.

Jonah handed his instructions to Cathy. 'Read this,' he said. 'I'm just going to check . . .' *The condition of the lungs, the ribs* . . . Not appropriate to say. Not for his grandma. 'I'm just going to check him, and see how we should progress.'

Cathy nodded. She turned away and started to read.

With care, Jonah undid the Velcro tabs at the neck and

shoulders of the one-piece and folded it back. Beneath it, the undertakers had placed a layer of waterproof padding. Jonah peeled it away from the skin.

The mark of the impact was obvious, across the left side of his chest, but the skin wasn't broken. He felt the ribs, and all were intact. The hospital report had been provided; no intrusive measures had been made in the attempt to save him. As Cathy had said, his heart had given out unexpectedly. It had happened a few hours after staff had stabilized him, with an expectation that he would make a good recovery.

A vocal revival would be straightforward.

He replaced the padding, then the one-piece, making sure it looked exactly as it should. He looked up to Cathy. She'd finished reading, and had been watching him work.

'You've read everything?' said Jonah.

She nodded. 'You'll attempt revival, and if you're successful, you'll indicate for me to bring Sara and Armel in. We should keep it short, and as soon as you think we're done you make it clear to me.'

'Yes,' said Jonah. 'People think the longer the better, but younger children get impatient. They can become upset, or even *bored*. That can be hard for the parents to deal with. As soon as I sense him going that way, we'll bring it to a close.'

'OK. Then I show them out, and you'll . . . finish.'

Jonah nodded. He pulled up his hood and got his seat ready. The room was brightly lit, and Cathy had positioned more subtle lighting around for the revival. 'Let's try it with the main light out,' said Jonah. She switched it off, and the lower light level seemed fine. 'I'm going to start, if you're ready?'

Cathy nodded.

Jonah took Grady's hand in his, then let out a long breath. The hand was so small. He thought back to some of the revivals he'd done in the past, those rare few where a child so young was treated as a witness. Those cases had been difficult, to say the least. Now, with Grady, he didn't have any of the fear he'd had then. This was to let the boy say goodbye.

He closed his eyes and readied himself for the first stage of the process, the part known as the *reversal*. Reaching out, finding the subject; sinking into the sensation of death that pervaded the corpse, allowing that coldness to fill him. When that was done, he focused, and Grady's injuries gradually reversed in his mind. He was aware of every contusion, every *scrape*, even the pinprick needle entry points of the lines the ER staff had put in the boy.

Jonah waited, focusing, as Grady's body became – in Jonah's mind – restored to the way it had been before death. The moment he reached that point, the second stage came.

The *surge*.

It was an unpredictable thing. The difficulty of the reversal was something you could tell just by looking at the state of the body. The worse the injury, the more time since death, and the harder it would be, the longer it would take.

The surge could be anything. At its best it could be a gentle sense of connection, going almost unnoticed. Jonah's first revival had been of his own mother, an accidental revival he wasn't even aware was happening until she'd taken that sudden gasping breath.

The worst surges were overwhelming. Memories of the subject, pouring into his mind; an avalanche of experience, images, emotions, battering him until he was ready to scream and give up, potentially rendering the whole revival a failure if he was to let go of the hand.

He tensed as the surge took him. It was intense, but manageable – he knew at once that he could ride it out. Jonah suddenly knew what his parents looked like. He knew what toys Grady preferred, what TV shows, what games. The boy felt like family, and with that his death hit harder.

He opened his eyes and watched Grady's chest. The essence of the boy was gathering itself. Jonah caught Cathy's eye, and nodded.

Grady took a breath. It was loud and uneven, and it sounded almost like he was choking, such was the struggle to take in that first lungful of air. Subsequent breaths – only needed when speech had emptied the lungs – would be quieter, less conspicuous.

Cathy was staring at her grandson, and Jonah could tell that this was the first time she'd seen a revival. He'd not even asked her that basic question, and he scolded himself for it.

'Grady?' he said. 'My name is Jonah.'

'Hi, Jonah,' said the boy's corpse. The voice came out as a harsh whisper. Jonah glanced at Cathy and could see unease there. It would fade, both as she accepted what was happening, and as Grady's voice softened.

'Do you know what happened to you?'

A few seconds passed before Grady answered. 'I guess I died,' he said. More often than not, children were almost matter-of-fact about their own death. Some thought this was because they didn't really understand the implications, but Jonah didn't agree. They just seemed more accepting of it. It made things difficult when a revival subject was in denial, but kids rarely were.

'That's right. I'm a reviver, Grady. Do you know what that means?'

With his lungs depleted, the boy didn't reply immediately. He took another breath, and it was already much less distressing than the first one. 'You'll let me say things, even though I'm dead.'

'Right again, Grady. You know your stuff. Can you tell me, do you remember what happened to you?' It would be unpleasant for Cathy, he knew, but he needed to get it out of the way. If he didn't get Grady to talk about it now, it could interrupt the boy's flow of thought later, and possibly make the revival stutter.

Grady's chest rose again; another breath. 'I think I ran into the road. Dad always told me to be careful, but I dropped my rubber ball and it bounced and I went to get it. Is the ball OK?'

'It's fine,' said Jonah. An outsider might think Grady's question was the kind of ridiculous thing only a child would ask, but adults did it all the time. They'd be worried if their car was damaged, say, or if their sneakers got dirty. 'Your grandmother's here, Grady. She's going to bring your mom and dad in, if that's OK?'

'Sure,' said the boy. Jonah nodded to Cathy, and made sure he was facing away from where the parents would be standing.

'Are they here yet?' said Grady, eager.

The door closed again, and Jonah could hear the shuffle of feet, and the sniffing. He felt a near-unbearable stab of empathy for Grady's parents.

'They're here, Grady. Do you want to say something to them? They can hear you, OK? You won't be able to hear them, but I'll tell you what they say.'

'OK. I'm sorry, Mom. I'm sorry I got killed.'

It prompted a gasp from his mother, and she immediately covered her face. 'I love you, Grady,' she said, in a rush of emotion.

'I love you,' said his father, hardly able to speak.

Jonah relayed it, his voice almost silent. Grady would still hear him loud and clear.

'I love you too!' said Grady. 'Is Remy here?'

His mother paused. 'Your sister couldn't come,' she said. 'She's just too upset. She loves you so much.'

'I love her too,' said Grady. 'Tell her it's OK. And don't forget to feed Chipotle!'

Jonah had a sudden memory: the odour of pine shavings, and the feel of a small fluffy animal. *Grady's hamster*, he thought.

'We'll look after him, baby,' said his mother. She was struggling to speak through her tears. 'And we'll tell Remy. We're going to miss you, honey. We're going to miss you *so much*.'

'You don't have to worry about me,' said Grady, after a breath. 'I'll be fine. Grandma, do you know if I get to meet Grandpa in heaven?'

'I don't think it would be much of a heaven if you didn't, now would it?' said Cathy.

It was nearly time, Jonah knew. There was only so much needed to be said; with adults and older kids, a private revival quickly became a time to reminisce, but with the youngest children that didn't happen for long. A parent saying 'Do you remember when . . .' would likely be met with a 'Not really' followed by a random question about ice cream.

That was just how kids were at that age.

He let them say how much they loved each other a few more times, in a few different ways, and then sent the parents and Cathy off. It seemed like such a small thing, to tell someone you loved them one last time. But it was everything.

The door shut.

'Do you know what it's like where I'm going?' said the boy.

'I don't know that, Grady.'

'I'm not scared. Is that strange?'

'No,' said Jonah. 'It's normal. I think that means there's nothing to be scared of.' He paused before saying it: 'It's time for you to go, Grady. Are you ready?'

Grady paused, taking a breath. Then he said: 'There's someone coming.'

'Who's coming?' said Jonah, suddenly wary.

'Someone for you.'

Jonah felt a flush of terror. 'For me?'

'You don't have to be scared, remember?'

Even though Jonah felt terrified, Grady wasn't frightened at all. 'I don't?' said Jonah.

It was a few more seconds before Grady took another breath; Jonah didn't breathe in those seconds either.

'Of course not!' said the boy. 'I think they got lost. Here, look!'

And suddenly, Jonah wasn't in the room any more.

*

He was standing, and Grady was standing beside him. The boy was wearing a little pair of jeans and a Pokémon T-shirt, and was holding his hand, smiling up at him.

'Where are we?' said Jonah, bewildered. Wherever it was, it was featureless. He couldn't even put a colour to their surroundings – it seemed to be every colour, and none.

'You don't know?' said Grady.

Jonah shook his head. 'This is new to me.'

Grady nodded a direction, and Jonah looked.

There she was. *Tess*. Sitting cross-legged, looking up to the sky above. She seemed dazed, unaware of their presence.

'Tess?' said Jonah. 'It's me. It's Jonah.'

He and Grady walked closer. Tess was whispering, and Jonah moved nearer and nearer until he could make it out.

Pandora, she was saying. Rapidly repeated, just that one word. She really wasn't aware of anyone else around her. Jonah passed his free hand in front of her staring eyes, and they didn't flicker.

'Is she OK?' said Grady. 'Does she not know where to go?'

Jonah had no answer. He looked around again, but the calmness of the boy eased the fear he was feeling.

'It's OK, miss,' said Grady. With his free hand, the boy took hold of Tess's. He looked at Jonah. 'Thanks for letting me talk to my mom and dad,' he said. 'I'll take it from here.' He let go of Jonah's hand and gave him a playful salute, smiling.

Jonah smiled back. 'Thank *you*,' he said, and the next time he blinked, he opened his eyes in Cathy's house again. He was still holding Grady's hand, but the boy had gone.

He stood and placed Grady's arm back by his side, looking at the boy's face for a few seconds, wondering what the hell had just happened. He'd been doing this for the best part of a decade, and nothing like this had ever happened to him before.

Once, he thought. *Maybe once.*

There was a knock at the door. 'Yes,' he said, and Cathy entered.

She looked overwhelmed. She nodded. 'I *think* that went OK,' she said. 'It was . . . strange. But I think Sara and Armel . . .' She shook her head.

'It'll help,' said Jonah. 'Trust me.'

'Thanks, Jonah,' she said. 'And again, I'm sorry. Asking you for this was unforgivable, no matter *what* you say.'

He smiled at her. 'Cathy, for the last year I've been no use to anyone. Tonight, I could help. So I did.'

As she showed him out, they both looked up. Barely visible in the dark sky was a slowly shifting green glow.

Aurora. Northern Lights.

'Jesus,' said Cathy. 'There must be some pretty significant solar activity for it to be at this low latitude. Got to be some kind of record. Green Bank will be grumbling, I guarantee you that. Too much interference.' She had a tissue in her hand, and wiped away tears.

'It's not something I've ever seen before,' said Jonah. On any other day, he imagined he would've been thrilled by the sight. Instead, it left him cold.

'I've seen an aurora plenty of times before,' said Cathy. 'They always looked miraculous. Not today.' She shook her head. 'Not with Grady gone. That just looks like the sky is sick.'

And Jonah realized that was part of why he felt wary of

what he was seeing. There was something about the shade of green that felt wrong, somehow.

He also realized the other reason for his wariness.

Tess had also been looking up to the sky, hadn't she? Looking up, and saying the same thing over and over again.

Pandora.

7

'How did it go?' asked Annabel when he came through the door.

'I think it was good,' said Jonah. 'It's not exactly a cure-all, but in the days and weeks ahead the kid's mom and dad will have one layer of regret taken away from them. They'll still endlessly go over how he died, what they could have done. All the last-minute changes to their day that would've meant they were somewhere else and none of it could have happened . . .' He sighed. 'That kind of shit. All the what-ifs will still haunt them, but they got to say goodbye.'

'How was the boy? *Grady*, wasn't it?'

'Yeah, Grady,' said Jonah. He thought of Tess, and what she'd said in his . . . What the hell was it? A dream? A vision? Annabel was watching him anxiously as he paused. 'He was strong,' he said. He put his hand to his head, feigning discomfort.

'You should lie down,' said Annabel.

'I will. Hey, did you look outside?'

She shook her head. 'Should I have?'

'There's an aurora in the sky.'

'What, Northern Lights?'

'Yeah. Faint, but there. Cathy reckoned it was some kind of record.'

Annabel went outside, and after a minute came back in with a smile. 'I'd always planned on taking a trip to see that. Just didn't get around to it.' She headed to the kitchen and turned on the TV. The news had nothing about it, although the picture was noticeably unstable, dropping out to black now and again, and Jonah remembered that Cathy had mentioned interference. Eventually, the story was picked up. Shots of the aurora came on, but they were unimpressively dim. 'They've not had time to do it justice,' said Annabel. She caught the look on Jonah's face. 'What's up?'

Jonah shook his head. He was still thinking about Tess, but the aurora had thrown him too. 'It feels like an omen,' he said. The TV picture dropped out again for a moment, and that didn't help. When it came back up, a female scientist was answering the anchor's questions about the aurora.

'. . . large solar flare that had been predicted, with an accompanying coronal mass ejection,' she said. 'In the past this could cause blackouts and communications problems, and even pose a risk to satellites, but we've had the ability to get advance warning of X-class flares for two decades now, and that early warning means we can cope with most of the issues that can occur. Satellites can be put into safety modes that protect their circuitry, for example. These things happen far more regularly than you might think.'

'You say these things happen regularly, so why has the aurora been so widespread?' said the anchor.

The scientist nodded. 'Chance plays its part, too. There's natural variation in Earth's magnetosphere and ionosphere, and an aurora can be brighter or dimmer depending on more than just the solar output.'

The anchor looked vaguely bemused by the answer. 'So in summary?'

'It's been a perfect storm of circumstances,' said the scientist.

The anchor nodded. 'A perfect *solar* storm, you could say!'

The scientist gave a pained smile. 'Indeed.'

*

Jonah made excuses about wanting some time to himself after the revival.

'You want me to make you a coffee or something?' asked Annabel, concerned.

'I'll grab a beer,' said Jonah. He grabbed four, and headed to a little office room he'd nabbed as part of his personal space when they'd moved in. He booted up his PC.

He thought about the place where he'd been with Grady – that curious region of nothingness, no colour, no *floor*, really, thinking back to it. It hadn't seemed like a dream, he knew that much. Afterwards, it was easy to dismiss it as imagined, but he didn't think that was true. Grady had been there with him, and it seemed reasonable to assume that Tess – or some part of her – had been present as well.

How was another question entirely. He'd been with Tess when she died. No attempt had been made at a revival. Even while alive she'd been unable to reveal much information from the entity she carried inside her, and there was no reason to think a revival would change that. Kendrick hadn't even *suggested* reviving her, though, and he wasn't the kind of man to let a chance at information slip by.

Jonah thought he understood. When the *Beast* was imprisoned, they stripped its power and locked it away somehow. The whole point of Winnerden Flats was to find a way to access that power, but all they had managed to do was open the door a crack. That process had involved Tess, but it had been interrupted before it could be completed.

Who knew *what* reviving Tess could have done? Opened the floodgates, perhaps. Without a compelling reason to do it, the risk was unacceptable.

Jonah could hear the voice of Andreas, the Beast speaking through him in Winnerden Flats, taunting: *The door is open now, Jonah. It will not shut . . . And I'm patient. Don't doubt me. Don't doubt that you'll watch all your friends perish, one by one.*

Those words had been foremost in Jonah's mind when he'd asked Kendrick to find a way for him to disappear.

He thought of Tess in that strange place, as Grady held his hand. She'd been looking up, and when he'd seen the aurora later, he'd thought it was too much of a coincidence.

He did the obvious thing: he googled 'Pandora'. A moon of Saturn. The home world of the *Avatar* movies. A few dozen businesses.

He'd half expected to find a link to one of the many companies of Michael Andreas, but nothing showed up. Eventually, he read about the most famous Pandora of them all.

The myth of Pandora's box.

He read the Wikipedia entry, knowing it was irrelevant

but happy for the distraction. It was intriguing, too, how little he really knew about it.

The Greeks had it that mankind really did start off as *man*-kind, an entirely male society living in perpetual bliss with no shortage of food and no need to work. When Prometheus stole fire from the gods and gave it to men, Zeus decided to punish the mortals by creating the first woman: Pandora, with 'a shameless mind and a deceitful nature'. Jonah couldn't help but smile at what Annabel would make of that – *shameless* was certainly an appropriate word for the tale as a whole.

Zeus gave Pandora a jar containing mysterious gifts, which turned out to be all the diseases and evils in the land and the sea.

The story Jonah had known as a child involved the infamous box, which Pandora was told not to open but then found too tempting. The original myth referred to a large jar, which Pandora opened the moment she arrived in the world of men, releasing all the evils to plague mankind for evermore.

In both versions, after the evils had been released, the only thing left in Pandora's box was *hope*.

What surprised him was that the meaning of the story, the moral, wasn't clear-cut. He'd always assumed that hope being left in the box was supposed to be a good thing – hope had remained to help humanity deal with the trials and tribulations that the evils of disease and toil had brought them.

It turned out to be much less straightforward.

Some scholars thought that the *hope* remained locked in the jar and was thus withheld from mortals. It was a nasty twist to the tale that all the evils were freed but hope itself was denied. He could understand why that wasn't the version taught to kids, as it was frankly miserable.

Then he read something that made him pause.

The argument about hope, and whether it was gifted to mortals or denied them, was rephrased by one author as the question of whether the jar itself was a *prison*. The author had used one phrase that jumped out at Jonah: *a prison for the dark things of all creation.*

A prison for the dark things.

Was it that simple? Was that why Tess had been saying it?

The Beast had been imprisoned, and Tess was one of those who had opened the prison. Whatever it was that Jonah had encountered during Grady's revival, a piece of Tess perhaps, or something that he himself had projected, *Pandora* was surely just a cry of despair. Tess had put herself in that role, as someone who had unleashed evil on the world.

He read everything he could find about Pandora, but came across nothing else that struck him as important.

He did think Annabel would find it amusing to hear about the myths, though, and their ingrained misogyny – the perfect world of men, ruined by vindictive women. Still, it was hardly restricted to the Greeks. The myth of Adam and Eve had plenty of parallels – the first woman causing trouble again. And although Eve was created as a companion rather than as some cruel and unusual punishment, she still took the blame for the end of the easy life: the eviction from Eden.

Jonah sat back from the monitor and glugged a beer.

The real mystery he needed to think about wasn't the word *Pandora*. Instead, the biggest question was what had made the revival of Grady so different? No revival he'd ever heard of had involved that kind of illusion of being in a different location. The *reversal* process sometimes had an element of it, certainly, and the reviver's surroundings receded while that first stage happened, but to feel fully and convincingly *elsewhere* wasn't a phenomenon he'd ever come across.

Except once. It hadn't been in a revival, though. It had been as he lay unconscious, shot in the chest and fighting for his life. He'd met Annabel's dead father, and he'd met his own mother, but ever since then he'd assumed the experience had been purely imaginary.

Perhaps it was more real than he thought.

*

He slept on it, but the next morning he was still thinking about his encounter with Tess. Annabel seemed to assume his distraction was entirely down to the revival, and Jonah wasn't keen to correct her. She had another meeting to get to, relating to a scandal brewing at one of the major for-profit hospital companies. It was a story she'd tried explaining to Jonah before, but it was one of those depressing ones where the sums involved were huge but the details were hard to follow, and hence tricky to get people to give a damn about.

A quarter of an hour after Annabel left, the doorbell rang. When he checked the door camera, Jonah wasn't surprised to see Cathy.

'Did you wait until Annabel left?' he said, smiling.

'Was it obvious?'

'Completely.'

She winced. 'I wasn't sure if she'd ever want to speak to me again, given what I did.'

'I don't think she'll hold it against you. Not for long, at any rate.' He gestured for her to come in. 'Can I get you a coffee?'

'Please,' she said, following him into the kitchen. 'I came to thank you, again, but I guess I also wanted to get out of the house. I spent all night trying to distract myself, but Sara and Armel are finalizing things with the funeral home for the service tomorrow. I started to feel odd being alone with Grady's body in the house.'

'There's no need to feel odd,' he said. He pointed to the coffee machine, putting a cup under the nozzle. 'Take your pick.'

'Thanks,' she said, pushing the button for a latte. 'Oh, I don't feel odd because of the revival. It's just the weight of it . . . Difficult days ahead, I guess. Difficult weeks. Every time I walk past the door, knowing his body's on the other side of it, it hits me hard. There are only so many tears before you feel emptied out.'

'How are his parents doing?' he said. 'I hope the revival helped them. I know it *will*, over time, but sometimes it can be too much for people at first.'

'They've been quiet, as you'd expect. Armel especially. He's an only child and both his parents are gone, and I think he's trying to hold it all together for the sake of me and Sara. He's got nobody else to unload on, so he's bottling it all up.'

Jonah nodded. He got himself a black coffee, no sugar. The bitterness suited his mood. After a few moments of silence, he said: 'Cathy, have you heard anything about last night's aurora?'

'Ah,' she said. 'I mentioned I was trying to distract my-self, and you got me. I was seeing what I could find out. There's been some chatter about the solar flare that triggered it. Well, triggered the geomagnetic superstorm, which then caused the aurora.'

'Chatter?'

'The low latitudes don't make sense. The coronal mass ejection that accompanied the flare wasn't anywhere near as powerful as it would need to be to trigger a superstorm like that.' She sipped some coffee. 'So naturally everyone's buzzing. One thing a scientist loves is stuff not making sense. Means there's something interesting happening!'

Jonah felt nervous. 'What *kind* of something?'

Cathy shrugged. 'I don't know that much about aurorae, I'll admit, but normally solar wind doesn't reach Earth's inner magnetosphere easily. A geomagnetic storm needs some kind of *door* to open; a "magnetic reconnection" is the term I've heard, but I don't know much about the details. Some are saying that the conditions weren't there for that to happen, so it's a mystery.'

He'd been bringing his cup up to his mouth as she spoke, and found himself freezing with the cup halfway. Something she'd said had shaken him, but he dismissed it; a stupid thought.

'It's not *that* well understood,' continued Cathy. 'Hence the arguments. How can someone say the flare wasn't strong enough, if we don't know much about the processes involved? Still, one thing's for sure: it's unprecedented. Whatever this is, it hasn't happened before, at least in the last few thousand years. People can sniff funding.'

'The news reports last night talked about communication disruption being unlikely. Is that true?'

She shook her head. 'Actually, the radio interference it generated has been unexpectedly wide-ranging, and long-lived. Trust me, the people I talk to online are *very* annoyed about it. Radio astronomers across the globe are twiddling their thumbs as we speak. Long-range radio is something I listen in to sometimes, to relax. Living here means lower-powered signals are less likely to be swamped by local noise. Last night I couldn't pick up shit. Solar activity is still high, so there could be more flares. We didn't get a full hit from the last one, either.'

She finished her coffee and headed to the door. 'I'd better get back,' she said, dejected. 'Thank you, Jonah. Talking about anything other than the obvious is exactly what I needed.'

'Any time,' he said, letting her out. 'Good luck with the service tomorrow.'

He let out a long breath when she was gone. When he'd frozen, it had been because of the words she'd chosen: *a geomagnetic storm needs some kind of door to open.*

Some kind of *door.*

However tenuous the link, the coincidence was chilling. On the same night, an unprecedented revival; an unprecedented aurora.

And the words of the Beast came to him again.

The door is open now, Jonah. It will not shut.

8

He didn't sleep well that night. He told Annabel that the boy's revival was responsible, and that it was nothing serious – the act of performing a revival after so long a break had just shaken him a little.

'Nothing to worry about,' he told her.

Tuesday's aurora was still making the news. Fringe theorists were picking up on the aspect that Cathy had mentioned, that the solar flare had been much too weak to create the observed aurora. On every news channel, experts in atmospheric physics were being interviewed and showing their excitement at the prospect of a good scientific mystery, but all too often the reporting would then cut to those with bizarre ideas to explain the mystery, ideas that ranged from government conspiracy to the Book of Revelation.

The irony didn't escape him, though. His own theory, the one that had been forming for the last few days, was surely the very definition of *fringe*. Cathy's mention of a *door* being opened was just unfortunate phrasing, but a door *had* been open. Ever since Winnerden Flats.

What had been missing was the *vessel* for the Beast's power to flow into.

It was Thursday, and Never had promised to come over for some more drunken pool. Jonah really didn't feel like it, and considered putting him off by citing Grady's revival as an excuse, but that kind of thing would guarantee that Never *would* come. All Jonah could do was hope that something else came up. He didn't relish having to spend the night putting on a social mask and acting as if nothing was wrong. At the very least, he couldn't risk drinking anything. If he did, he'd spill his guts at the drop of a hat, as always.

*

'Greetings, stranger,' said Never when Jonah opened the door that evening. 'How's tricks?' He had a mini cask of beer with him. 'I bear gifts. Well, *gift.*'

Jonah smiled in spite of himself. 'Come in,' he said. 'It went fine, by the way. Just to get that dealt with.'

'Good,' said Never. 'I wasn't going to ask.'

'Like hell you weren't,' said Jonah. In the kitchen, he fetched glasses while Never opened the cask.

'Naturally. So, when you say fine, you mean . . . ?'

'It was emotionally draining but positive.'

'Where's the missus?' said Never, as they flopped onto the couches with their drinks.

'Saving the world from dubious medical accounting,' said Jonah. 'She's on her way back.'

'Cool,' said Never. He downed some beer. 'I look forward to failing at pool again. Oh, another flare is predicted for tomorrow. You see that?'

'No,' said Jonah.

'I heard it on the radio on the way here. Could be a big one. NASA's Solar Dynamics project gives it a sixty per cent chance of being the biggest in a decade, if it hits us full on. CNN did a survey to see how people felt about it, and you know what the biggest concern was?'

Jonah shook his head.

'The impact on access to social media,' laughed Never. 'Seriously. That's, like, the *least* worrying thing that could happen. Second was whether cellphone service would be affected, which, actually, is more of a likely problem. I think fifth was the world being burnt to a cinder. Tenth and last was satellites failing, and that one's the most likely by far.'

'Priorities!' said Jonah.

'Actually, I think there *was* an impact,' said Never. 'An impact on revivals.'

Wary, Jonah looked at him. 'What?'

'The ENFRI posted up some figures,' said Never. The ENFRI was the French equivalent of the FRS. 'From late Tuesday night, success rates took a tumble. The call went out for other groups to check their own stats. I mean, these are the kinds of blips we all see locally from time to time, just chance effects, so it's only when you gather up nation-wide figures that anything will show up, but . . .' He paused.

'OK, tell me.'

'I rang round to get some FRS figures. Comparing esti-mated chances of success to actual outcome is usually within five per cent, on average. The FRS success rates on Tuesday were thirty per cent lower than the estimates. Yesterday, it was back to normal. Interesting, right?'

The last thing Jonah wanted to hear about was another link between revival and the aurora. 'Sure,' he said.

'Oh, come on!' said Never. 'There hasn't been anything

interesting in revival research for years, and all you can say is "sure"?'

Jonah sighed. 'The last big revival research effort was at Winnerden Flats, Never. Let's just say I'm not *that* keen on anyone starting up another one.'

With a grimace, Never nodded. He absently rubbed at his chest. 'Fair point.'

'Uh . . .' said Jonah. 'Was there anything else odd at work?'

'Like?'

'I don't know. Anything strange being reported by revivers, during cases?'

'Nothing I heard,' said Never. 'I'm in on Saturday so I'll ask around. Do I get any clues as to what I'm asking around *for*?'

Jonah shook his head vaguely. 'The revival with the little boy on Tuesday . . . it ended strangely. I kind of hallu-cinated. I had an image of Tess.' He shrugged. 'That was all.'

'Mmm,' said Never, looking deeply suspicious. 'That was *all*. OK.'

On the wall of every room was a small security panel; on the one near the TV, a light went red. Having spent the first few months living here with everything still seeming like a threat, Jonah saw it at once – it meant that a vehicle was coming along the drive.

'Annabel's home,' he said, getting up.

'I'll keep drinking,' said Never. 'Bring some grub on your way back?'

Jonah was at the door ready for her.

'Hey,' she said.

'Evening. Never's here already.'

'Why am I not surprised?'

Then the hairs stood up on Jonah's neck. In the distance, he could see another vehicle coming towards them. A black van, it looked like.

'Get inside,' he said to Annabel, urgently.

'What?' she said, turning. She saw it too. 'Shit.' She hurried in. Jonah went to the security panel nearest the door and pressed a button.

Lockdown.

The main focus of the alterations that had been made by the previous owner – all that concrete and cinderblock – had been to turn the building into something where every entrance could be secured. Slowly, metal shutters wound down on the windows and doors.

The cacophony brought Never to them. 'What's happening?'

'We have a visitor,' said Annabel. She pointed to the screen near the door, showing the camera feed from outside. The black van pulled up behind Annabel's car.

'Oh,' said Never, anxious. 'It's definitely not FedEx.'

The van door opened. Out stepped Sly, and the three of them relaxed.

'Yay!' said Never. Then he frowned. 'Sly turning up out of the blue. Good or bad, do you think?'

'Bad,' said Annabel. Jonah nodded.

Sly was at the door shutters. She knocked.

Jonah pressed the intercom. 'Password,' he said. They may have dispensed with most of Kendrick's precautions by now, but it was probably better not to let Sly know that. Whatever she said next would indicate whether she was under duress or not.

'Fuck off,' said Sly. All clear. Jonah started to raise the shutters, wondering why they'd let Never pick the responses.

With the shutters raised, he opened the door.

'You two gentlemen with me,' said Sly, turning and walking back to the van.

'Is a hello out of the question?' mumbled Never, following.

As Jonah moved, Annabel put a hand on his arm. 'Be careful,' she said. 'Something's wrong.'

Jonah nodded. He could feel it, too – Sly coming here unannounced was concerning enough, but there was something in the way she'd spoken that didn't sit right.

She'd seemed *shaken*.

She and Never were now at the rear of the van, its doors wide open. Both were silent as Jonah reached them. He followed the line of their gaze, and saw it.

In the back of the van was a body bag.

Jonah felt his blood boil. He'd told Kendrick many times that this was a line he'd not cross – interrogating corpses that Kendrick needed information from.

'I told Kendrick I wouldn't do this kind of thing for him,' he said. 'He agreed.'

Sly gave him an unusually cold look. 'Take it up with Kendrick,' she said. 'He's the one in the bag.'

*

They set the bag down on the hallway floor and went through to the kitchen.

'Get me something to drink,' Sly said to Never. He filled a glass of water and put it in front of her, getting a severe glare in response. That wasn't the kind of drink she'd meant.

'Drink it,' he said. 'You need to. I'll be back in a second.'

Sly sagged visibly and picked up the glass, downing the contents without a pause. By the time she was done Never was back, a bottle of vodka in hand. He passed it to her, and she poured out a third of a glass.

She sat, taking long deep breaths.

Jonah, Annabel and Never waited, glancing to each other. Jonah also kept glancing to the door that led to the hall, where Kendrick's body was. The FRS had plenty of rules, and one of them was as obvious as they came: you didn't revive a subject you had a connection to. Part of the reason was to remove any possibility of bias from the resulting court evidence, but private revival firms had the same rule. It just wasn't a good idea.

Almost three years before, Sam Deering had been stabbed. It had been touch and go for a time, and Jonah had stayed in the hospital overnight waiting for news. Sam's wife Helen had been there too, of course, and at one point she'd spoken to Jonah about the possibility of Sam dying.

Sam had revival insurance, she'd explained, but they'd not been able to afford the *best*; the chance of failure was high. She'd asked Jonah the question that he'd been fearing since the moment she'd started talking to him.

Promise me, she'd said. *If it comes to it. Let us say goodbye.*

Just the *thought* of it had sent Jonah into turmoil. Sam had pulled through, thank God, but even with everything that had happened afterwards – all the horrors he had faced – Jonah still found himself waking some nights with that moment being replayed in his nightmares.

He'd not known Kendrick anywhere near as well as Sam,

of course, but he'd come to respect the man more than he'd ever thought possible. His heart was already racing, thinking of what Sly had – surely – brought his corpse here for.

Finally, Sly spoke. 'He didn't tell me what he was doing,' she said. She talked with a slow, precise voice that suggested she was struggling to keep calm. 'He didn't always, though. Sometimes he followed hunches at short notice, and he knew I hated that. It was too cavalier, and he'd taught me that *cavalier* was dangerous. But he'd set up what we call an *overdue*. A message you have to cancel once you're done and safe, or else it gets sent, and the person who gets it knows something went bad.' She took a punishing gulp of the vodka. 'I got his overdue. He'd gone to a place out in Arkansas, to see a source he'd mentioned to me but not given me much detail about. The overdue had the location and the name, a man called Virgil Drayton. I called a contact I have in the State Police, to see what he knew about Drayton. Rich guy, it turned out. Reclusive.' She had another drink and met Jonah's eyes. 'Died in a fire three days before. I met my contact at the site yesterday. The recluse lived in a decaying mansion with one servant. Both men were found dead in the burnt-out building. The servant was in the hallway near the source of the blaze. Drayton was in the basement, tied to a chair.'

Jonah saw Annabel's eyes widen, her face paling. Her own father had been found tied to a chair, dead for weeks.

'The building was unsound,' said Sly. 'A full search was delayed. Forensics concentrated on the areas around the two bodies. Both men died from smoke asphyxiation. The servant was set to inherit a decent amount of money. The working hypothesis was that he'd tried to engineer his boss's death, but had screwed it up. When I got there, I could tell the fire was Kendrick's doing. But there was still no sign of him. So I went looking. In the basement, the ceiling had collapsed. This basement was stone-built, and should have been solid as anything, so with it compromised they knew at once how unstable the building must be. They'd not searched beyond the collapse of that ceiling yet, too risky. In I went. Place nearly came down around me, I think, but at the end of what remained of a long corridor I found a set of rooms, piled high with charred filing boxes, and on the floor—' She stopped talking, and looked to the hall. To the body bag. She took a drink. 'I have no idea what the chances of revival are, Jonah. I didn't have another option.'

'I thought you had access to other revivers,' said Jonah.

Sly shook her head. 'Maybe he gave you that impression, but no. He knew you didn't want to do any revival interrogations, but if you'd known he had no others to go to, you might have felt obliged.'

'I didn't think he gave a damn,' said Jonah.

Sly raised an eyebrow. 'When he got to know people, he did,' she said. 'Besides, if you'd been willing, then *he* would have had the option too, right? To take it to the next step.'

Jonah frowned. 'Kill someone just to interrogate them.'

'Exactly. I don't think he wanted to go there again, if he could avoid it.' She finished her vodka and thumped the glass down on the table. 'Well?' she said. 'Are we going to do this?'

Jonah closed his eyes and nodded.

9

Jonah and Never carried the bag down to the lower basement, and cleared a space on a table by the wall. If Jonah
decided to go ahead with the revival, the body would be at a
good height there for what could prove to be a very long
process. He still had what was left of the standard med pack
he used with Grady; the wide range of pill strengths meant
that there was just enough left to meet his dose, although
again he got Never to work it out for him.

'I assume we want this to be recorded?' said Never.

'Yes,' said Sly.

'OK.' He turned to Annabel. 'You got any stands? Cameras?'

'One camera and a tripod,' said Annabel.

'Fetch them,' said Never. 'Power lead too.'

Annabel nodded and went off to get the equipment.

Jonah gritted his teeth and unzipped the body bag. The
smell hit first, of course – the stale smoke, undercut with the
unmistakable odour of spilled blood, and meat gone bad.

'Fuck,' said Never.

What they needed from Kendrick was information, so
Jonah had already been planning to attempt a non-vocal

revival – with no requirement for *evidence* as such, non-vocal would allow a faster flow to the revival even with Jonah repeating aloud everything that Kendrick said.

Looking at Kendrick's body, though, it was clear that a vocal revival would have been impossible anyway.

Kendrick's throat had been torn out.

The wound was ragged and brutal. His torso had suffered badly too, pierced and ripped around the ribcage, clothing tattered. Some of the ribs were probably broken, Jonah thought. There were deep lacerations to the abdomen. Adipose tissue and part of the lower intestine protruded in several places, worsened by the body having been transported.

There were signs of the fire, too; that was the most concerning part, as far as revival odds went. Cooked bodies didn't stand a chance.

'I know burns are bad news,' said Sly. 'The rest of it doesn't help.'

'It depends how deep the fire damage is,' said Jonah. He looked at Never and pointed to a box at the back of the room. 'There are medical supplies in there, should be some latex gloves. Throw me a pair, would you? And scissors.'

After a brief hunt, Never came back and Jonah put the gloves on. For the revival – if a revival proved possible – he would have to have direct skin contact with Kendrick's corpse, usually by taking the hand.

He began his examination.

The man's face had suffered from fire damage, certainly. The left eyelid had retracted unevenly, and there was blackening around that side of the face, but the eyeball itself was intact. Jonah reached out and palpated the orb. It still had some give, and the iris and pupil were clearly visible. The cornea would have been opaque if significant heat damage had penetrated. A corpse's hair was a good indicator of where flash-heat had reached, and the hair on the right-hand side of Kendrick's head showed little sign of it.

The clothes were singed in multiple places, probably where burning debris had fallen.

'Was he covered by anything when you found him?' asked Jonah.

'There was charred paper mainly,' said Sly. 'Boxes of documents had tipped onto him. Stonework and a burnt piece of timber were over his legs. I cleared it myself.'

Jonah nodded. 'How established do you think the fire in the basement got?'

'The collapse wasn't under the main fire in the house, but the basement held so much paper it was inevitable some of it would go up.'

'Paper can be good and bad,' said Jonah. 'Thick stacks of it tend to smoulder rather than flare, especially if the throughput of oxygen is restricted.'

'The *heat* was severe, though,' said Sly. 'I could tell from the surrounding area.'

'Paper can also insulate. That may be why the flesh isn't as badly scorched as you might have feared.'

Annabel returned with a plastic bag and unloaded a handful of cables, a tripod and a camera. She started to set them up; Never stepped over to help.

Thus far, Jonah hadn't highlighted any of Kendrick's more gruesome injuries. Now that he was satisfied that the heat damage wasn't immediately disastrous, the other wounds needed to be looked at closely.

Penetrative wounds were a mixed bag when it came to revival. Even a bullet in the brain wasn't always that much of a problem, yet multiple piercing injuries to the chest could prove surprisingly difficult to handle in the reversal.

He took the scissors and cut Kendrick's shirt to expose the damage. He sensed movement above him, and in the corner of his eye he noted Sly turning away as he continued his examination. He was glad, given what else he needed to do.

Wound by wound, he pulled the flesh apart and dug around inside with his right index finger, like a surgeon exploring an incision to locate a piece of shrapnel. Familiarity could help during the reversal; he was trying to get a sense of the depth of penetration, and the internal damage caused. The injuries seemed consistent with a bladed weapon, yet the throat looked more like the result of an animal attack.

One thing he *didn't* see was the cauterized edges to the wounds that had been an indicator of attacks by the shadow-parasites, and for that he was glad. Then Sly spoke.

'I smelled something I recognized down there,' she said.

Jonah looked up, questioning.

'In that basement,' she said, looking wary and shaken. 'That acrid vinegar scent that we got in Winnerden Flats, when the shadows died.'

Jonah said nothing for a few seconds. Anxiety was in danger of flooding him, and he tried to focus on his breathing. 'You think they were attacked, maybe?'

Sly shook her head. 'I don't know. Drayton was helping Kendrick find anyone with an interest in the shadows, so maybe they'd been compromised.'

'But the shadows hadn't shown up,' said Annabel. She

shot an urgent look at Jonah. 'There'd been no sign of them, right?'

Jonah said nothing, but Annabel must have seen something on his face. She gave him a curious look, as if she knew he'd been holding out on her.

'Drayton was tied up,' said Sly. 'By Kendrick, for all we know. I didn't get to see the police photographs. If I had, I'd know by the way he was tied whether or not it had been Kendrick who'd done it. So, Drayton could have been conspiring.'

'And the smell you got suggests a shadow perished there,' said Jonah. 'Drayton may have been a host.'

'Exactly,' said Sly. 'We knew they were out there somewhere. It was just a matter of time.'

'Speak for yourself,' said Annabel. 'I was still hoping they'd all died when Andreas did.'

There was an awkward silence, and again Annabel gave Jonah a look. It was left to Never to puncture the moment. 'Camera's all good to go,' he said. 'Ready when you are, Jonah.'

Jonah nodded. 'May as well get on with it,' he said. There was an office chair in the far corner. He removed his gloves and walked over to it, wheeling it back.

'This could take a while,' he said. 'Maybe an hour or more. You don't have to hang around for the boring part, but if you do, you should get comfortable.' By 'the boring part', Jonah meant the reversal – it was a long and uneventful period for onlookers, and anything *but* uneventful for the reviver.

'I'll stay,' said Never. 'Of course. Keep an eye on the camera. I won't start recording until you succeed, though, OK?'

It was normal FRS practice for the entire revival process to be recorded, but in this case there would be little point. 'That's fine,' said Jonah. He looked to Annabel, glancing to Sly and hoping that Annabel got the message – Sly needed a break, but saying it aloud wouldn't be helpful.

Annabel understood. 'Come on,' Annabel said to Sly. 'May as well sit it out until it's worth being here.'

Sly seemed hesitant, but she nodded. She looked at Jonah and Never. 'The moment anything happens, you get me, understand?' After a nod from Never, she and Annabel left.

'Well,' said Never. 'It's been a while, right? You and me, on a case.'

'I'd rather be anywhere else than here, doing anything else than this,' said Jonah. He looked at Kendrick again. 'I don't think this will be easy.' He sat in his chair and adjusted it until he felt comfortable. He looked at the tripod-mounted camera Never had set up. There was a natural urge to state his name, the formal way all forensic revivals began, but he ignored it and took Kendrick's dead hand in his own.

Then he began.

*

The moment he closed his eyes, he could feel the death flowing into him, filling his senses. It hit the way it sometimes did, like a physical liquid covering him, clogging his nostrils with rank fluid. He held his breath until he got used to the sensation, enough to convince his body that he wouldn't choke when he took another breath.

He breathed it in, the sensation of the gore and the clotted rotting blood; breathed it, and let it seep through his pores and into his own flesh. A decade of experience had taught him how to control the panic that threatened him, but it was difficult. He was drowning in death, drowning in decay, yet he knew it for what it was, and knew it posed no real threat.

After a few seconds, he'd mastered it. He was only dimly aware of the room now; in his senses, he inhabited Kendrick's corpse. He sought the injuries, and in his mind he healed the damage. The ragged stabs to the torso knitted together, from the deep flesh outward to the skin, the intestinal protrusions returning back into the protection of the abdominal cavity; the ribs, shattered in places, were forged whole; the devastated throat flexed and gathered itself.

It all took time, and the damage was significant. Eventually, there was little left to attend to – just the scorched flesh, the eyelids, the myriad abrasions.

The physical corpse was unchanged, of course, but the body Jonah inhabited in his mind was whole once more, pristine, ready for the blood of life to flow again.

Ready for the *essence* of the man to return to it.

The reversal was almost over. Jonah reached out into that unfathomable void, searching, waiting. Then his hand was taken, and he pulled.

It was time for the surge, and he was dreading it. Kendrick's traumatic fate would, he expected, make for a particularly challenging surge. He was right.

He felt himself plummet through darkness, falling and falling, waiting for the sudden rush of memory and image that would come. It hit him hard – anger and fear and adrenaline and *urgency*, images of desert and city and ruin and street; gunfire and blood, shouting and panic. Then: a man, horribly burnt yet somehow still alive, facing him in a glaringly white room. Then: Jonah's own face, his chest bleeding profusely. Then: Sly, younger, her face full of rage and sorrow.

And then darkness again, the eyes of a *child* staring out of the black. He heard a voice: *the perfect vessel isn't easy to find*, it said.

More, more, *more*, the images came too fast even to see, with sounds that grew ever louder. He felt *pummelled* by it, beaten by the sheer force of experience. He held on, though, and at last it subsided.

He opened his eyes. It would take a few more moments before the dead man spoke. 'He's here,' said Jonah. 'How long was it?'

Jumping up from where he'd been sitting on the floor, Never checked the time. 'Seventy-three minutes,' he said. 'You OK?'

'Tired,' said Jonah. 'But I'm fine. Go get them.'

'Will do,' said Never. He ran, returning quickly with Sly and Annabel in tow. They got settled, and Never started to record with the camera.

There was no movement from the body, even as Kendrick started to speak. Non-vocals weren't always like this. There was often twitching of the muscles of the face, spasms from limbs, but not now.

'Jonah,' said Kendrick. 'Good. I wasn't sure my body would even be found. I wasn't sure there'd be anything left to *revive.*'

It didn't surprise Jonah how easily Kendrick had come to realize he was dead. One of the things Kendrick had done in his long career was to develop revival as a means of interrogation – including methods that amounted to torture. To counter his own work, he'd also devised training that taught operatives how to resist. How to *be revived* without being compromised.

'Sly found you,' said Jonah.

'How is she?'

Jonah wasn't sure how to answer that. 'She's safe,' he said. 'She's here. Annabel and Never, too. This is non-vocal, so I repeat everything you say.'

Kendrick was silent for a moment. 'Understood. Tell Sly I'm sorry. I got careless.'

Jonah passed it on. Sly nodded. 'Ask him to report,' she said. 'We may not have long.'

'Yes, *sir*,' said Kendrick when Jonah told him. 'Virgil Drayton. He was my link to a network of people obsessive enough and paranoid enough to see what the rest of the world might miss. I told Drayton what to keep an eye out for, and we found them. People connected to Andreas, planning anything unusual. From those I saw, none of them were hosts to those shadows, those parasites. If anything, that was their goal – they dreamed of becoming hosts, to creatures they knew almost nothing about.'

'You killed them, I assume,' said Sly once Jonah had finished repeating it. She spoke with a matter-of-factness that was chilling, if unsurprising.

'Yes,' said Kendrick. 'That kind of interest . . . I wanted to excise it. I used fire when possible, to make sure that if there were any shadows, they would perish. There's a file, Sly.'

'I looked in the usual places,' said Sly. 'There wasn't anything.'

'It's not in a usual place,' said Kendrick. 'The picture of your parents. The one you always keep. I slipped a note into the frame a while back. It'll tell you where to look.'

Sly didn't reply, but she nodded. Her eyes were wet, Jonah saw.

'Drayton got in touch,' continued Kendrick. 'He said he had more to tell me. I'd decided to rig his house, just in case, so I'd brought the goods and I had the chance. I planted a device where I knew it would be devastating. Drayton had an assistant called Ferris. A butler, I guess. He told me Drayton was in the basement, in his precious archives, and I was to go down there.

'I should have been more careful. Drayton was tied to a chair. He told me he had a shadow on him, burrowing into his flesh, trying to *take* him. Drayton said they brought it here, the thing the shadow came from. The source of it. Ferris started to mock me over a PA. He admitted to having a shadow, said that there weren't many of them, but there were enough. When the vessel perished, those shadows that didn't die managed to hide. He said they'd struggled to find a new vessel. But they had done it. A blank slate, he said. A tabula rasa. Uncorrupted by something as mundane as morality. Free of a sense of humanity. The perfect vessel isn't easy to find, he said.'

The words Jonah had heard in the surge. 'The vessel was the thing Drayton had talked about?' he asked. 'The source of the shadow that was on him?'

'I assumed so. Drayton told me where it was. I went to the door, and I could hear something on the other side. I opened it. There was a long corridor, almost dark. I could see movement at the far end, and the smell that hit me . . .

my God. Death, shit, decay, blood . . . nothing I say could do it justice. I'd brought a second incendiary, and I knew that was my only chance. I backed away from the open door, and slowly the thing started to come towards me. It lumbered out into the light and, Christ, it was an abomination. The flesh was the glistening black of tar, limbs with joints that almost seemed random . . . It was the height of the ceiling, roughly shaped like a man, but from its flesh things pro-truded – claws, teeth. Angles and blades, that was what I saw, but it made little sense to me. Then I saw its face, and I saw its eyes, and I felt a fear I've not felt in my whole life.

'I threw the incendiary and detonated it. I watched the burning fluid cover it and spread, but it shook itself. The fire should have stuck to it, but instead it was like a dog shaking off water. It screamed, raging, and it looked hurt, but it wasn't burning any more. It ran towards me blindly, shield-ing its face. Around the doorway to the corridor, the fire was taking hold. I saw my chance. I ran, making it through the door and pulling it closed. I'd been burnt, I could tell, and the fire was already inside that corridor, but the creature seemed wary enough of it not to follow through at once. I hoped to find a way out before it regrouped.

'The fire was taking hold. I could hear it rage. But all I got were dead ends. No way out. I could hear it coming. It must have been fleeing the worst of the blaze, but perhaps it just wanted *me*.

'It didn't take long before it found me. I raised my gun. Raised it to my *head*. But it was quick. The gun was knocked away—'

Kendrick paused, long enough for Jonah to think he was fading, that the revival was coming to an end.

'The smoke was thick,' Kendrick said at last. 'I could feel myself losing consciousness as it attacked.'

Another pause. He was definitely fading now.

'What Ferris had said came back to me,' said Kendrick. 'The perfect vessel isn't easy to find. A blank slate. I saw its eyes again, saw them up *close*. I saw the *youth* in those eyes. I saw delight. I saw wonder. The eyes of a *child*.'

He stopped.

Jonah let him be for ten seconds, twenty, but Kendrick was fading fast. 'We don't have long,' said Jonah, prompting. 'You need to say your goodbyes.'

'Sly,' said Kendrick. There was a mountain of regret and sorrow loaded into that one word. 'It's been an honour.'

'You're damn right, boss,' said Sly. 'But I'm going to miss saving your hide.'

'It's time,' said Jonah.

'Do it. Let me go.'

Jonah did.

But instead of seeing the room around him, and Kendrick's corpse to his side, he found himself looking out through something *else*'s eyes. With horror, he realized what it was. The images he saw were full of flame, and then suddenly there was a man in front of him: Kendrick, bringing a gun to his own head. With a flick, the gun was gone from his hand.

Behind Jonah's viewpoint, behind the *creature*, the crackle of fire was growing. Jonah suddenly realized he could sense this creature's thoughts. It knew it would have to leave soon. It didn't have time to send the shards of its being out, to try and *commune* with the man before it. There was time for *something*, though.

The creature began to tear at Kendrick's flesh, savouring each moment: the spray of hot blood, the cracking of fragile bone. It relished the pain it caused. It delighted in the screaming.

It was just starting to learn about the world.

*

Jonah opened his eyes with a start, breathless and terrified.

'What?' said Never, eyes wide. He stepped forwards and put a timely hand on Jonah's shoulder, just as Jonah felt himself start to black out.

'Shit,' he said. He looked around; Sly and Annabel were clearly as concerned as Never. 'What just happened?'

'You said it was time,' said Never. 'Then you went quiet and started to slump.'

'I saw it,' Jonah said. 'I *saw* the creature.' He shook his head. 'No. I was looking out of its eyes.' And knowing what it was *thinking*. When it had known it had to leave, and get away from the fire, it had thought of the *ceiling*. 'Sly,' said Jonah. 'The collapse you mentioned. The one they assumed meant the building was unstable. You said there was no fire above it?'

'There was,' said Sly. 'Just not the most intense.'

'Could that fire have come *up* from the basement?'

Sly shrugged. 'I'm no expert. Why?'

'I think it broke out. I think it tore the ceiling down, and broke out.' But outside? Wouldn't that be the worst place it could put itself? The shadow parasites couldn't survive long in sunlight, and surely this creature would find it unbearable too. 'What time did the fire happen, do they know? Was it *dark* outside?'

Sly nodded. 'It was late evening. Yes, it was dark.'

Jonah took a long breath. It would have had all night to find shelter. Tess's words came to him: *The Beast is coming.* It was already here.

10

Sly was keen to leave at once, to find the file Kendrick had told her about, but Annabel managed to talk her into staying over and getting some food and sleep. Annabel whipped up some pasta for Sly, which she wolfed down as they sat on the games-room couch catching up on the news about tomorrow's expected solar flare, and the likelihood of some impact to power and communications.

'Any problems may take *days* to resolve,' said the anchor in a grim tone, and Never scoffed.

'I know they like to big these things up,' he said. 'But *please* ... The worst problems people might see is their lights dimming for a second, or more of the interference on TV signals.'

'Less catchy,' said Annabel. 'People love their news to be frightening and doom-laden.'

About to reply, Never stopped. He'd just noticed that Sly had fallen asleep. He stood and took one of the blankets folded at the side of the couch and carefully placed it over her. He half expected her to snap awake and break his nose, but she slept on.

'She needs it,' said Annabel, softly. Then she looked at

Jonah, and her expression hardened. 'So, Jonah,' she said, 'when Kendrick mentioned the shadows, you didn't seem quite as stunned as I might have expected. Anything you want to tell me?'

Jonah had been half expecting this. 'Ah,' he said. He glanced at Never, who clearly recognized the impending awkwardness.

'I think I'll head home,' said Never. 'Give you two some peace.' He made a hasty retreat.

'Well?' said Annabel once Never was out of earshot. 'Are you going to tell me?'

'Not here,' said Jonah, nodding to Sly. He stood and went to the door, and Annabel followed.

She shut the door behind her. 'Out with it,' she said.

'When she died, Tess told me something. She said that the Beast was coming. She said to be ready.'

Annabel sighed, and nodded. 'So all this time, you've just been waiting for the inevitable, and not saying anything to me?'

'That's about it.'

She glared at him, then punched him in the shoulder in frustration. It was just hard enough to hurt. 'We're a *team*, you fucking idiot. You tell me these things.'

'I didn't want to give you anything more to worry about.'

Annabel groaned. 'I know. That's exactly why I've not talked to *you* about it either. You seemed so adamant that the shadows were all gone, I thought you really *believed* it.'

Jonah looked at her and frowned. 'Didn't *you* believe it?'

'I'm a journalist,' she said. 'I have a nose for these things.' She paused for a moment, then shook her head. 'Although, to be fair, it did help, you seeming so certain. It meant I could let myself hope, when I needed to.'

'So you forgive me?' he said.

She smiled and gave him a hug. 'Just don't do it again.'

His shoulder was still smarting from her punch. 'At least Never didn't *hit* me when I told him.'

She took a step back. 'You told Never about this? Before you told me?' She shook her head. 'Shit. Now you *are* in trouble.' From the games room came an indistinct moan. They opened the door quietly; Sly was still asleep, but restless. 'Scratch that,' said Annabel. 'We're *all* in trouble. Kendrick and Sly always seemed immune to fear. Did you see how hard this has hit her?'

'Of course,' said Jonah. 'She's always looked like she could walk through Hell without breaking a sweat. Tonight's the first time I've ever found myself *worrying* about her.'

'You need to sleep too,' said Annabel. 'It's been a tough night for you. I'll stay down with Sly and make sure she's OK.'

Jonah nodded. He turned to go, then looked back. 'I'm sorry,' he said. 'For not telling you everything.'

Annabel kissed him. 'Go,' she said. 'You're forgiven. Sleep.'

But sleep didn't come easily for him.

Jonah had long been used to having Annabel in bed with him, and having their bed all to himself tended to upset his sleep anyway. The revival had left him both exhausted and overstimulated. He tussled for an hour. The images still in his mind from the surge were unsettling. Memories of a subject could linger for a time, in spite of the medication he took, but in the hours immediately after a revival they were freshest. Kendrick had lived a life on the edges of morality, pushing the boundaries of what was acceptable in the defence of a country, and some of the flashes of recall that Jonah experienced underlined that.

By far the worst thing, however, was when he remembered the feeling of looking out through the eyes of the creature in the basement. *Sensing* its thoughts.

Sleep eventually came, but it was fitful, and shattered by a dream: he was in the same void he'd been in when he saw the vision of Tess. There she was again, but standing and looking right at him.

'*Pandora*,' she said. She held out her hand to him, and he approached. She put her arms around him, and began to squeeze until it was painful. He couldn't breathe, and still she squeezed harder.

She let him go, a look of malice on her face. Then she opened her mouth, wide, *wider*; she looked to the sky and placed her hands on her top and bottom teeth, then pulled until the jaw cracked wide. She kept pulling, her flesh tearing down her neck. Inside, gore-streaked, was Annabel. She smiled at him and opened her mouth just as Tess had done. Jonah screamed as Annabel placed her hands in the same way and began to *pull*.

He woke with the sound of cracking bone still ringing in his head.

*

For Never, the rest of that night didn't hold the same kind of sleep disturbance as it had for Jonah, but he did find himself restless when he got back to his apartment. After so long without the threat hanging immediately over their heads, the cautious peace-of-mind he'd known for the last year – which had come at the price of Jonah's 'death' – was utterly gone. *Hope* had gone.

He'd set foot on the Dead Road again, and he wasn't sure if he'd be able to think himself off it. His grandmother would *not* have been pleased.

He drank a little more, vaguely wishing that he had thought to bring the opened mini-cask back with him as consolation. He thought about Kendrick, and Sly – whose relationship had always been mysterious, and unbroachable. He'd tried more than once with indirect questions, probing how the two had met, and how the close bond had arisen. Watching her there, with Kendrick's body so mauled, had been strange. Heartbreaking, in a way, but he had no real insight into what went on in Sly's mind. Kendrick could have been her real *father*, for all he knew, or simply a close colleague.

Still, it underlined why any kind of relationship between himself and Sly couldn't work. She was emotionally sealed off in a way that Never wouldn't have been able to deal with. He liked to think that was one of the reasons she wouldn't countenance anything happening between them. And sure, that notion made it easier to deal with than a simple 'She's just not into you', but he figured he was due a break.

The next morning was Friday, and he wasn't at work – hence why he'd suggested the previous night for a marathon pool/beer session. His few consolation drinks from the night before had hit him harder than they had any right to, which seemed unfair. Hungover, to add to his newfound sense of pessimism about the future of – well, of *everything*.

Cruel.

118

He decided to watch old comedy movies all day, but the phone rang mid-morning. It was Tabitha, one of the tech team at the office, complaining that the work he'd done on the backup comms hardware had already failed and could he come in and fix the damn thing.

He was about to suggest that *she* fixed it, but then he remembered going slightly ballistic the month before when he'd realized someone had changed the settings on those servers without telling him. He'd *kind of* suggested that if anyone touched them but him, he'd fire them on the spot.

In other words, he'd asked for this.

That didn't stop him cursing Tabitha's name as he drove.

On the way to work, news broke of another failed sub-oceanic cable and the ensuing war of words between likely culprits trying to deny blame. Worse, a delay in repairing the damage was inevitable as, of the five repair ships in the area, two were already engaged in other cable repairs, and the remaining three were all in dry dock for ship repairs or maintenance work. This was bubbling just under the headlines, however, which were all focused on the likely timing of the predicted solar flare's arrival – or, more correctly, the arrival of the coronal mass several hours subsequent to the flare. Whether it would cause significant effects on Earth would only be known when it hit NASA's ACE Probe, and until then the best they could give of its ETA was roughly five hours.

He saw Tabitha as soon as he entered the office.

'All right,' he said. 'I'm here.'

Tabitha frowned. 'Good. There's a second link down.' She paused. 'I'm sorry I called you in, Never, but it's been a busy one today, and I know you like the comms stuff *just so.*'

'Not a problem,' said Never, feeling slightly bad about cursing her name. Across the office, he saw Lex and caught her eye. She waved and came over.

'Hey,' she said. 'Thought you were off today?'

'They called me in to, uh, fix some stuff,' he said, suddenly finding he couldn't speak in intelligent sentences in front of her. 'How was your revival yesterday?' He winced a little, remembering that it had been a gruesome one that she'd almost certainly not want to talk about.

'I don't want to talk about it,' she said. 'It was a bit grim.'

'Right,' said Never. An awkward silence ensued.

'Oh!' said Lex. 'Yeah. Some of us are out for drinks later. Maybe you could come along?'

Feeling his face form into an idiot-grin, he nodded. 'Will do!' he said. Lex went, and he wondered if she'd just sort-of asked him out. Great timing, what with the end of the world on its way.

He went to the comms room in the basement and got on with his work, chiding himself for being such a dour bastard. Yes, Kendrick was dead, and yes he was killed by something terrifying, but it could be decades before their little 'pet' was all grown up, and there was surely plenty that could happen between now and then to stop it. Sly, for one. It was personal now, which made Never feel anxious for her. She would commit to the cause even more than she already had.

'OK,' he said to himself, running through the first tests on the hardware. The link he'd fixed was down again, as well as one other on the same secure government network that ran on dedicated lines, called FMRC. The hardware tests came out fine, though. He frowned. The two downed links were on two separate parts of the government network. He called the data centres and asked them to check their end, which took fifteen minutes. They came back with the all clear on their hardware, but one of them said something that made Never fret. As the phone was hung up, he just caught a few words of conversation with a colleague: 'looks like another one'.

He called the Chicago FRS and asked for a favour – could they check their own secure links and backup comms?

'Funny you should ask,' came the reply. 'Our only running backup comms are to private data centres right now. All the federal ones are silent.'

'All of them?' said Never, incredulous. Then he looked at his own, and saw that now he had exactly that problem. He rang upstairs and asked Tabitha to come down. 'You know much about the FMRC system?' he asked when she arrived.

She shrugged. 'Enough,' she said.

'OK, so what would make for a countrywide FMRC outage?'

Tabitha screwed up her face. 'What kind of question is that? The redundancy means you can't really have that happen. Like the Internet, shit can slow down and *sites* can go offline, but it doesn't *die*.'

'The whole FMRC is down. I called around.'

Tabitha shook her head. 'You called everyone?'

'Not *everyone*,' said Never. 'But enough to be worried.'

She looked at him like he'd sprouted an extra nose. 'What? It's probably innocuous. A fuck-up, yes, but short-lived.'

'I don't know,' he said, but he *did* know. It bothered him that there were so many simultaneous breaks in communications cables, and that the repair ships were out of action, and that a supposedly failure-proofed communication net-work had failed.

All *before* the supposed effects of the solar flare hit them. He thought about his chat with Jonah, mentioning how governments or business might want to take advantage of an unusual situation by making it much worse.

'They'd better make sure it's back up soon,' she said. 'Someone's head will be on the block for this.'

'Yeah,' said Never. 'I think I'll, um, head on home maybe. Our kit's all fine, so there's nothing I can do about it.' He went back upstairs to his desk and checked out the news. The flare's arrival had been narrowed down to the next half-hour, but it was now confirmed as one of the most powerful on record to hit head-on. Communications, it was noted, might be affected.

But just not *yet*, he thought.

'Hey, Never!' called someone across the office. He didn't even look up to see who it was. 'Do we have to switch any-thing off for this flare thing?'

'No,' he said. 'Circuit breakers will deal with any unex-pected surges. It's unlikely we'll see any impact.' He was starting to wonder about that. He put on headphones and brought up a live news stream about the flare, and found a NASA site that showed its ETA: still another twenty-eight minutes to go. Then he hunted around in the FRS emer-gency contact list for an FMRC phone number. It was engaged. He kept trying. He tried an alternative number, and it was engaged too.

And then the words the Chicago FRS had used came back to him: *all the federal ones are silent.*

It was ringing a bell, and he didn't quite know why.

Silent.

He thought of Lex, and the question she'd asked after their revival in Durham: *Don't you ever follow up old cases?*

'Shit,' he said. He called up the records they had on that case, because he'd had a sudden sense that something important had been staring him in the face.

John Trent, Patti Trent's husband, had set himself on fire rather than take a gun to his own temple. He'd not been himself for months, and when he *was* acting like himself, he'd killed his wife, poured gasoline over his head and lit a match. They'd assumed the fire was so he could avoid being revived, but it wasn't just revival chances that fire destroyed . . .

Just ask Kendrick.

He suddenly realized why *silent* had rung a bell. It was what Patti had alluded to.

He said he didn't want me to be around for the silence. He said he wanted to spare me that.

Silence. What *kind* of silence?

John Trent's records came up on screen. *John Trent*, it said. *AT&T Telecommunications Engineer.*

He picked up the phone again, ready to try every damn FMRC number he could find.

Then, simultaneously, the live-news stream froze and his phone line went dead.

The hum of activity in the office didn't miss a beat, but Never's heart did. He reached into his pocket for his own phone. There was no signal showing.

He stood up. 'Hey,' he said. 'Can everyone check their cellphones? Anyone got a signal?' Infuriatingly slowly, a few people checked. Nobody had a signal.

With perfect timing, the power went off, prompting a complaint from everyone in the office. He stared at his blank monitor, feeling vaguely like his *brain* had short-circuited.

Enough was enough. He clapped his hands together as loudly as he could manage. 'Can I have everyone's attention, please?' Some conversations continued. '*Hello!*'

The office fell into total silence. Even Hugo came out of his corner office, his face somewhere between scowling and bemused.

'Everyone should get home,' said Never. 'And stay there until everything is back up.'

Hugo came over to him and spoke in a lowered voice. 'You can't just order the office to close, Never. It's the solar flare they predicted. The news said it might hit the power in some places, but it won't last more than a few hours. It'll probably be back up in a minute.'

'One problem with that,' said Never. 'The flare doesn't hit for another half-hour.' Hugo had no response. 'Go home, Hugo. I mean it.' He raised his voice again, and was aware of how shaken he sounded. 'I *mean* it. I don't think it's just here.' Everyone stared at him, baffled and uneasy. What the hell could he tell them, that wouldn't make him sound crazy? 'Go *home*,' he said. 'Before it gets dark.'

He took his coat and left.

There was only one place to go. As he drove, negotiating the streets where all the traffic lights were off, he saw people standing outside shops and buildings, looking around themselves and examining their phones. There was a sense of curiosity written on their faces, many of them smiling as if they were kids who'd woken to snow. Shrugs and laughter, faced with something that was unusual, but just a brief inconvenience.

He looked up to the late-morning sky. No aurora was visible, but he imagined it would be too dim to see against the bright blue.

It would be daylight for another nine hours.

He had a terrible feeling that it would all change when night came.

11

When he pulled into the drive at Annabel's, Sly's van had already gone. He knocked on the door.

'Hi, Never,' said Annabel, with a little frown. She was surprised to see him, but he supposed that his agitation was pretty apparent.

'Sly's gone?' he said.

'She went to find the file Kendrick mentioned.' She led him inside. 'Power's out, by the way.'

'No shit,' said Never. 'Where's Jonah?'

'In the kitchen. What's up? You look tense.'

'The power's out,' he said. 'Doesn't that worry you?'

Annabel shook her head. 'It'll be back on soon.'

'Fuck that! *Everything* went off. Everything. Internet, landlines, cell networks, power. All of it went off, *before* the flare hit.'

'I thought the flare happened hours ago,' she said.

He shook his head. 'The news was saying—'

'You're both right,' said Jonah, appearing. 'The flare happened hours ago, but peak effects don't happen until the solar wind reaches us, the coronal mass ejection. The geomagnetic storm's what takes out power, and they were predicting for –' he checked the time – 'about now.' He looked at Never and shrugged. 'When the power failed I just figured the estimate was off. Richmond's affected too?'

'*Everywhere* is affected, Jonah,' said Never. 'Look, before the power went, the landlines went down, cell networks went down, Internet went down . . . They're all different systems and, if anything, the power should have gone *first*.'

Jonah and Annabel shared a long look. 'What are you saying?' said Annabel.

'I'm saying that someone was making damn sure the communications failures happened. I'm saying maybe *they* got their timing off.' He was thinking about the drone submersibles they found on the undersea cable. A thought struck him. 'How easy would it be to block satellite communications?'

'No idea,' said Annabel. 'But I know someone who will.'

*

As Annabel drove to Cathy's place, Jonah grabbed a flashlight and brought Never down to the lower basement. After his dream of Tess and Annabel, Jonah had felt uneasy all morning. With Never's arrival, and his insistence that *everywhere* was affected, he'd fallen into an oddly numb state. He felt like he was going through the motions of living, but it was already too late.

'What makes you think it's *everywhere*, Never?' he said.

'Don't you feel it? Nobody's going to know what's coming. Nobody will know, even when it hits them, because there'll be no warnings.'

Jonah tried to swallow his fear. He'd brought Never down here because power generation had been something he'd been sure to deal with early on, at least as far as *purchases* went.

'We have two options for power,' he said. He pulled out a box.

'Ah, you *did* get the spares for the generator,' said Never, delving inside. 'You just didn't do anything about actually *fixing* it.'

'OK, OK,' Jonah said. 'But we have another option.' Not wanting to bring in someone from outside to do the installation, he'd told himself he would get around to it. Thus far, he'd failed. As with the generator, the idea that there was no immediate *hurry* had been too appealing. 'Here it is,' he told Never, pulling away a sheet that covered variously sized boxes.

'Oooh,' said Never, pulling out one of them as if it contained treasure. Which, for Never, it did. They were solar panels and high-capacity batteries, the latter too heavy for one person to move, but they weren't the ordinary run-of-the-mill variety. When your girlfriend was wealthy, why skimp? 'These are pricey! Why haven't you put *these* up yet? They're simple. Come to that, why the hell didn't you mention them to me? I'd have done it for you.'

Jonah frowned. 'What, tell you I was prepping for global disaster? I didn't want to give you something else to worry about. I told you I was happy letting you think it was over. That was why I didn't mention what Tess told me.'

'Did you tell Annabel yesterday?' said Never.

Jonah nodded. 'I told her what I told you. But Tess said something else. I told you I had some kind of vision, after the little boy?'

'Here we go,' grumbled Never. 'Tell me.'

'She said one word. *Pandora*. She just kept saying it over and over.'

'Pandora? Like the box?'

'Like the box.'

'Do you think it was just in your head?'

'No,' said Jonah. 'At first I wasn't sure, but I think she really sent me a message. Somehow. So far, I have no idea what the hell she meant by it, though.'

'Great,' said Never, pulling out more of the solar panels. He gave Jonah a particularly sarcastic look. 'If you see her again, ask for more details.'

*

It didn't take long for all the necessary boxes to be brought up to the courtyard, ready for installation.

'And by installation,' said Never, 'I mean propping up at a bit of an angle.'

'There's some timber in the storage shed by the garage,' said Jonah. 'I got that to make frames to fix the panels to.'

'Right,' said Never. 'Let's consider that to be gilding the lily, OK?' He started to read through the instruction manual.

'It was the connection to our electricity supply that I was worried about doing.'

'That's pretty easy,' said Never. 'Especially now that there *isn't* one. I'll have it all up and running in half an hour, trust me. It's a clear day, might even have the batteries well-charged by nightfall if we're not drawing much in the meantime.'

Jonah heard the approach of Annabel's car and left him to it.

He was surprised to see Cathy in the passenger seat, and

there was something in the rear of the hatchback, the seats folded down to accommodate it.

'Jonah,' said Cathy. She looked exhausted, but she gave him a tired smile.

'You go on inside,' Annabel said to Cathy. 'Jonah and I will start bringing your gear into the house.'

When Cathy was out of earshot, Jonah said: 'What did you tell her?'

'I asked if she had a satellite phone.'

'Living here in the Quiet Zone, that'd be damn close to Original Sin,' he said.

'It was just to start the conversation. I said we were worried that the power cut was wider than people realized.' She paused. 'OK, I said *you* were worried. I also may have pulled a face and implied that you're a little bit paranoid.'

'Thanks.'

'Well, I didn't see I could go all out and tell her the crazy stuff. She would've slammed the door in my face.' She opened the rear door of her car. Inside were two large cardboard boxes full of electronic equipment.

'What's all this?' he asked.

'Cathy's been a radio skulker for decades.'

'A what?'

'She sits and sifts through the airwaves for anything interesting. It's a hobby. Living in the Quiet Zone means she can get weak signals that'd be swamped otherwise. She said if she had power, she'd be able to find out how widespread this was, hence . . .'

'You brought it all here! Good. The power won't take long to be up, according to Never. Did Cathy have an opinion on the flare causing the power outage?'

'She did,' said Annabel. She looked at the sky. 'I asked if the lack of an aurora was odd, but she pointed out that the *previous* aurora had been the strange one. She mentioned some figures and said it could easily have triggered black-outs if the power companies underestimated the strength of the flux, as they might have to shut parts of the grid down in a panic and spend a while checking for damage before they put it back on. We have a bet as to whether we'll get her radio set up before the power returns.'

'You'll collect on that one,' Jonah said. 'How much?'

'Ten dollars. Now grab the end of this and let's get it inside. Who knows? Maybe everything will be fine in twenty minutes.'

'Who knows,' said Jonah, absently. He reached into the car.

*

'I hope my daughter's OK,' said Cathy. She was assembling her equipment with the kind of practised grace that came with years of experience.

'She might be better coming out to stay with you,' said Annabel. 'She's not far, right? An hour's drive or so? I can take you if you'd rather not go alone.'

Cathy considered it, but frowned. 'This is all going to be fine,' she said. 'We'll be laughing about it in an hour, trust me.'

At that, Never came in and flicked on a light. 'Ta da!' he said, turning it off again. 'We're good to go with power. Although it's drawing a fair bit, so if you'd be so kind, Jonah, and scoot around the house unplugging everything? Fridge and freezer should be OK to leave.'

'OK,' said Jonah, and he started to go from socket to socket around the room.

'I'm Never,' said Never, extending a hand to Cathy as his eyes took in the jumble of equipment she was configuring. He didn't need to ask her what it was. 'Good to meet you. Anything I can do to help?'

'There's an aerial in that box in the corner,' she said. 'It's a spare of the type I've got set up at home. Takes a little care to put together, but I'm sure you're up to it.'

'Right,' said Never. 'Should it go anywhere specific?'

'On a roof, if possible.'

Annabel spoke up. 'The garage has a flat roof, if you've enough cabling to reach it.'

'My dear,' said Cathy, 'I have enough cabling to reach the *coast*.' She smiled. 'My husband used to tell me that, anyways.'

As he walked over to the box of aerial parts, Never paused. 'I was thinking, are any of your neighbours old, or vulnerable? It'd be worth asking if they'd want to stay here.'

Jonah, pulling the last plug from its socket, stared at him in shock.

'I'm allowed to be thoughtful,' said Never. He frowned. 'Aren't I?'

Jonah came closer. 'I was thinking more about privacy,' he muttered.

'I think the time for privacy has passed,' said Never. Jonah grumbled and went off to unplug things elsewhere in the house.

'Philip is a retired surgeon,' said Cathy. 'Right up the far end of the valley. Next to him is Petro, but they're both pretty independent souls. You folk really should try and relax. It'll be fine.'

Jonah came back. 'It occurred to me to try the TV,' he said. 'I figured they should have their own generators. Nothing.'

Cathy shook her head. 'They'd not necessarily have power for their broadcast beacons. Are you terrestrial or satellite?'

'Both,' said Jonah. 'Nothing's showing.'

Cathy frowned. 'That's digital for you, see. A geomagnetic storm creates a mountain of interference. With digital, you either get a usable signal and a basically perfect picture, or it drops below threshold and you get zip.' She plugged one final cable in. 'OK, Never. Get the aerial up. We'll find out what we can hear.'

*

Jonah joined Never as soon as he'd finished his trip around the house. There were a few things he knew would be drawing power – various chargers, for example – but it was only once he'd done the whole house that he remembered the shelter below him. Outdated batteries, essentially automotive, which were trickle-charged from the mains supply.

He went down the tunnels to the shelter and cut the power supply to the batteries, making sure to kill the tunnel lights once he was back in the basement. When he returned, Never confirmed that the drain he had complained about had vanished.

Once the pieces of the aerial were laid out, Never seemed to get into his stride. Much of it slotted together without a fuss, and soon they were lifting the part-assembled pieces onto the garage roof ready for final assembly.

'We'll want to anchor this down,' said Never. 'Maybe some guy lines too. Later, though. Lily, gilding.'

Jonah gave him a grim smile. 'Cathy's under the impression we'll be taking it apart almost immediately.'

'I hope she's right,' said Never, but neither of them believed it for a moment.

Jonah looked at the sky, and thought he could see the faintest hint of green wisps fluctuating up there. 'Is that the aurora back?' he said.

After a moment of squinting, Never shook his head. 'I can't tell. It's not as clear as last time, if it is.'

Jonah nodded. He wasn't sure either – the human mind was hungry for pattern, and it simply could have been his brain filling in something that wasn't there.

They went back inside, Never feeding out the cable from the aerial. Cathy had plugged her equipment in, and she held out her hand for the loop of cable. As soon as it was attached, she switched the receiver on and started to tinker. A single speaker rested on top of the equipment, and from it came a continuous hiss.

'Ongoing interference,' she said. 'A flare gives you an initial burst of trouble, then when the coronal mass ejection reaches the planet you get the more serious problems. The problems keep going as long as the geomagnetic storm lasts.' She played with the dial for a minute, but Jonah could see a frown forming. She flipped a few switches and tried again. All Jonah could hear was the static, but from time to time Cathy paused and went back and forth across the same frequencies. She grabbed a pair of headphones she'd brought but not connected, put them on and plugged them in, cutting off the speaker. She had an increasingly intense expression on her face, very carefully shifting frequency. Occasionally she paused, refined the position and listened again.

After a few minutes, Cathy took her headphones off. 'There's quite a narrow band that's less clouded with interference,' she said. 'Getting some signals, but they fade in and out. The folk at Green Bank could probably learn something interesting from that, given time. The rest of the spectrum is just a mess. Unusual atmospherics, I think.'

'The aurora might be back,' said Jonah. 'I couldn't be sure if I was really seeing it, so it's very faint if it's there at all.'

Cathy nodded. 'An aurora can create plasma layers that reflect radio signals better,' she said. 'It can vastly increase the distance signals travel, but the same goes for the noise.' She unplugged the headphones, and the speaker crackled into life.

Jonah strained to hear anything different from it, but couldn't – then he realized he could just make out something underneath the static. Perhaps it was simply his mind again, creating meaning out of noise, like the old EVP tapes that TV shows about hauntings loved so much, so-called electric voice phenomena – supposedly hearing the voices of the dead, when nothing was really there.

Cathy was poised at the volume control, and when the static dropped lower she turned it up. With a startlingly loud click, a male voice came on: 'Were there any signs of spiking? Check for that, see if . . .' It faded back into static.

She turned it down again. 'That's reasonably local,' she said. 'From what I listened to before, it's a couple of power company guys talking. No idea if they chanced on the frequency or had the skill to look, but it's all been shop talk. Drowns out weaker signals, though.'

'Have they had anything much to say?' asked Annabel.

Cathy shook her head. 'I didn't get much detail. A few equipment failures were mentioned, but it sounded like they were grasping at straws and really don't understand why the power's gone. I'm going to try and filter out the stronger signals and see if there's anything else we get. It'll take a few minutes.' She plugged her headphones back in and got to work.

The others drifted to the kitchen.

'Any chance I can steal some power to make a coffee?' Annabel said to Never.

He frowned. 'If you're desperate, eat it raw,' he said. 'If the batteries get full while the sun's still shining, *then* you can have some.'

Jonah shrugged and took some cans of Coke out of the fridge, then handed them out. 'So this is happening,' he said. 'Exactly what the news spent all day yesterday saying *couldn't* happen. And people think it's just temporary.'

'What's coming, Jonah?' said Annabel. 'The thing Kendrick saw . . . I mean that can't really do much harm, can it? Quickly? And all this . . .'

'Does it need to be quick?' said Never. 'In a few days, things will get very nasty indeed. We're only ever four meals away from anarchy, isn't that what they say?'

'They knew this flare was coming,' said Jonah. '*It* knew. It must have known for a long time, for its people to set everything else up. Making sure to cripple everything that could be crippled.'

Annabel nodded. 'Destroying the communications infra-structure means nobody can find out what's happening,

THE DEAD ROAD

nobody can plan. Everything falls apart and there's no way back.'

Jonah couldn't help but picture the Beast, striding across the landscape. 'It feeds off souls,' he said. 'And it enjoys it. Maybe it wants to relish all of this. In a week or so the people of the world will be at each other's throats for the last scraps of food, or fuel. It's in no hurry.'

Cathy came in. 'I picked up another couple of transmissions, one from Pittsburgh and one from Louisville, sounded like civilians comparing notes. Joking, almost. Power's out across the country.' She looked at them with a sour expression. 'You were right about that. I owe you ten dollars, Annabel.' She shook her head. 'I think your suggestion of bringing my daughter and her family here makes a lot of sense.'

Annabel nodded. 'As I said, if you'd rather not go alone I can go with you.'

'I'd appreciate it,' said Cathy.

Jonah handed her a Coke and they all returned to the radio. Cathy put it back onto speaker, and there was currently nothing but a very faint hum. 'The dropout is where the stronger signals swamp it, or the interference had strengthened,' she said. 'We just need to wait.'

As they listened, Jonah had the same sense he'd had before of his mind creating voices from nothing.

Then he heard it.

Almost buried by static, a voice was talking rapidly in a foreign language he couldn't place. The voice was agitated, desperate.

'Record it,' Annabel told Never urgently. He rushed to take his phone out, and hit record.

137

It faded, came back, faded again. Short bursts of sound, and then a long section, uninterrupted, the female voice joined by a male one, equally agitated.

When the voices faded again, they waited but heard nothing else.

'What language was that?' said Annabel. 'Russian, maybe?'

'Might have been,' said Cathy. 'Eastern European, if not. Petro is originally from Ukraine, we should ask him if he can translate it.'

Annabel nodded. She swapped her phone with Never's. 'You two, keep listening. If you hear anything else, record it, OK?'

They nodded.

Jonah wanted to go with them, but he wasn't sure he was ready to hear what Petro would have to say.

Something had cut through the language barrier already. The people in that recording were *terrified*.

12

Petro's house was three hundred yards further up the road.

'What's this guy's story?' said Annabel, driving. 'I called by a couple of times when we moved in but nobody answered.'

'Petro's fairly shy,' said Cathy. 'You wouldn't think it when you meet him, but he is. If he doesn't know someone, chances are he'll just ignore them. Used to be a civil engineer, smart guy. US citizen since '95, but he still talks like a mix of Schwarzenegger and Dolph Lundgren.'

Annabel smiled. 'Well, you met Never. You'd think he left Belfast a week ago, not fifteen years.'

Cathy returned the smile, but it faded. 'He cuts a lonely figure, Petro. His partner of thirty years died, what, seven or eight years ago. He's only mid-fifties, but it took a heavy toll on him. He has no other family, and his partner was the social one of the two. There's been a joke we've had around here for a while now: on this road, we're all leftovers. Until you moved in, everyone was on their own. Me and Petro are about the same age, and my son-in-law keeps trying to suggest we pair up.' She raised her eyebrow. 'My son-in-law means well, but I'm the wrong gender.'

They parked in the drive, and by the time they got half-way to the house, a tall burly man, balding with short-cropped hair, had opened the front door. He hurried over.

'Cathy!' he said. He gave her a long hug, his expression almost distraught. 'Philip told me about your grandson. I didn't know whether I should come and say something. Such a shock. Such a shock.' His emotion was genuine; his eyes looked wet.

'It was,' said Cathy, but she was clearly not eager to talk more about Grady. She looked to Annabel, instead. 'Petro, this is Annabel. She moved in to Harlan's place last year, she called by but you didn't appear. I guess you were out.'

Petro looked uncomfortable. He reached out a hand, which Annabel shook. 'Good to meet you,' he said. 'Come in, come in!' He led the way inside to his living room, turning back to Cathy as he walked. 'Are you OK with this power cut? You need help at all? How long before all this crazy shit stops, huh? You should know, of all people.'

'Well, that's why I'm here,' she said. 'I've been listening for radio transmissions, Petro. I heard people across the country talk about the power being off. It's everywhere.'

He frowned. 'Everywhere?' He sat in a well-worn leather armchair, and gestured for Cathy and Annabel to take the couch.

Cathy nodded. 'Then I heard this. I wondered if you could take a listen.' She nodded to Annabel, who held up Never's phone and played the recording.

Petro listened to the frightened voices, and as the recording played on, he grew pale. When it was done he stared at Cathy. 'Is that real?' he said, and Cathy nodded. 'Jesus.'

'What did they say?' asked Annabel.

Petro told them.

*

They brought him back to the house, where Jonah and Never had been listening to nothing but static.

'Anything come through while we were gone?' asked Cathy.

'Not a jot,' said Never.

'OK,' said Annabel. 'This is Petro. Petro, this is Never, and Jonah.'

Petro shook Never's hand, but Jonah declined. 'I'm a reviver,' he said.

To his surprise, Petro smiled. 'Ah! My partner's cousin is a reviver in Quebec. I know, I know, the funny feeling thing, right?'

'Chill,' said Jonah, nodding.

Annabel got them to sit. 'Petro listened to the recording,' she said. 'If I play it again, Petro, can you translate so Jonah and Never can hear what was said?'

Petro didn't look happy. 'If I must,' he said.

Annabel played it.

Petro spoke over the top as the fearful voices began. 'This part,' he said. 'Confusion about what happened. Hard to hear. "Tidal wave," someone says. Broken transmission. Very weak.' He listened. 'Here: "People are fleeing the city in darkness." "Tell them what you saw." "A sea of . . . of poison rose up. The dark rats came." I say rats, maybe vermin is the better word. "They tried to get into my car, but couldn't get to me. Seal yourself inside." The woman says something about mist, but it gets lost.'

141

Annabel paused. 'That was the first part. Then we had the longer sequence, clearer. Ready, Petro?'

He nodded, and Annabel continued the playback.

'"We are reporting to those able to hear us",' translated Petro. '"An attack . . ."' He shook his head as static cut in briefly, then continued. '"Soon after night fell, the power failed. The sea itself attacked us in the dark. We are reporting from Gatchina."' Another voice began to speak. '"People have returned to the city to see what's happening now. Nobody has come back yet. Nobody else is willing to go into the city until morning." Someone asks: "Are people hurt?" "My God yes, my God yes. And the . . ."' The static returned. 'That's all,' said Petro.

'Gatchina?' said Never.

'Gatchina is south of St Petersburg,' said Petro. 'Twenty miles or so.'

'So it's Russian?' asked Never.

Petro nodded. 'Yes. It doesn't make sense what they say, but these people are scared. You can hear that already. What's going on? Do you know?'

Jonah and Never shook their heads, but Petro was watching them with a wary eye.

*

Annabel and Cathy got ready to leave, to bring Cathy's daughter, son-in-law, and their other child back with them.

'You want me to go with you?' said Petro. 'I have a gun at home, maybe things will be bad by now?'

Cathy patted his arm, with a smile. 'I think society's breakdown isn't quite here yet,' she said. 'We'll be back long before dark.'

Annabel shared a glance with Jonah. He knew she'd had a gun in her car ever since Winnerden Flats, but her father had always been vociferously against them. Pulling a weapon, he'd said, was like trying to put out a fire with napalm. 'It won't be that long before people start to hear that this is across the country,' she said. 'People will be doing what we're doing – getting family, going somewhere they think is safe, but some will be driving a few hundred miles to do it, and they'll see that everywhere's the same. Word will spread, and panic will spread with it. Looting *could* start tonight, but I guarantee people will be hoarding by tomorrow.'

'Sooner we go, the better,' said Cathy.

Annabel nodded. She looked at Jonah. 'Keep listening. Record anything you hear. We'll be back in two hours.'

*

Jonah, Never and Petro sat by the radio.

'I should have gone,' mourned Petro. 'Here, what use am I?'

Over the past hour, there had been the occasional break-through from the radio, but it had all been local transmissions. People were finding the gap in the shortwave static and making use of it, but it meant that the more distant signals were being overpowered.

Annabel's pessimism about the way people would behave in the situation was preying on Jonah's mind. 'What the hell do law enforcement agencies do when something like this happens?'

'Something like this?' said Never. 'They'd have to ad-lib. It'd be a mishmash of post-nuclear planning and natural disaster strategy. Except with no significant casualties to deal with. Well, not *yet*.' The other two were looking at him. 'Uh, I've spent too much time around Sly. We've talked about this, trust me.'

'Sly's a friend,' Jonah explained to Petro. 'She works in national security.' And while that may have missed out a vast range of important aspects of Sly's background, it was basically true. He turned back to Never. 'Any other insights to offer?'

'Like I said, me and Sly have talked about this,' said Never. 'It's very different for short- and long-term problems, but I reckon for this it'd be mainly a widespread natural disaster strategy. That's when little or no help from outside is expected for a period of days. Stabilize the area, maintain visible police presence for reassurance and information. When communications are compromised, they maintain contact by shuttled physical messenger. Essentially Pony Express.'

'And the post-nuclear stuff?' said Jonah.

'Yeah,' said Never, almost with a wince. 'The problem there is that the rules change completely. The moment they decide to adopt those plans, it's shoot-to-kill for looters and the expectation that everyone will go fucking ape-shit.' He sighed.

The radio had been nothing but static so far, but suddenly they could make out something more. There was a definite signal in there somewhere, although nothing clear yet.

'Shit,' said Never, scrambling to get his phone recording again.

'Hurry up,' said Petro.

'*Trying*,' said Never. Finally, he got it going.

There was very little they could make out, mostly brief fragments of speech. It was enough to tell that the people speaking were terrified, just as those in Gatchina had been.

Then a panicked voice came on, speaking in accented English: 'It killed them! It came out of the water and . . . oh, God, oh my *God*, it was over everything, it covered *every-thing*. It tore . . .'

The impenetrable static returned.

The three men stared at each other for a moment.

'What language was that at first?' said Never. 'Spanish?'

'Portuguese,' said Petro. 'I think. And I'm sure I heard them say Lisboa.'

They waited a little, until they were sure there was no more coming, then played the recording back.

'Lisboa,' said Jonah. 'I heard it too.' He caught Never's confusion. '*Lisbon*,' he said. 'Your geography's not *that* bad, surely?'

'Do you have an atlas?' Petro said.

Jonah thought about it and shook his head. 'No.'

'Ah,' said Never. 'Because *Internet*. Who needs physical maps?'

'Exactly,' said Jonah, then he remembered something. 'Wait.' He went to the kitchen and came back with a mug that had an antique world map on it.

'Seriously, fuck off,' said Never.

'Do *you* have a better atlas, wise one?' said Jonah as he gave the mug to Petro, but Never ignored the comment.

'OK,' said Never. 'Where's St Petersburg?' Petro pointed

it out. 'Really?' said Never. 'Wow. My geography does indeed suck. Although Lisbon is about here, right?'

Petro nodded. 'Both coastal cities. The St Petersburg witnesses described the sea as being the attacker, whatever that means.'

'So, St Petersburg,' said Never, marking it with his finger. 'Then Lisbon. Twenty-four hours for the whole thing, so that little bit is, what, about four hours as the world turns? Then . . .' He moved along the same distance. 'East Coast USA. South America. Canada.'

Jonah stared at him. 'What do you mean?'

'I mean, what's next?' said Never.

Petro nodded. 'Big city by the coast,' said Petro. 'Take your pick.'

'New York,' said Jonah. 'Miami.' He thought of Sam Deering, down in Florida. At least he was in Ocala, about as far from the sea as you could get in the state.

They heard a vehicle's tyres scrunching on the gravel outside. Jonah jumped up and went to the door, relieved that Annabel was back, but it wasn't her. It was Sly. 'Hey, Never, your girlfriend's here.'

In a flash, Never was beside him. 'Don't *ever* say that around her,' he muttered. 'She'd murder me.' He frowned, looking at her van. 'God, I hope she offloaded Kendrick's body.'

'Don't say *that* around her either,' said Jonah.

She came in with a laptop bag, and held out a USB memory stick. She handed them both to Never. 'Make a copy of this, fast as you can. And put Kendrick's revival footage on there, too.'

'Hello,' said Never, pointedly. He took the memory stick and the laptop through to the kitchen.

'I hate to bring bad news,' she said to Jonah. 'But this power cut is widespread.'

'We're aware of that,' said Jonah. 'We've been listening to radio transmissions. There are things you need to hear.'

'Where's Annabel?'

'Our neighbour wanted to fetch her family, Annabel went with her.' A sudden fear hit him. 'Are things still safe out there?'

Sly raised an eyebrow. 'Safe? I think you'd better get me up to speed. Fast.'

Jonah took her through everything they knew, and in return she explained that the memory stick held a full record of Kendrick's files. She wouldn't say where she'd been to get them, just that the roads had seemed normal enough, just quiet.

'I stopped at a gas station on the way here,' she said. 'Their pumps were off, but they were still open for cash sales of everything else. The power had been off for five hours by then, and wherever people had come from they had the same story.'

'Were they worried?' asked Jonah.

'Mostly about their frozen stock,' she said. 'A few others I talked to had the same kind of deer-in-headlights look, basic denial that this would last much longer. No signs of panic, though.'

A moment later, Never reappeared. He handed Jonah his phone. 'I've copied the recordings of the radio we picked up from St Petersburg and Lisbon onto the USB stick,' he said. 'You should play them for Sly while I make a backup of the rest.' He went back to the kitchen.

Jonah played the recordings, and Petro translated again. Sly listened in silence. When the recordings finished, she looked at Petro. 'Write it down,' she said. 'I need your translation.' He did as she asked.

'All done,' Never said, returning. He handed her the USB stick and the laptop. 'What are you going to do with them?'

She took a deep breath and shook her head. 'I have an old friend to meet. Jesus, I'd thought we'd have more time . . .'

'What's in Kendrick's files?' asked Never.

'Detail,' she said. 'Lots of detail that seems a little pointless right now, but I have a duty to tell them what I know. The revival footage is more important, and now the radio transmissions. I don't know if I can convince them. I don't know if it would make any difference anyway.'

'I'm coming,' said Never. 'I'm a witness to the revival. Might help your case.'

'No,' said Sly. 'I go alone.'

But Never wasn't having it. 'You're in strung-out shape, Sly. If you want me to stay in the van I will, but I'd be happier if you had some company.'

She looked at him for a long moment, then nodded. 'Company would be good.' She opened the front door and started walking.

Jonah looked at Never. 'You sure?'

'Mainly I want to guarantee she doesn't just fuck off somewhere,' he said. 'If shit happens, she'll be worth her weight in gold.' He ran through to the kitchen and returned with his jacket in one hand, and the video camera in the other.

'Be careful,' said Jonah. 'Sunset's not far off. Don't take risks.'

'I have personal protection,' said Never. 'What could go wrong?'

13

'It's getting dark,' said Never. He could hardly stand still. He'd been watching the sky since the moment he and Sly had left Annabel's, watching as the aurora became unmistakable, growing increasingly clear as the sun made its way down to the horizon.

They were in Washington DC, standing overlooking the Potomac by Long Bridge Park. Behind them, the Pentagon skulked. Above, the darkening sky was showing off the aurora in almost its full glory now.

'He'll come,' said Sly. 'I spoke to him this morning, before I went for the files. Before the power went.'

The Pentagon was one of the few lit buildings in the city, and even then most of the windows were dark. That had been where they'd tried first, only to be turned away by the guards at the main entrance after ten minutes of waiting. The response Sly had got had seemed like a simple rejection, but she'd explained to Never that it had merely been a way to establish where to meet. She'd driven over to Long Bridge Park and taken Never to where they'd been standing since. Her allowing Never to leave the van and tag along had come as a surprise to him, but she was visibly exhausted and wanted an extra pair of eyes, even if those eyes belonged to Never.

That had been forty minutes ago, and time was ticking.

'How long do we give him?' said Never.

'Feel free to walk home,' she said. There was an edge to her impatience, Never knew. She didn't suffer fools at the best of times, but he could tell she was thinking exactly the same thing that he was: they should have left the city already. She just didn't appreciate Never banging on about it.

He couldn't help it, though. By day, anxious as he was, there had still been a *theoretical* edge to what was happening. Now he looked at this city he'd known for so long, and he couldn't deny that everything about the situation was utterly alien. The green sky; the near-deserted streets. It was a dark city, devoid of street lights, the buildings dead. The silence was broken from time to time by the short squawk of a police vehicle announcing its presence, a basic reminder to the inhabitants that they'd not been forgotten. There was no sign of the looting or unrest that had seemed a clear possibility. Whether that was down to the police visibility or not, he didn't know, but he reckoned there was a good chance that the residents were feeling the same sense of *portent* that he was, even if they could have no idea why.

He switched the video camera on and started to capture the scene.

'Put that away,' scolded Sly.

He let the camera fall to his side, casually continuing to film as a man in black jeans and black jacket walked up the park steps to where they stood.

'Sly,' said the man.

'You took your sweet time,' said Sly.

'Who's this?' he said, nodding to Never.

'A friend,' she said. 'Harmless. I got the files I told you about. I got some more you should know, too.'

'I'll take a look when things settle down,' said the man. 'If you hadn't noticed, we have a situation.'

'This situation is the *same thing*.'

The man shook his head. 'Like hell. Look, Sly, I'd like to help, but none of Kendrick's *hobby* has ever been sanctioned. None of it has ever been *believed*. Trust me.'

'They believed it enough to vaporize Winnerden Flats.'

The man shook his head. 'They didn't know what the hell that was. Can I remind you that Kendrick changed his story repeatedly? And he hasn't even got the decency to come here himself. He sends *you*.'

'He didn't *change* his story,' she said. 'A virus was cover, that was all. He made that clear. Here.' She passed him the USB stick. 'Kendrick's dead.'

The man said nothing.

'All his files are here. So is footage of his revival. He *saw* it. He saw the creature, alive again in a new body.'

The man shook his head. 'Shit, Sly, I'm sorry. But they gave your boss the benefit of the doubt all this time, and look what happened. Nothing.'

'You call *this* nothing?' She gestured to the sky.

'Take this,' said Never, reaching out to the man. He had a piece of paper in his hand.

'What's this?' said the man, taking it.

'A frequency to monitor, and a translation of what we've heard so far,' said Never. 'The files Sly gave you include a recording from St Petersburg. And Lisbon. They—'

Sly interrupted, and Never realized she'd noticed something in the other man's expression.

'You already *know*,' she said. 'You know something's
coming.' She shook her head, smiling in a way that was
loaded with anger. 'I assume everyone important is at Mount
Weather by now.'

'I can't answer that,' said the man.

She drew in a sharp breath. 'Aren't you planning on
warning people? You realize New York is probably next, yes?'

The man scoffed. 'Warn them about what?' Sly said
nothing. '*Exactly.* You want to create panic?' He took a long
breath, and looked at the USB stick in his hand. When he
spoke again, he sounded drained. 'You really think this is
connected? *That*'s what this is?'

Sly nodded.

The man gave her an urgent look. 'Then tell me that
there's an *answer* in these files, not just ramblings.'

Sly closed her eyes for a moment. 'I don't know if there's
an answer here,' she said. 'But I think it's the only place we
can look for one. *Christ*, why didn't you people listen to
what we were telling you? We're out of time.' As she spoke,
Never could see her fist clenching. 'What do they think this
situation is? Tell me.'

The man seemed wary, but he relented. 'Information is
sparse. What we do have makes no sense, but the inter-
national tensions that were spilling out this past week are
based on something, Sly.'

'The cable sabotage?' she said.

'Exactly. The submersible drone they found wasn't just
chance. There had been rumours for days in advance.'

'Rumours of what?'

He looked reluctant again. Sly glared at him. 'OK, OK. Have you heard of QNB? Or BZ?'

Her mouth almost dropped open. 'No way.'

They were silent for a moment, until Never found he had to speak. 'Can someone explain, for fuck's sake?'

'It's a drug,' said Sly. 'Developed as a weapon.'

The man took over, looking at Never. 'We don't think this is QNB exactly, but that's our best bet. A neurochemical weapon with effective aerosolized distribution. QNB is an incapacitant, essentially – it creates stupor, confusion and confabulation. Causes hallucinations, OK? People make shit up. The effects can last for weeks. The reports you've heard, yes, we've heard them, and the reason they sound like a nightmare is that they probably *are*. This is war, but not war like we've ever known it. This isn't about taking territory, Sly, this is about fucking *everything* up and using the effects of the flare to mask it.'

'Who do they blame?' said Sly.

'They wanted to strike North Korea,' said the man. 'The prime candidate for aggressor.'

'They wanted to *launch*?' said Sly, appalled. 'So what happened?'

'They did launch,' he said, matter-of-factly. 'And nothing hit. At least, nothing *detonated*. We can still detect nuclear explosions seismically, and none were detected.'

'Are you saying our nuclear capability has been compromised?'

'It could be anything,' said the man. 'Finding out what will take time, and time is not what we have.'

While they'd talked, Never had been biting his tongue,

but there was a question he needed to ask. 'Uh, does Pandora mean anything to either of you?' he said.

Sly looked at him. 'In what way?'

'I don't know,' said Never. 'A project name, maybe? A weapon? It's just . . . Jonah had some kind of dream . . .' He shook his head, knowing how weak it sounded. 'He thought it was important. I don't know.'

The man sneered. 'A fucking *dream*? Jesus.'

'Don't dismiss it,' said Sly. 'Trust me.' She shook her head, though. 'I don't know of a Pandora weapon, Never.' She gave her colleague in black a pointed look.

'Me neither,' said the man, without disguising his disdain. 'Look, Sly, this is bad, but it's not some fucking *demon* that's coming. Best advice I have: get supplies, hide, wait it out. So unless you actually have information we can use, then we're done here.'

The man's attitude infuriated Never. 'Did you tell people *anything*?' he said.

'To stay indoors,' said the man. 'What else could we do? We can't protect anyone but ourselves.' He put the USB stick in his pocket. 'Take care of yourself, Sly.'

He walked away.

*

Sly looked vaguely ill. 'When I mentioned Mount Weather, did you see that twitch?'

'No,' said Never. 'And Mount Weather is . . . ?'

'Emergency Command and Control hub,' she said. 'It's where senior figures would gather, but I don't think they're there. Nobody high up the command chain, at any rate.'

'Where, then?' said Never. He was still quietly fuming about the way he'd been treated.

'You heard the man,' she said. 'They're leaving the people to fend for themselves. The top brass have decided to cut and run, until they see how bad this gets. I'd be willing to bet they're all in Cheyenne. Hiding deep in a mountain.'

'Meaning . . . ?'

Sly sighed, and Never saw her clench her fist again. 'It means we're on our own.' They stood in silence for a moment. 'Let's go,' said Sly. She started back to the van.

He looked to the sky. The aurora was brighter than he'd ever seen it, and he lifted his camera to film the slowly shifting forms. Now that he could see it so clearly, the pattern of the lights seemed odd – shot through with a secondary branching structure, like dark veins in a corpse. And while the lights gently fluctuated and rippled, this structure seemed stable, yet growing . . .

He used the camera's zoom to take a closer look. He stared at what he saw: there was a *pulsing*, he was sure of it, in the darkness. A gradual widening and shrinking of the dark lines, which was all heading in the same direction. As he watched, a small region of pure black formed high in the distant sky, then bulged. Slowly, the bulge stretched down in a thin black line, until it was out of sight.

He started to back away. The column of darkness was widening by the second.

'Come *on*, Never,' said Sly. 'We need to . . .' She drifted off, as she saw it too. 'What the hell is that? Is that a . . . a water spout?' Her expression changed suddenly, becoming fearful.

'How far away do you think that is?' said Never. 'Over Chesapeake Bay? Nearer?'

The veins in the sky thickened.

'We need to leave,' said Sly, but Never felt dazed at the sight.

'Coastal,' he muttered. 'So we thought New York. On the other hand, Washington DC and Baltimore are almost on top of each other. And both are beside water.' The proximity of the Potomac suddenly felt like a threat.

'We need to leave *now*,' said Sly, grabbing his arm.

As she did, the dark column suddenly collapsed inward, and at the same instant the aurora surrounding the black nexus brightened enough to leave an afterimage.

They both stared. A few seconds later, a dull rumble reached their ears. It was like thunder, but the rumble didn't simply fade. It kept going, and seemed to grow louder.

Nearer.

They ran to Sly's van and jumped in, Sly starting the engine and pressing hard on the accelerator before Never had even shut the door. When they reached the I-395 there was another sound underneath the rumble – a higher-pitched noise, a curious *hissing* that took Never a moment to place.

'That's water,' he said. 'The *river*.' He looked behind them, to where the top floors of the Pentagon were still visible past the rise in the road. Something dark rose up behind it, silhouetted against the green-tinted clouds to the north. A shapeless mass, it rolled forward to engulf the Pentagon. He thought of Petro, translating the report from Gatchina – *a sea of poison rose up*. The lit windows on the building were obscured now, and he could see the same black form rising further up and down the river.

'What is it?' said Sly, focusing in the road. 'What do you see?'

He faced front. 'Drive,' he said. 'Just drive.' He thought of the road they were on, and it occurred to him that it ran parallel to the Potomac. 'Shit,' he said. 'Get us off this road. Get us away from the river.'

Sly said nothing. She slewed the car across to the next off-ramp, heading for Lincolnia and along the Little River Turnpike. The screaming of the engine still wasn't enough to drown out the rumble and the hiss that seemed to follow them. The road was almost empty, the few drivers bemused and angered by Sly's speed. They passed houses that were dark, save for the flicker of candles and the beams of flashlights. There were curious faces at the doors, though – the rumbling, hissing sound was drawing attention.

'How far will it come inland?' said Sly. 'How far away do we need to get?'

'The first report came from Gatchina,' he said, trying to remember. 'Petro said it was maybe twenty miles out of St Petersburg. That gives us an upper limit, I guess.'

'Jesus,' said Sly. 'We're outpacing it, though? Right?'

'Yeah,' said Never. He had no idea. Although the darkness had seemed to rise slowly to consume the Pentagon, he'd not seen what kind of speed it was advancing at now. For all he knew they would see it any moment, crashing over the rooftops beside them.

They kept going down the turnpike, and just as they passed a gas station on the left, another vehicle hurtled out of the road to their right, the driver's face a mask of panic.

Sly swore and swerved, slamming on the brakes, but she hit the traffic signal post on the corner. Airbags fired and the engine died.

When Never gathered his senses, for a horrible moment he thought he might have blacked out for a time. 'Sly?' he said, unclipping his safety belt. He reached across. She was slumped, unconscious. Her door window had smashed into tiny fragments, letting in the roar and hiss, louder than before. It took a few seconds for the situation to really dawn on Never.

They weren't going *anywhere* now.

'Oh shit,' he said. He jumped out to the road and looked back along the turnpike. The drivers in the few cars that passed them looked terrified, glancing behind them, but none stopped to check on them or offer help after their impact. He looked around. There were only a couple of car lots and empty shops nearby. Nowhere to hide.

In the distance, the road was *moving*. Cars headed that way were stopping suddenly, and turning back. He watched the furthest of them, as their headlights simply vanished, swamped by the dark tide.

He thought of the report from Gatchina, and how someone had mentioned shutting themselves in their vehicle. With the window smashed, staying in the front of the van wasn't an option. But this van had a metal divider between the front seats and the rest of it. Maybe it would be enough.

He ran to Sly's door and yanked at it. The impact had clearly shifted the frame slightly, but the door creaked open with a little force. He leaned across her and unclipped her belt, then pulled her out and dragged her to the back of the vehicle. He opened the rear doors. Kendrick's body bag was still there, the van's internal light glinting off the black plastic. He hoisted Sly up and bundled her inside, all the while horribly aware of the rising volume and the realization that, as the sound grew nearer, he could hear a chitinous, insectile *click* underpinning the hiss. As he climbed into the van, the camera strap around his shoulder tangled on the latch. He turned back, looking along the turnpike again, and shuddered to see how close the dark had got. He pulled the doors, but the lock wouldn't engage – the camera strap was blocking it. He opened the doors again and yanked with all his strength to free the strap. It was snarled, though, and he couldn't quite tell how to get it cleared.

He could see what the *flood* consisted of now, dim-lit by the green sky: dark spider-legged *things* covering everything in their path, closing down, closing down . . .

A car screeched to a halt by the van, and the panicked driver shouted at Never through his open window: 'What the hell *is* that?'

'Close your fucking window!' screamed Never, still work-ing at the strap. 'Close it!'

The strap came free, as the river of shadows engulfed the rear of the other car.

He closed the van doors. The lock held.

The van shuddered as a thousand legs scratched and scraped over the metal, the hideous sound unbearable in the confined space. He wanted to cover his ears, but he didn't dare release his hold on the doors, just in case, just in *case*.

He could hear something else underneath the roar of movement, and he was sure it was screaming.

14

Never dreamed of a dark river, flowing through all the waterways of the planet – a slow, tar-like morass of hatred, moving with intent, *alive*. The land was dry; the few trees and sparse vegetation along the banks were struggling to hold on, and as the black waters reached them, the poison was drawn into their sap, spreading up inexorably through to the veins of the leaves. Once the contagion had taken each plant, it collapsed in on itself, then tumbled to the earth and fell apart into pulsating wet masses. Eventually, those masses dragged themselves to the dark water and joined the vast flow.

Sly's voice woke him. 'Get up, Never.'

He opened his eyes, wincing at the daylight coming in through the van's open doors. Sly had a red mark across her face where the airbag had hit her. He sat up sharply, amazed that every part of him wasn't in pain after the van's impact. His hands, though, ached like hell. No wonder. He'd spent an hour holding the van doors closed, even though they'd latched, even once he'd seen the internal lock-snib and clicked it up. He couldn't bring himself to let go. A long hour, with things from a nightmare continuing to flow over the vehicle, and – God help him – audibly *testing* the structure. Scratches that seemed more than just a scrabble over the roof.

Looking for a way in.

An hour was a guess, though. It had seemed like eternity before the sudden drop in the intensity of the sound, and a gradual dissipation of the claw-rain that surrounded him. At last, in the silence, he'd slumped to the floor, drained. He could hear Sly's breathing, and he'd called to her without a response. Eventually, he must have fallen asleep. It astonished him that sleep could have come at all.

The camera, whose Judas-strap had almost been the end of him, was sitting beside him on the floor of the van. He looked outside. The light that had made him wince was the light of dawn, the edge of the sun barely above the horizon. The road was dotted with cars, but he saw no movement at all.

Sly was standing by the car that he'd seen stop last night, the driver of which had called out to him in fear – the driver he'd yelled at to close his window, moments before the dark swallowed him. He thought of how long an electric window took to shut, cold electronics with no notion of urgency. No sense of danger.

He got out of the van and walked over to Sly. The driver's body was face down on the asphalt by her feet.

'Did you pull him out?' he asked.

'Don't look at him,' she said, as she opened the car's rear door.

He felt his blood go cold and went back to the van. He remembered all the times where footage of the aftermath of disasters had been taken by people; all the times the perpetually outraged had bemoaned how someone could *document* rather than *help*, as if documenting a catastrophe had no purpose. He fetched the camera and started to record. Someone had to.

'I said don't *look* at him . . .' said Sly, as he turned the body over.

He stumbled back. There was a hole in the man's face where his eyes and nose should have been. He made himself record it, then panned the camera around. Other cars further away, other bodies, slumped over steering wheels, faces obscured or just too far away to tell.

To tell if the same had happened to them.

'Give me a hand with Kendrick,' said Sly, and when he just looked at her, she scowled. 'I'm not leaving him here, Never. I'm not fucking leaving him.'

His hesitation had merely been confusion, though – he'd not understood what she'd been talking about. *Of course*, he thought: the van was done for, and here was a car they could use.

Together they carried the body bag from the van to the back seat of the car.

'Get in,' she said.

Movement caught his eye further down the road. Someone was walking out to one of the cars, where a body was sprawled across the hood.

'Can't we help?' said Never.

'We're going,' said Sly, cold. 'Get in the fucking car.'

He was about to protest when the distant figure took hold of the body's arm and started to drag it slowly away from the vehicle and across to the sidewalk. There was something about the lumbering way it was done that made

Never decide that getting out of there was the only sensible thing to do.

He got in the car, raising the camera to record as Annabel drove. There was no damage to buildings that he could see, but roadside vegetation looked trampled every- where he looked, small trees broken, larger ones cleared of most of their leaves, the branches stripped and snapped. His dream came back to him, and he shivered.

Scattered cars littered the road, as did occasional bodies. Many of them were clearly mutilated, with the same bloody crater where their face should have been.

That could have been *him*. If he'd lost consciousness after the crash, or taken two seconds longer to get the van doors shut. He felt numb at the thought. He'd saved himself, and he'd saved Sly, but instead of relief he felt nothing. The same blank shock was on the faces of the few living people he saw as they drove, a total incomprehension of what had gone on here. Most people still seemed to be inside, and after the horrors overnight he supposed it was still early for them to pluck up the courage to venture outside. He im- agined people cowering indoors, peering through curtains.

When they reached Chantilly, sixteen miles from the river, the trampled vegetation petered out.

'Stop,' said Never. Their car slowed to a halt.

From here on, the road looked clear, but the only person around was an elderly woman sitting on a bench. He got out of the car and approached her, lowering the camera but con- tinuing to record.

'Ma'am?' he said. She looked up at him, deeply anxious, keeping a firm hold of a metal walking stick. In one hand she held a bible.

'You stay back there,' she said. 'Till I get a good look at you.'

He nodded and kept his distance. 'Did you see what happened here?'

'I saw some of it,' she said. 'I saw a river come up the road, and I saw it was full of *devils*. I got in my cellar and I prayed. Seems God took pity on *me*.' She said it with a hint of contempt, looking back down to the few bodies visible on the road, then she looked at Never with suspicion. 'What about you?'

'We were caught in it. We shut ourselves in the back of a van.'

She nodded. 'My neighbour packed himself and his family into their car, half-hour back.'

'Leaving the city,' said Never, but the woman shook her head.

'Others did, but not him. They were going *into* the city. He said they'd be safest there, but his kids looked at him like he was crazy.' She fixed her eyes on Never. 'He was *something*, but I don't think he was crazy.'

'What was he?' said Never. He wanted to hear it from someone else. He thought of the person he'd seen, dragging a body to the roadside. Perhaps they'd simply been traumatized. Perhaps. Or perhaps they were getting on with a task. A *clean-up*.

The old woman was watching him closely. 'I don't know what he was. Changed, that's for sure.'

Sly called to him. 'Let's get going,' she said.

'Two seconds,' said Never. He turned to the old woman. 'Have you got people here? Do you want to come with us?'

She watched him for a few seconds, then gave him a cold

look and shook her head. 'You go on your way, son,' she said.

She didn't trust him, he realized. He nodded, then looked back down the road. Who could blame her?

*

When he heard the car, Jonah was outside clearing leaves and other debris from the surfaces of the solar panels. The wind the previous night had been strong, although not strong enough to mask the noises they'd heard soon after dark – what started off like distant thunder had grown into something far more disturbing, and the sky itself had seemed to pulse with some kind of hideous life until the early hours. And all that time, Never and Sly were out there.

It hadn't been long after the two of them had driven off that Annabel had returned, and Jonah wondered how he would have coped if she'd not been back, either. As it was he'd spent an uneasy night in the living room, sometimes listening in to the radio to see if any transmissions came through, but the static was complete. Even local transmissions were overwhelmed.

The rest of the time he tried to sleep, jumping at any noise in case it was his friend coming back.

Or something else. He'd lowered the shutters overnight.

He went to the door and, although he didn't recognize the car, he could see Sly and Never through the windshield. He couldn't help but run out to them, yanking Never's door open as the car came to a halt.

'Thank Christ,' he said, and Never got out. He was trembling slightly, Jonah thought. 'What happened?'

'We were there,' said Never. 'We saw it.'

'Saw what? We heard what seemed like a thunderstorm in the distance, but nothing like any of us has experienced. I didn't know if it was—' He stopped talking, seeing the urgent terror in Never's eyes.

'The attack was on DC,' said Sly, getting out of the car. 'Maybe Baltimore too. Depends on the radius. At least twenty miles from the Potomac in this direction, but who knows how far it could reach?'

'It?' said Jonah. The picture in his mind was of the *Beast*, vast and triumphant; striding across the landscape with a terrible screaming *roar*. He looked at Never, who held up his camera.

'I don't know how much I got,' said Never, 'but I got some.'

'Uh, what are all these?' said Sly. She gestured to the newly arrived vehicles in the driveway and Jonah nodded.

'Annabel went to fetch the family of one of our neighbours. She came back with more than she bargained for.'

He led them into the house. Annabel appeared, grinning with relief. She hugged them both.

'My *God*, we were worried,' she said, but her smile faded as she realized how wary they all seemed. She reached out a hand to Sly's red-marked face. 'Are you OK?'

'I crashed the van as we were escaping,' said Sly. 'It might be hard to believe, but Never saved my life.'

Annabel shot her a bemused look. 'Escaping?' she said. 'What do you mean?'

Sly summed it up. 'Something happened. Something bad.'

A ten-year-old girl strolled past them, wiping sleep from her eyes, getting a raised eyebrow from both Never and Sly.

'OK,' said Jonah. 'Let's take this somewhere private, huh?'

*

He took them to his office space and shut the door.

'So who was that kid?' said Never. The camera was hanging from its strap around his shoulder. He took it and removed the memory card.

'Remy,' said Jonah. 'Grady's big sister.'

'How many strays have you managed to collect?' grumbled Sly.

While Jonah booted up his PC, Annabel answered. 'Three neighbours. Petro you've met. Philip, a seventy-two-year-old retired cardiovascular surgeon, and Cathy, our resident astrophysicist. Cathy's daughter Sara, Sara's husband Armel, and their daughter Remy, who you just saw.'

'Remy's younger brother Grady died a few days ago,' added Jonah. 'Just so you know.' A horrible thought crossed his mind – the possibility that, when all was said and done, little Grady might have been the lucky one.

'Is that the lot?' said Sly.

Annabel shook her head. 'No. Sara is neighbours with her best friend, and when we arrived and explained, she went next door. So they're here too – Jansin, her husband Mark, two kids. That's it. So far.'

'Sara explained to her friend?' said Never. 'What exactly did she explain?'

Annabel shrugged. 'Just that the blackout was widespread, and it might be better out of the city.'

'And how does that affect your supplies?' said Sly. 'Having the extra mouths to feed?'

'We're fine,' said Jonah. She and Kendrick had known that Jonah was half-heartedly setting up the place as a well-stocked bolthole, even if assembling and installing any of the kit he'd bought had tended to fall by the wayside. 'We have our own bore for water, food for a month, and that's without raiding our neighbours' stocks too.'

'A month,' said Sly, half to herself. The despairing way she said it made Jonah anxious to know what the hell had happened.

'What did you see?' he said. 'Can't you just tell me?'

'Best you see it yourself,' said Never. Jonah logged on to his PC. 'Let me drive,' said Never, and Jonah stood to let Never take the seat. He put the memory card into the PC; it took a few moments for him to open the card's folder. 'Sly took us to meet someone. What was he Sly, NSA?'

'Something like that,' said Sly.

'Here we go,' said Never. He played it back – the view of the aurora, the camera lowered to give a shot of the stranger's lower legs. The audio was a little muffled, but they could get the gist of the conversation.

'Pause it,' said Sly, and Never did. 'I thought we knew more than they did, for a moment,' she said. 'But they sure as shit knew something cataclysmic was on the way. They knew about St Petersburg and Lisbon, but they thought the confused descriptions of what had happened indicated the use of a neurotoxin. Biochemical warfare. Something that would create chaos, a hallucinogen. The way they saw it, a hostile agent was taking advantage of the problems caused by the solar flare, and ensuring communications failed more completely than would have been the case without their *help*.

169

Then this unknown enemy attacked with the biochemical agent to complete the job.'

'Why?' said Jonah. 'Why the hell did they think anyone would *do* that?'

'Somewhere like North Korea?' said Sly. 'Imagine if the rest of the world could be turned into a disaster zone, something they were prepared for and could cope with easily. They'd suddenly be the strongest nation around. And you know what? For a moment, I wondered if maybe that could be it. I forgot about what Kendrick saw, and I hoped . . .' She shook her head. 'OK, play it, Never.'

In the audio, they heard Never and Sly's exchange, where she mentioned Cheyenne; Never paused it once more.

'Tell me again what that is, Sly,' he said. '*Cheyenne.*'

'Imagine if an asteroid was coming,' said Sly. 'Imagine it was about to wipe out the country and there was nothing anybody could do about it. Cheyenne is the place to be. The bunker to end all bunkers. Started out as a command and control facility, like Mount Weather, but over the years they just kept expanding the place. All those mystery Defense-budget dollars.'

'What's its capacity?' said Annabel. 'How many people?'

'Five hundred for ten years,' said Sly. 'So I heard. Might be more. I imagine all the *guests* are already there. They don't know what this is, but they know it's bad.'

Playback resumed. Jonah and Annabel watched with rising dread, as the black patterns in the sickly green aurora appeared and gathered; as the column stretched down in the far distance, and the terrible thunder began, the hiss; as Sly and Never hurried to the van, and the darkness could be seen covering the Pentagon.

Turning off the interstate. The crash. A moment of silence, before Never moved again, and got Sly out. The panic as the strap caught, the camera juddering and capturing only the sight of Sly lying prone.

The other driver's voice, and Never's response.

And then, as Never triumphantly went to close the van door, the camera swung round on its strap and caught one last glimpse of the scene: green-lit creatures, the front line ever nearer, the dark river stretching out to the horizon. The doors closed; the sound of the flood covering the van poured from the PC speakers.

Playback stopped. 'Then an hour or so of that fucking *sound,*' said Never. He opened the next recording, which started with the shot of the body of the driver. Annabel and Jonah gasped as the body was turned over, then watched the rest in silence – the abandoned cars. The bodies.

'Any questions?' said Sly. 'Because I don't think we have answers.'

15

Annabel insisted on getting Sly and Never checked over by Philip. She had managed to introduce herself to the retired surgeon when she'd first moved into the area, although it had been brief. He'd appeared at his front door and had given her the shortest of polite greetings. He'd seemed pleasant enough, though he certainly hadn't come across as wanting much of a relationship with his new neighbour. That had suited her fine back then, but this time Annabel had made far more of an effort to break the ice.

He turned out to have a gentle sense of humour, which was a good sign. When she asked him to take a look at her friends, Philip didn't hesitate.

'Been a while since I worked ER,' he said. 'But it's all in here, if I can dredge it up.' He pointed to his temple.

She'd left Sly and Never with Jonah in his office, and when she and Philip entered, the two patients had a quiet desperation in their eyes that Philip seemed to pick up on right away. He gave Annabel a wary glance – she'd told him almost nothing about what had happened to them.

'Annabel tells me you two had an accident,' he said. 'Tell me the details.'

'We crashed in a van,' said Never.

There was a pause, Philip clearly expecting more. 'What speed?' he asked.

'About thirty,' said Sly, and again there was a pause.

'I see,' said Philip. 'I may be rusty, so bear with me.' He produced a pen and held it up in front of Sly, then moved it around. 'Follow the pen. OK, good. Now turn your head fully to the left. And to the right.' He nodded, and turned to Never. 'Now you.'

He repeated the same instructions, which Never dutifully followed.

'OK,' he said at last. 'Did either of you lose consciousness?'

'No,' said Sly, and Never looked at her at once.

'Yes you did,' he said. 'You were out cold. You didn't stir the whole time the—' He paused, and looked at Philip. 'Uh, you didn't stir.'

Sly frowned. 'Shit,' she said. 'I can't really remember.'

Philip put his hand under her chin and looked carefully at her, moving her head gently. 'Rapid deceleration,' said Philip. 'I see the marks from the airbag on your face. We'll need to keep a close eye on you. Concussion's a real danger. Headache, dizziness, not thinking straight. You too, uh, sorry, Annabel *did* mention your names, but I . . .'

'I'm Never,' said Never. 'She's Sly.'

Philip nodded. 'Never. Sly. Kids these days . . .'

'Ha!' said Never, smiling at last. '*Kids*, he says.'

'Son, when *you* reach eighty, you'll realize I meant it. We need to watch you both, but Sly especially. Most important thing is to rest.'

'Thanks, Philip,' said Annabel. There was something else

she wanted from him, though. 'Look, uh, I was going to ask you for some advice.'

'Sure,' he said.

'Something big happened,' she said. 'In DC. But I don't know what to tell everyone. I don't want to give people more than they can handle.'

Sly looked at her. 'What do they know already?' she said.

'*They*, huh?' said Philip, raising his eyebrow. 'Well, Cathy already told us that the power cuts are widespread, and there have been attacks of some kind on cities near the coast in Russia and Europe.'

'She did?' said Annabel.

'While you were asleep,' said Philip. 'The kids were sleeping too. Of everyone, I think they're the ones we should be most careful about.'

'Agreed,' said Annabel. 'What else did Cathy say?'

'That we're taking shelter, just in case. We've tried to limit speculation, and with the kids awake we've agreed not to talk about it.' He looked from Sly to Never, and back. 'A good doctor can see the ghosts in a patient's eyes. Fear can't hide when you really *look* at someone. I'm guessing that things have taken a turn for the worse.'

'We owe you the full story,' said Sly. 'You can—'

'Not so fast,' he said, interrupting her. He gave her a kind smile. 'Look, I'm not a religious person. My wife was, even when she was being eaten alive by cancer. Not even fifty, and she still thought God was the *bee's knees*.' He shook his head. 'It made me angry, the injustice, but I hid it because I knew it would just be toxic if I didn't. You see, I don't think a *lack* of God would have done her any good.

Sometimes ignorance is a terrible thing, the *worst* of things, but there *are* times when it's a blessing.'

'You don't want to know what happened?' said Sly.

He nodded. 'If you think knowing what's out there will help, then by all means tell us. Otherwise, keeping it vague suits me fine. And for God's sake, we all have to pretend everything will come out good in the end. Kids pick up on more than you think.'

*

'So what do we do next?' said Annabel. Philip had gone, and nobody had spoken for an uncomfortably long time – Never and Sly seemed a little shell-shocked, naturally, but Jonah had an air of dismay about him that she didn't like, partly because she could feel that same dismay herself. If she succumbed to it now, she didn't know if she'd recover.

She looked at Jonah, silently begging him. *Pull it together*, she thought. *For me. For all of us.*

'We move everyone into the tunnels,' said Jonah. 'The upper cavern. We shutter the house at night, go into the cavern and lock the door. The security systems will tell us if anything comes near, but we'll be safe either way.'

Sly shook her head. 'This can't be it,' she muttered. 'Hiding.'

'Survival is what comes *first*,' said Jonah. 'Today we move all our supplies down below. We stay safe.'

Sly looked exhausted. 'And then what?' she said.

'Then?' said Jonah. 'Then I find a way to win.'

He smiled and slapped Sly gently on the back, and gave Annabel the briefest of looks. Of all of them, Annabel hadn't pegged Sly as the one to need false hope, but Jonah was trying his best.

*

Letting Sly and Never rest, Annabel and Jonah got on with some basic preparations. They fed the cable from the radio aerial downstairs and into the cavern, and brought the receiver into the little wine cellar so that they could monitor it overnight. The narrow frequency range that had been typically static-free was noisier than ever, and local traffic was all they had been able to get since the night before. Even then, most of it tended to be unintelligible.

There was a single remote unit they could use to monitor the house security and control the shutters, which Jonah left beside the radio. He also brought in the two sunlamps he'd bought, old models that had long been discontinued because the light they produced was above legal limits. They were the same type which Kendrick had used in the safe house he'd kept Tess in, and although they'd not proved as effective as had been hoped, they'd certainly been useful when the safe house had been attacked, and had bought precious time. The parasites could physically detach from their hosts and attack, but sunlight severely damaged them.

'Do you think the things Never saw are the same?' asked Annabel. 'Are they like the parasites?'

'I think so,' said Jonah. 'When they have a human host to draw from, they can get much bigger.' He plugged the lamps in and gave them a brief test, wincing at the heat and light that came from them. 'They'll drain the power pretty fast,' he said. 'But in the morning I'll feel a lot better if I can put these on before I open the tunnel entrance and come out into the basement.'

Soon, Never came down to the basement and insisted on helping.

'You should be resting,' Annabel told him.

'I *tried* to rest,' he said. 'Sly's out for the count, but I can't sit still.'

Annabel left them to it and went back upstairs. She insisted on giving Cathy and Petro the option of hearing what had happened in DC, telling them both how Philip had felt. Cathy decided that she also didn't want to know, and as a result opted out of listening for any more radio transmissions. 'If I don't stop, I'll hear something bad,' she said. 'Something I won't be able to keep off my face, and Remy will pick up on it. That's the last thing she needs.'

'What about Remy's mom and dad?' asked Annabel. 'Should we talk to them?'

Cathy shook her head. 'They're hurting so much right now.' She leaned over and gripped Annabel's arm. 'If this is going to be the end of it all, I'd rather they had no idea. If they thought it was . . . They need hope, Annabel. Hope for their daughter.' She thought for a moment, then added: 'Jansin is Sara's best friend, too, and the same applies to their kids. You don't tell her or her husband, not yet.'

When Annabel spoke to Petro, he was keen to know everything. At his request, she took him to Jonah's office and showed him the footage from Never and Sly's road trip. Grey-faced, he turned away from the screen when it was over and looked her in the eye. 'Don't they say, "Share a burden, lose a burden"?' he said.

'Something like that,' said Annabel.

'Well, I'm glad to help take some burden. Perhaps we'll listen to the radio, and hear something good soon.'

She hoped he was right.

She returned to the basement and discovered Jonah and Never unboxing half a dozen tents she'd had no idea existed. Jonah had had a proactive phase of buying all kinds of equipment early on, before sinking into the depression that had dragged him down.

It became something of an adventure for the children, and for their parents, taking the tents into the cavern, placing the cushioning mats Jonah had bought, working out the baffling intricacies of the fibreglass poles and the tent material. The stone of the cavern echoed with laughter, and laughter hadn't been something she and Jonah had had much of in the last year. She couldn't have imagined old Harlan, the house's previous occupant, ever having been one for laughter either.

With food supplies and quarts of water, airbeds and sleeping bags, blankets and flashlights, there was a feeling of readiness for the night. Down here, things would be the same, whatever the sky contained, be it bright sun or flickering aurora.

Or the blackening veins, and the *flood*.

*

By late afternoon, preparations were almost complete. The three children were chased out of the courtyard garden by Never, anxious about the solar panels and their less-than-robust mountings. In the wine cellar, Petro was taking a turn listening to the radio, a duty he shared with Never, Jonah and Annabel. Sly was still asleep on one of the games-room couches, exhausted, with Never popping his head in from time to time to make sure she was OK.

Jonah, meanwhile, shut himself in his office and looked at the footage Never had captured. The first time he'd viewed it, he'd thought he'd noticed something but hadn't been sure. Now, he knew he'd not been mistaken.

Just as Never had been about to shut the van door, the camera happened to sweep up and capture several frames of the distant sky. And there, silhouetted against the green-tinted clouds, was a shape from Jonah's nightmares.

It was tiny in the shot, but he knew how far away it had to be, and hence how vast it really was. A dark figure, arms reaching to the sky.

The Beast itself.

There was a knock on the door. Jonah hid the image as Never looked in. 'Petro's heard something on the radio,' said Never, and Jonah followed him down. Annabel was there already, and they kept their voices low. The occasional excited yelp from the children playing in the cavern filtered into the wine cellar.

'The transmissions have become crowded,' said Petro. 'Overnight there was just too much static, presumably an effect of . . . of what came. Someone managed to bring a kind of order to the chaos, basically by bossing everyone around to take turns on what little space there was. Making people use identifying handles, time allocation and emergency call-outs. So, I've heard plenty from the neighbourhood, nothing much to add to what we know except that Baltimore *was* affected, and people are advising everyone to stay out of the cities. Nobody who goes into them comes back.'

Annabel nodded. 'The Gatchina broadcast said the same thing. Could be all kinds of bedlam there, panic and looting.'

'And other things,' said Never. They looked at him. 'I don't know . . . I saw people this morning acting the way you'd expect, distraught and scared. But there were others who just seemed to be getting on with something. Too purposeful, given what had happened.' He turned to Jonah. 'How fast can they take someone? How fast can the shadows take *hold*?'

Jonah shook his head. In Winnerden Flats, one of the parasites had tried to attach itself to Kendrick after its host had been killed. It had been a move of desperation, as the creature couldn't survive long without a human to drain life-force from – given Kendrick's sheer stubbornness, he was always going to put up a hell of a fight. Yet even with that challenge, Jonah had come to realize that it would either be a matter of time, or end up in the death of them both. The natural revulsion a person felt was the most important factor in preventing the creatures getting a foothold, but the revulsion would fade. He thought back to Lucas Silva, a man who had been a target Kendrick had selected when they were still trying to get some idea of what was really going on at Winnerden Flats. He'd been identified as someone who possibly carried one of the shadow parasites, so Kendrick had taken Jonah to get a good look at him, and verify it one way or the other.

And Silva did indeed have that pulsating grotesque creature clinging to him, its tendrils like ancient dead fingers digging deep into his breastbone, its central mass pulsating like a dead heart, its skin the colours of a diseased slug.

Then Silva's wife and child had shown up, and Jonah

had panicked when he'd seen that they too had something clinging to them – the smallest of *buds*, something they were surely unaware of, burrowing its way into their souls.

But how fast could it be done?

'I don't know,' said Jonah. 'But it's the *bodies* I've been haunted by since I saw them on that footage. Those people weren't being sought as hosts for the shadows. They were *fodder*, pure and simple.' The Beast had gone by many names; Eater of Souls was one of them. Was that what the ripped-out faces lying in Washington DC indicated? That the Soul Eater was feasting?

'There was something else I heard,' said Petro. 'Rumours, that's all, but . . .'

'Isn't everything?' said Annabel.

'I guess,' said Petro. 'An explosion in St Petersburg. A massive one, the size of the city itself.'

'Nuclear?' said Annabel.

'That's what people seem to think.'

A nuclear explosion, thought Jonah. Given the way the shadows reacted to intense light, it was surely something the Beast would fear. 'Wait,' he said. 'When was this?'

'Overnight, for us,' said Petro. 'Daytime for them. Reports say that someone had planned it for when the darkness that attacked them came back, but it went off during the day.'

'Why did they think it was coming back?' said Jonah. 'If it was like DC, it had been *decimated*. Better to move on to untouched cities, right?'

Petro shook his head. 'I don't know why they thought it was going to return, or when, but that's the story I heard.'

Jonah frowned. 'Perhaps it makes sense that it *would* come back,' he said. 'No resistance. No rush. It could enjoy itself with those left behind.' Part of him wondered if the mutilated victims would have given it much satisfaction; if, indeed, it hadn't just killed those it sensed it couldn't *drink* from, the way it had surely drunk from Silva and the others.

'So the people of St Petersburg were ready to hit back,' said Annabel. 'And their bomb went off too soon. What does that say to you?'

Petro shrugged. 'It says sabotage. It says there were collaborators.'

*

An hour before dark, they got everyone into the cavern and closed the heavy entry door, which locked from the inside with long-armed metal latches. The lighting, strung along the cavern walls, was bright enough to see by without draining too much power. The kids were reading by flashlight. Sly had remained in a low mood since she'd roused from her earlier sleep, but Philip had given her another check and was confident she would improve, albeit slowly.

Meanwhile, Jonah had transferred almost all of the smorgasbord of equipment into the cavern, including significant medical supplies. He showed them to Philip, who was a little taken aback.

'Wow,' he said. 'That defibrillator might prove handy for an old goat like me.' He smiled. 'You got yourself a basic field hospital right here.'

Jonah felt oddly proud.

As midnight approached, people started to settle down to sleep. Jonah went to relieve Petro from his most recent stint on the radio. Petro almost jumped out of his skin when Jonah put a hand on his shoulder.

'Sorry,' said Jonah. 'My turn. You should get some sleep.'

'You scared the Jesus out of me,' said Petro, taking off his headphones. 'So I heard your friend Never say, when I took *his* turn. Not heard that before.'

'It's *be*jesus,' said Jonah. He smiled. 'And if you hang around Never, you'll hear plenty you've not heard before. Anything to report?'

Petro shook his head. 'No more to add to the list,' he said. On the pad by the radio, they'd been writing down a list of suspected attack sites, but it had been impossible to tell rumour from fact. Rio de Janeiro, Shanghai, Mumbai, Cape Town . . . The list went on. The only thing they had much certainty about was that only DC and Baltimore were being mentioned as far as North America went. So far, it seemed, the country had been spared a second catastrophe.

The earlier report about St Petersburg, and the idea that they'd been expecting a return of the destructive forces, played on Jonah's mind as he listened to the static-laden fragments. He wondered again *why* they would expect it to come back. He wondered also about his assumption that a blast of any kind, even nuclear, would really cause that much damage to the Beast, but another thought occurred to him: it simply might *know* if there was something like that waiting for it, and go elsewhere.

Or have one of its *puppets* deal with the situation.

The static hiss lulled him into a doze.

He woke with a start, immediately realizing that he'd been asleep. For how long, he didn't know.

He was in darkness. There was no hiss from the radio now, but it wasn't because the static had cleared – the radio was off, just as the tunnel lights were. He realized he'd not brought a flashlight with him. He was about to stand when he was sure he sensed movement nearby.

'Hello?' he whispered. He heard no sound, but he was sure *something* was there with him. For a moment he couldn't move. Then, slowly, he edged out into the main corridor, feeling his way past the wine bottles protruding from their drill-holes in the wall. He could hear voices ahead of him now, people waking perhaps, or who hadn't been sleeping; they were too far away for him to hear what was being said, but he couldn't hear any panic. Anxiety, perhaps, but no panic.

He could see a dim light ahead, enough for him to navigate to the cavern. As he reached it, someone was walking towards him with a flashlight.

'Jonah?' It was Sly. She seemed a little groggy. 'What's happened?'

'I don't know,' he said, but something occurred to him. 'We should check the door.'

He turned back and down the tunnel and got to the main entryway, Sly close behind him. The door was closed, the lever latches still in place, but something about it didn't sit well with him. He stared at the latches. He'd been the one who had locked the door, and he was certain he'd pulled the levers fully into position. Now, they weren't quite pulled all the way. Secure, yes, but . . .

He put a finger on the locking edge of the lever, where it crossed the narrow gap at the edge of the door. A sudden image came to him, of a blade coming through that gap and lifting, *shoving* the lock out of place. He reached to the lever and put it into its fully locked position.

'What?' said Sly. 'What's wrong?'

Jonah leaned forward, putting his eye to the crack at the edge of the door, closer, closer . . .

He had that same sense of movement again and backed away. He fetched the chair from beside the radio and brought it out, lodging the headrest tight under the door lever.

'I think something might have tried to open the door,' he said. Was he imagining things? Maybe someone else had adjusted the levers after him, that was all . . .

He looked back down the tunnel. The *dark* tunnel, and the dark cavern beyond.

If the locks weren't secure after all, if something had got inside and locked the door again after . . .

'We need to wake everyone,' he said. '*Right now.*'

By the time they reached the cavern, more flashlights were on. Annabel and Never were both there, as was Petro, and they'd placed some of the lantern-style lights around on the floor. Jonah's eyes were darting to every dark corner, his adrenaline high enough to make him feel sick. He picked up one of the lanterns.

'Get everyone awake,' Sly ordered. 'Try not to alarm the kids. Jonah thinks something might have been at the entrance.'

'No alarms went off,' said Annabel. 'Why do you think something was there?'

Jonah shook his head. 'A feeling.'

'We can't risk panic, just for a feeling,' said Annabel.

'The door might have been opened,' said Jonah. 'I can't be certain. But the power didn't go off on its own, that's for damn sure.'

'Actually, that's entirely possible,' said Never. Jonah saw

that he was looking around uneasily too. 'It's possible the main circuit breaker in the house tripped.'

Jonah pointed his flashlight right in his face. 'Clutching at straws, don't you think?'

'I mean it,' said Never. 'It's new kit up there, and, um, maybe I got something wrong. I mean, that's *rare* but it happens.'

'And the door, Jonah?' said Annabel. 'Why do you think it was opened?'

'The latches were only halfway over,' said Jonah. 'Like it had been locked in a hurry. I made damn sure I pulled those levers all the way.' Saying it aloud made him certain that he wasn't being crazy.

'Couldn't one of the kids have wandered in the night?' said Never. 'Opened it by mistake?' Jonah shook his head. 'OK, OK. Straws.'

'We need to check on everyone,' said Jonah. 'Make sure nobody's acting strangely. Then we'll look around.'

Annabel stared at him. 'You don't think . . .'

'God forbid,' said Jonah.

'But if *something* managed to get inside,' said Annabel, 'you'd be able to sense it, yes? See it, if it was—' She paused, searching for a way to phrase it. 'If any of us was in trouble?'

'I think so.'

Annabel woke Cathy, and got her help in waking Sara, Armel and Remy, before moving on to Jansin, Mark and their two boys. Everyone was a little shaken, which made it hard to tell if anybody was *too* shaken: shaken enough to suggest that something dark was trying to attach itself.

To *burrow* inside.

They spread out and walked the cavern, using their

flashlights to search. There was no sign of movement, but there were plenty of nooks and crannies where something dark could hide.

'This is *not* good,' whispered Never.

Annabel frowned. 'Shouldn't the shelter battery feed these lights with the power off?' she said.

Jonah's mouth dropped open. He'd forgotten all about turning off the feed to the shelter batteries. It went both ways. 'Fuck,' he said. 'I switched it off.'

'*Why?*' said Annabel.

'So it wouldn't drain the power coming from the solar panels.' He turned to the tunnel that led down to the lower cavern and the shelter. That was where he'd need to go, to switch the lights back on. If it hadn't been put out of commission already. He took a deep breath. 'OK. Who's coming with me?'

'Down there?' said Never, warily looking at the dark entrance to the lower tunnels.

'I'll come,' said Sly.

Jonah looked at her. She still seemed groggy. 'You should stay here,' he said. 'Petro? Stay with Sly and the others, OK? Annabel? Never? You two come with me.'

'Cheers,' said Never. 'Remind me to stop being your friend.'

16

Jonah had been down this tunnel many times in the past year. The shelter, with its stash of notebooks that he'd hidden from Annabel as if it was porn, had been his place to go and think, certainly in the early months. *Think* was perhaps a kind way to put it, of course; *obsess* was probably more accurate.

It was an entirely different tunnel now.

The thin cable of lighting had been able to turn a dark, cool stone passageway into an extension of his home. With the lights out, the eerie shadow play of the flashlight beams made it an alien place to be, a hostile place.

He had confronted shadow-creatures before, but those had been the vast, powerful parasites that had skulked on the shoulders of Michael Andreas's immediate circle of acolytes, his most trusted followers. When those creatures separated from their hosts, they had *considerable* power, something he couldn't hope to stand against. Yet when one had attempted to latch onto Kendrick, he'd been able to wrench it from his flesh before it took hold, and Jonah had sensed how the thing *feared* him, lashing out but finding that Jonah was poison to it.

The things that had swamped DC the night before were vastly weaker, he thought. He *hoped*.

'Nothing's down here, right?' whispered Never. 'If something did get in, why the hell would it hide down here?'

'The important thing is that none of us are on our own,' said Jonah. 'When a shadow tries to attach itself to someone, I think the victim is terrified. That's why we had to wake everyone. We'll be able to tell.'

'Right,' said Never, sounding anxious. 'So there's nothing down here. No chance.'

'Let's just get the lights on,' said Annabel.

They walked in silence down the gentle slope of the tunnel. At last, they entered the lower cavern, smaller than the first, and saw the shelter at the far side. There was a faint red glow from within, giving the whole cavern a slight red tint. An allusion to Hell that was about as unwelcome as anything could have been.

Jonah tripped, startling himself and the others, but they soon reached the shelter. Jonah put his hand on the switch that linked the shelter batteries to the mains, half expecting that nothing would happen.

The lights came on.

Annabel and Never laughed quietly with relief.

'How long will the lights last?' said Annabel.

'They'll last until dawn,' said Jonah. 'But we're not here just to put the lights on. We're here to search.'

'Oh,' said Never, his eyes widening.

'There's probably nothing there,' said Jonah. 'Keep your eyes open all the same.'

*

They spread out and cast their flashlights around the cavern and started to make their way back to the others. They saw nothing as they entered the tunnel.

When they reached everyone else, the return of the lights had been enough to calm nerves. The children, Jonah was glad to see, seemed to get back to normal quickly and settled down to sleep. The adults were more shaken, but none of them gave any sign of the outright *fear* Jonah was watching for.

When morning came, the shelter batteries were running low. Jonah got everyone together at the cavern entrance.

'Wait here with your flashlights on,' he said. 'We're going to get the shutters open, it might take the last of the power.' He took Petro and Annabel with him along the tunnel to the basement door and used the security remote to open the shutters up top. Then he positioned the sunlamps facing the doorway. He looked at Annabel. 'When I say, turn these on.'

'You think there are things out there?' said Petro.

'Sunlight hurts them,' said Jonah. 'So if there are any, these should at least let us know.'

He unlocked the door. The sunlamps took what was left in the shelter batteries, but it gave them a brief burst of light. It was all they were going to get, but Jonah was just playing safe, because he didn't think anything *had* been there overnight.

An idea had come to him, and he didn't like it. He was eager to take another look at the footage Never had captured the day before.

Everyone was relieved to get out into the sunshine, the tension of the night palpably dissipating. Jonah followed

Never as he hurried to find the reason for the power failure. It didn't take long to identify, and it wasn't a tripped circuit. Four of the six solar panels had been trashed, a single brick on the ground nearby the likely weapon. The batteries, those glorious pieces of tech-porn that Never had found so appealing, were charred ruins.

'Single nail,' said Never, poking through the debris. 'Hammered into them. That would've created one hell of an arc, then an impressive fire. *Brief*, but impressive.'

'What about those two panels?' asked Jonah, nodding to the ones that seemed undamaged. They'd been tossed to one side, but they'd not had the brick hurled into them to shatter the sensitive photovoltaics.

Kneeling down, Never gave them a quick check. 'They might be OK,' he said. 'That one's cracked at the edge, but it could still work.' He pointed across to the batteries. 'The problem is that the power inverter unit was beside the fire. It's toast. I'd have to run a separate cable down to the batteries in the shelter to charge them, and without the inverter the current loss would be huge.'

'So we spend the rest of the day getting the generator fixed.'

'My thoughts exactly. How much fuel do we have for it?'

'Some,' said Jonah. 'Plus whatever we can get out of the vehicles.'

Annabel came out, wincing when she saw the damage. 'No power, then?'

'We need to repair the shelter's generator,' said Never. 'The bigger question is, who or what did this?'

'The people you saw acting strangely out there,' said Annabel. 'Maybe they've been spreading out, sabotaging survivors. But we have another problem.' Jonah and Never looked at her. 'Sly's been freaking out. She's told people what they're up against. In detail. And that we have no hope of surviving it.'

'Shit,' said Never. 'Has Doctor Phil taken another look at her?'

She nodded. 'Fear response after an accident; he says it's common enough with minor concussion. Just fucking unfortunate.'

Jonah shook his head. 'Fear response? Philip has no idea what kind of fear Sly is used to.'

'I'm not so sure,' said Annabel. 'Kendrick's death might be the catalyst. Her mentor, or whatever the hell he was to her. Whatever the reason, she's got everyone spooked that something nasty is still down in the cavern, and the kids are terrified. *Nobody* wants to go back into those tunnels, let alone spend another night down there. Right now, the discussion is about whether everyone should even stay *here*, or move on.'

'Where the hell are they going to go?' said Never.

'Sly's talking about safe houses she knows,' said Annabel. 'I think we'd be wise to get Sly to lie down for a few hours. Away from everyone.'

Jonah sighed. 'All right. Here's our to-do list. Annabel, convince Sly to get some rest. I'll suggest to everyone that we spend tonight in the basement with some sunlamps set up, while Never takes a look at the generator.' He looked at Never. 'Maybe ask if anyone has much mechanical expertise to offer, to help you. *If* they'd be brave enough to venture into the depths.'

*

Jonah went to his office. He had a backup power supply for his PC that gave four hours of use, and he planned on using some of that right now. He powered it up and waited.

He wanted to look at the footage again.

Annabel's question, about whether he would *see* one of the shadows if it was trying to attach itself to someone, had struck a chord with him. When Kendrick roped him into trying to look for a shadow-infested host after Winnerden Flats, Jonah was the only person who had been able to see them while they were attached, and even that had needed a specific state of mind, a kind of honed *fear*, which he'd found relatively easy to conjure up.

The truth was, Jonah hadn't wanted to find a shadow. Could that simply have led him to overlook things? To miss clues that he should have spotted? Back when he'd been able to see them, the shadows had had no reason to think that they were vulnerable; now that they knew they could be seen, surely they would have been more cautious?

A specific thought had been brewing in his mind. There were things he needed to check before he talked to Annabel.

The footage Never had captured. The final frames, where the Beast itself had been caught on screen. He opened the file and found the position, then did something he'd not done before. As the camera fell away from the shot of the horizon, he kept playing it, until Sly came into view – unconscious, and vulnerable.

He played it again, one frame at a time.

Looking.

When he saw it, he closed his eyes. It was the only thing that made sense, really, but that didn't stop the feeling of defeat.

He opened his eyes again and looked at the image, blurred by the motion of the camera. Captured just before the van doors closed, a darkness was visible in the gap. It was easy to miss, caught against the backdrop of dim-lit road, but he could see its shape, the darkness *within* the vehicle.

The wave of creatures in the background hadn't been the first of them, after all. Some must have got slightly ahead of the front line.

And one of them had made it inside before Never closed the doors.

*

He went to speak to Philip, first. There was something very specific he needed to know, and even though Philip was wary to begin with, the answer eventually came. Next, he went to see Annabel. She listened to him with a grim expression, but she agreed with what he was saying.

He found Never with Petro, working on the generator in a ring of flashlights down by the shelter.

Petro was visibly jittery. 'Hey, Jonah,' he said. 'It was not hard to fix. Not as bad as you thought, yes? You needed to clean it up, mostly!'

Jonah realized that Petro's hands were filthy, while Never's were basically clean.

'So was Petro much help to you?' Jonah asked him.

Petro gave a hearty laugh, and Never scowled.

'Look, uh,' said Jonah, reluctant. 'I need to talk to you, Never. Once the generator's working.'

'OK,' said Never. 'How long d'ya reckon, Petro?'

'We'll not be long,' said Petro. 'We switch it on now, right? Then tune a little and tidy up.'

Jonah waited.

When Petro kicked the generator on, he laughed loud enough to create an echo as the tunnel and cavern lighting came on. Beside him, Jonah saw, was one of the sunlamps from the basement, and it now burned bright. 'I finish up here,' said Petro. 'You go. Now I feel safer. Also, more tanned!'

Jonah led Never away, down the tunnel that, lit, felt like part of his home once more.

'What's up?' said Never.

'I've got news, and you're not going to like it.'

'OK. That sounds ominous.'

Jonah stopped walking. 'I was looking over the footage from the van, when the shadows reached you. One of them got inside, Never.'

Slowly, Never's face fell as the implications sank in. 'No.'

'Sly was unconscious,' said Jonah. 'And she's not been herself. We've all noticed it.'

'No way,' said Never. 'You're saying she did all that? She trashed the power?'

'More than that. She's been stirring up a desire for us to get out of here, to some random safe house that may not even exist. She gave us a threat, she made us scared to be down here.'

'I don't believe it,' said Never. 'I thought you said these things had to *fight* to take you? She'd not give in so easily.'

'I was thinking about Lucas Silva again, and his son. His wife. I didn't think they knew those things were on them, Never. Maybe that's the alternative. If it can't take you fast enough, maybe it doesn't need to. Maybe it nudges you one way or the other, whispers to you. Maybe you don't even know you're doing it.'

'Shit,' said Never. 'So what the hell do we do?'

'I asked Philip. The medical supplies have some intravenous sedatives, enough to knock her out for a few hours. You'll have to help me. You know her, and I think she trusts you more than anyone else here.'

'I'm not sure she'd agree,' said Never. 'But I'll do my best. Then what? Can you remove it, the way you did for Kendrick?'

Jonah shook his head. 'I don't know. When the shadow tried to take Kendrick, it was just starting to burrow into him. This has had plenty of time, and we *know* it has some level of control over her, even if it's only like a form of sleepwalking. We just have to hope.'

'She's going to hate me for this,' whispered Never.

'We're going to say that she needs rest, OK?' said Jonah. 'She's sleepy, but if she overreacts, we'll have to hold her down.'

'No shit,' said Never.

'You'll have to hold her arm secure either way, understand?' said Jonah. 'The others will help too. You ready?'

They walked through to the lower basement, then upstairs, and Jonah could see Never's anxiety written all over his face.

Sly was lying down on one of the couches. Annabel, Philip, Armel and Mark were all there, Philip kneeling next to Sly's arm with the two men ready to hold down her legs.

'Sly,' said Philip. 'You're going to need plenty of rest, all right?' He was ready with a syringe. 'This will help.'

'Hey, Sly,' said Never. He got down next to Philip. Her eyes were already closed. 'Everything's going to be fine.' He looked from Sly to Jonah, who nodded, so Never took hold of her arm and held it tight. 'Quick,' he said. 'I think she's exhausted anyway, but hurry the—'

That was when Philip put the needle in his arm.

'But . . .' started Never. He didn't get to the next word.

17

When he opened his eyes again, Never's head hurt like hell. So did his wrists. And, when it came down to it, his arse wasn't exactly *comfortable*, either.

He was in the nuclear shelter. The bunk beds had been removed – he could see where the bolts had been undone, leaving rusty circles and a line of old paint. The table and chairs (*comfortable* chairs, he seemed to remember) had gone too. The shelter's main room was twenty feet by thirty, and all it contained was the small basin area near the door, and the bank of control switches currently half covered by a sheet of opaque yellow plastic. The video camera he'd used in DC was on a tripod just in front of it. It was recording.

He was in a heavy seat he recognized from the garden – wrought-iron sides and teak slats. The chair was old, the slats warped. It was absolutely *fucking* uncomfortable, and his wrists were tied to the bastard thing. His feet, too.

He rocked left and right to test it. And yes, it was as sturdy as it was uncomfortable. He was really very *deeply* annoyed.

'Hello?' he called. He tried to work out what the hell he was doing in there, and it came back to him in a rush. Jonah had asked him to help sedate Sly, but Sly had – he realized now – been sedated already.

They had *both* been the target.

'Jonah? For fuck's sake, talk to me.'

The shelter door clunked and opened. In came Jonah, not making eye contact. 'I'm sorry about this, Never,' he said. 'I really am.'

'Oh *good*,' said Never. 'I'm so glad you're *sorry*. Just tell me one thing, OK? What the *fuck*?'

'We sedated Sly, Never. With you down here working on the generator, out of the way. I figured I needed time to be able to see the shadow on her shoulder. That maybe it was hiding, and I just couldn't see it.'

'You made sure I was out of the way?' said Never. He took a long breath. 'You weren't certain it was her.'

'Oh, I was pretty sure,' said Jonah. 'It fit too well. But there was a chance I was wrong. There was also a chance that more than one of the shadows had got into the van. Imagine if you'd been there watching as I looked at Sly, and I realized I was wrong. Do you think that if you had a shadow on you, then it might just have decided to *react*? If it suspected it had been found out, could it have pushed hard? What might you have done? What effect could it have had on you? There was no point risking it.'

'So you didn't see it on Sly?'

'No,' said Jonah. 'And I took my time. I think I would have seen it, if it had been there.'

'And now you're here to check me over.'

Jonah looked away, just for a second. That brief pause was enough for Never to feel horribly wary. 'I came and got you,' said Jonah. 'I thought, maybe I was completely wrong.

Maybe I wouldn't see one on you, either. But even then, there'd be a chance they'd learned to hide too well for me to detect them, and that would have been an altogether different problem.' Jonah looked at him with an expression that spoke of a deep weariness, bordering on despair, and suddenly Never felt a fear growing within him. A hot, dangerous fear. 'That's not how it's turned out.'

'You've already checked,' said Never, slowly. 'You've already seen it.' He felt sick. He looked to his left shoulder, then to his right. 'Where is it?'

Jonah looked a little nauseous too, he saw. 'Before, they were always up high on the shoulder. Their *fingers* going down under the collarbone. Yours is on your back. Under your left shoulder blade, over to the side.'

His mouth felt appallingly dry. 'What does it look like?' he said. But did he really want to know?

'It's small,' said Jonah. 'Three, four inches across maybe. Flattened against the skin. The tendrils, or fingers, whatever they are . . . they spread outward, four in all.'

'Colour?' He *did* want to know, he realized. He wanted to know what this fucking thing was that had dared to *infest* him, that had made him scare the living shit out of his friends and put everyone at risk. He needed to know his enemy.

'They're not really black,' said Jonah. 'They're mottled, grey, sickly things. Like something dredged up from a dead river, a rotting *mollusc*. It pulsates slowly, but the rhythm is close to your own heartbeat.' Jonah looked Never in the eye, at last. 'It's part of you now.'

'Enough,' said Never. He closed his eyes. His lip was trembling. God, he felt *cold*. His breathing was getting faster as his dread grew. 'I didn't know, Jonah. I swear, I didn't know.'

'When you were unconscious, I took your shirt off and there it was. I saw it right away, no trouble at all, and I checked Sly again. She was clear. We had to do something with you, and I'd had time to think already. Getting this place cleared, making space so we could bring you here and ensure the thing couldn't get out. Whatever happens.' Jonah shook his head. He went to the door and opened it again. Annabel entered. She didn't make eye contact, either.

'Why is she here?' said Never. 'It's not safe for her. It's not safe for *you*. Leave me here, leave me tied up.'

'I'm not going to leave you,' said Jonah. 'The longer it's on you, the deeper it'll take hold. It doesn't have you yet, Never. You say you didn't know it was there, and I believe you. I think I can still help.'

'Why the hell do you think that?' he said.

'You still seem like yourself,' said Jonah. 'I think—' He broke off, and Never could see tears in his eyes.

'You can't trust anything I say. Just leave me. Lock me in here.'

'We deal with this,' said Jonah. 'Here and now.'

'Annabel, please,' said Never. 'Get out. Take Jonah, and get out.'

'I volunteered,' she said, still without looking him in the eye. 'Jonah needs help with this. And if you think we're just going to abandon you . . .'

'Please,' he said. '*Please.*' He was starting to understand that Jonah was wrong, that he *had* known, deep down. He thought back to the van, holding the damn doors for so long, slumping to the floor in exhaustion and fear. Something had been nearby, and he'd *known*, but it had been too late.

He'd known. But every time his mind went there, every time he came close to remembering, he lost track of his thoughts. He didn't recall destroying the panels or the batteries, but he did remember talking to Sly during the night, after the chaos had settled down. She'd been confused then, drifting in and out of sleep, and he'd whispered to her, making sure the others were out of earshot. He'd talked of how dangerous it was to stay here, and how – surely – she knew better places to be.

He'd set her up.

He'd done it, and then it was gone from his mind. He was like a dog distracted with a thrown stick. And now that he was aware of it, it was *still* trying to throw him off the scent.

'I can feel it,' he said. Jonah looked at him, pain and fear in his eyes. 'I can. It wanted you all put at risk, outside. Ready to be offered up.'

Jonah's eyes narrowed. 'Offered up?'

'Shit,' said Never, appalled that he *knew* this. 'Yes. Offered up. Prone. Defenceless. You wondered how anyone in St Petersburg knew the Beast was coming back.' He stopped for a moment: when he'd said *Beast*, he'd felt an odd sensation. A pleasurable one. Nausea swamped him at the thought. 'Someone like me, like me but *stronger*, must have held out enough to be able to tell them. It *will* come back, and there'll be enough shadow-hosts to protect it. No, not just protect . . . *Prepare.* The others I saw in DC, they'd been taken easily, and *completely*. No need for them to pretend to themselves that everything was fine.' He shook his head. 'I'm stalling you, aren't I? Just get on with it.'

Jonah looked to Annabel. She nodded.

'This is probably going to hurt,' said Jonah. He walked towards him, then around behind him. He was carrying scissors, and he pushed Never forwards gently, cutting his shirt away.

'I liked this shirt,' said Never. He tried to smile, but he was crying now. 'I think . . . I think I might try and hurt you.'

'I know.'

'Annabel, you shouldn't be here.'

'I'm staying,' she said.

'Signal for them to lock the door, Annabel,' said Jonah.

She nodded and turned, then Never heard a clunk. She turned back. 'Done.'

Petro's face was at the window, emotionless.

'They're under orders not to open up under any circumstances, until we're finished,' said Jonah.

'You're fucking crazy,' said Never. He pulled at his restraints again, and he realized that while part of him wanted to test that they were secure, there was another part of him that wanted them to be weak, to *fail*.

He couldn't understand why Annabel was risking herself like this, or why Jonah was *letting* her. 'Please! I can feel the fucking thing now. It's angry, don't you see? It's trying to burrow in deeper. I feel it scratching at my fucking *mind*.'

'I can do this,' said Jonah. 'Trust me. Try and hold still, if you can.'

As Never closed his eyes, he could feel something now, where Jonah had told him the creature was – a cold *twisting* in his back. His breathing was becoming more rapid, and shallow. Panic was flowing through him.

'I'm going to try something now,' said Jonah. 'Just . . .'

Pain coursed through Never. He yelled, and when the agony subsided he was out of breath. He looked up. Annabel was staring, her hand over her mouth.

'Jonah?' she said. '*Jonah?*'

He turned his head as far behind him as he could, and for a second he didn't know where Jonah had gone. Then he saw him on the floor, motionless. 'What happened?' he asked Annabel. He was trembling all over, now, and felt colder than he'd ever felt in his life.

'He went to touch it,' said Annabel, terrified. 'He just collapsed.' She started to walk towards him.

'Stop!' cried Never. 'Annabel, I can *feel* it. I think . . . Oh God, I think it's trying to come away . . .' It was what they did: when bonded to a host, they could detach, coalesce into something tangible, something *dangerous*. The sensation was appalling, like a limb pulling from its joint.

Surely Annabel could see the desperation in his eyes – she turned and pounded on the door, calling to be let out. After a moment she turned back, pale. 'They won't open it,' she said. 'They won't let me go.'

'*Let her out!*' screamed Never. '*For fuck's sake let her out.*' He could feel it leaving him – no, not *leaving*, not like that. It wasn't letting go of the hold it had, just loosening the grip, venturing off on a long leash. His breath hitched. He closed his eyes again, and gasped when he could still *see*, his point-of-view low down, dropping to the floor . . . 'Oh Jesus, Annabel. I can see what it sees. I can feel what it *feels*.' And what he could feel sickened him. The anticipation, watching

Annabel back away from it, horror on her face because she could actually *see* the thing now that it had detached from him, see it pulsate and glisten as it slowly slouched towards her.

It was the first time it had detached, the first time it had walked, and suddenly Never understood how ancient this shard of darkness was – and what it had once been. The Beast took the souls it consumed, but only the ones it had truly taken its time with were truly corrupted, transformed into mirrors of itself. The rest were mere fodder.

This had been a soul, once, but what it had been so long ago no longer mattered to it. It worshipped its new god, and in Never it had found another to convert to its unholy faith. But first, it would feed. It would *enjoy* feeding. The woman ahead of it, shrieking now as it drew nearer: she would suffer, and once the Beast had taken this world, it would be free to return to the corruption of its master's heart, and bring the new proselyte it had found back, transfigured into darkness.

'Please, Annabel,' said Never, barely above a whisper. 'Please get out. *Run.*'

Too late, he thought. *Too late.*

Tears poured down his face. He forced his eyes open, ripping himself out of the creature's viewpoint, and now he could see it fully, midway to Annabel, *lurching* along on its newborn limbs. He could sense the tendril that still connected him to the pulsating horror on the floor.

'Annabel . . .' he mumbled. His strength had gone, and he knew why. The creature was draining him in its efforts to *form* itself from the fetid shadow-flesh it had, to congeal and harden its legs, and ready its barbed claws from noxious excretions, preparing the newly forged muscles to *leap*.

But worst of all, worse even than the horror burnt into Annabel's expression, was the simple fact that he could feel its *enjoyment*, its anticipation of the pain it would inflict on its victim.

He could feel it, and it felt *good*.

'God forgive me,' he said. He screamed it: '*God forgive me!*'

It had almost reached her. The creature rocked back and forth on its rapidly strengthening legs. It *hissed* through a sham of a mouth, relishing the terror it was creating. And then, just as it was about to leap, Never had a simultaneous rush of utterly conflicting emotion as he realized that Annbel's expression held not just horror, but a stolid anticipation of her own.

She was waiting for something, and it made Never rejoice and rage all at once. The creature, tied to him, realized it too. Something was wrong. It hesitated, uncertain.

Too late, Never thought again. His love for Annabel collided with the hatred the creature felt for her, as she reached to her side and yanked at the yellow plastic sheet beside her to reveal what it had been hiding.

A sunlamp, that burst into terrible, *beautiful* light.

He felt an appalling pain rip through him, and he screamed. Every part of him was on fire, it seemed; the agony grew and grew, spreading out from his back, and gathering within his head, building as if his skull would explode with the intensity of it.

Suddenly he was aware of movement behind him. He managed to turn his head enough to see Jonah standing, *reaching*, and he could feel it as Jonah took hold of the tendril that connected him to his abhorrent offspring.

Jonah twisted it around his arm, gathering it in.

The creature backed away from the light, its grey-black skin blistering. It turned and hissed, then ran towards Jonah and launched itself at him.

18

Jonah grabbed it as it leapt.

This had been the plan, of course: to feign his own collapse, and use Annabel to lure it out, to force it to take on physical form. That was when they posed the greatest threat, yes, but it was also when they were at their most vulnerable.

Seeing it on Never's back had been a terrible shock at first. He'd had several minutes of angst before he realized that there was hope. This creature was small. It wasn't like the powerful shadows he'd faced before, powerful enough to withstand the burning light a sunlamp gave out.

And he'd managed to kill one of those, in the darkness of Winnerden Flats, as it had tried to attach itself to Kendrick. Back then, the creature hadn't had time to gain a deep hold on its victim, and Jonah had grasped the thing, pulling the creature out by the roots.

He knew that the same approach might not work with Never. His shadow, small as it was, had burrowed deep already. He hadn't had long to formulate a plan. While the shelter was made ready, he devised their strategy.

Lucas Silva was the key.

When Kendrick had arranged for the capture of Silva, he

had also devised a series of tests, experiments to ascertain the weaknesses of the creature. Exposed to the light of a sunlamp, it had rapidly returned to its host for protection.

Draw it out, he thought. Draw it out, attack it, and try to prevent it from rejoining the host.

Annabel had been horrified at the idea.

'These things can kill when they're physical,' she'd said. 'They can kill *easily*, Jonah.'

'The lamp will hurt it, trust me.'

'And what if it doesn't come for me? What if it attacks you straight away?'

'These creatures are very wary of me,' he told her. 'When I ripped it off Kendrick, the shadow was weakened just by my *touch*.' Perhaps all revivers had the same effect, but it didn't matter. He was poison to them.

'You can grab it from Never's back,' she said. 'Grab it and hold it, that's all it will need. I'll be ready with the light, and I'll move in quickly when you tell me.'

'I'll try and apply what I did with Kendrick. I'll make Never *fear*, make him feel *sick* at the thought of it, and then I'll make my move. But if that doesn't work, Annabel . . . You know what to do. Getting it as far as possible from Never is crucial.'

'It won't come to that, OK? You'll be able to do what you did with Kendrick, just peel it from Never, peel it away and watch it shrivel and die.'

There was one more thing she'd insisted on. As the shelter was prepared, she'd sent Petro to his house to retrieve heavy-duty rigger gloves. Jonah agreed to wear them, if the first approach failed.

With Never tied to the seat, terrified of what was to

come, Jonah had reached out with his bare hands, suppressing his revulsion as his fingers closed in on the sickening, pulsating darkness that had taken root. He'd grasped it, and he'd pulled, and at once he'd understood that this wouldn't work. He'd had an overwhelming sense of the *depth* of those roots, the moment he took hold.

He'd had no choice. He'd fallen to the ground, as planned, and Annabel had switched seamlessly into her new role. She was the bait, and the creature fell for it.

The plan progressed. Jonah took its life-tether and gathered it in; the creature turned and leapt. But there was one small change Jonah had made.

He'd decided not to put on the gloves.

*

The moment Jonah's skin touched it, he could feel the sting. It was desperately trying to get back to its host, and its physicality was fading rapidly, thank God, but there was enough left to draw blood and slicken his hand. There was a sudden danger that it could wriggle free of his grasp. While he'd managed to gather up the strange *tether* that linked it to Never, he didn't want it getting out of his grip.

'What's happening?' said Annabel, sounding utterly terrified. 'I can't see it any more. Shit, Jonah, your hands are bleeding.'

'I still have it,' said Jonah. 'It's weakening. I don't think it can do much more damage to me.' Its legs were thinning out now, becoming the corpse-like 'fingers' that wanted *so* much to embed themselves back into Never's essence. 'Bring the light nearer, but be careful.' He took a few steps to come around the front, so that he could see how Never was faring.

Not well. He was shivering, and pale as a long-drowned corpse. He was staring ahead of him. Jonah thought his stare was aimed at Annabel to begin with, but his gaze didn't follow her as she moved closer with the light. His breath was rapid, almost panting. His nose started to bleed, a single drop gliding down over his lips and onto his chest.

When Jonah had dealt with the creature trying to attach itself to Kendrick, he'd not had the advantage of the sun-lamp, but that creature hadn't been able to draw on its host's resources the way this one seemed to be doing. Before, the creature had shrivelled and perished without its host to thieve from, even in the darkness.

He tried to take hold of the tether and *squeeze* it, hoping that might somehow stem the flow, but he might as well have tried squeezing string. Its struggles were slowing, how-ever.

'Stay there,' he said to Annabel, and she stopped her advance with the lamp. Any closer and she might be in range of a sudden lurch from Never, if the creature still had much control over him while detached. The gentle thrum of the generator outside the shelter was reassuring, and he could see Petro's anxious face peering in through the window in the entry door.

It would drain Never until there was nothing left, he thought. There was only one thing he could think of to try. He could hold the creature easily now with just his right hand. He was *aware* of the insubstantial tether he'd swept up and wrapped around his left arm more than he was actually able to see it, but he gripped as best he could and tugged. With each pull, more seemed to emerge from Never, and Jonah turned his hand to gather it up. The creature was almost still, and he was keeping a close eye on it, in case it was faking its lethargic state.

More tether came. More. Finally, he sensed resistance. He pulled gently, and Never cried out.

He pulled harder. The slow drops of blood, which had been falling steadily from Never's nose, became a sudden torrent.

'God,' said Annabel, and Jonah could *feel* that she was eager to step in and help somehow.

'Stay back,' he said. 'Wait until I tell you it's safe.'

He pulled again, even harder. This time it brought a cry of such *agony* from Never that he almost recoiled at what he was doing. There was blood coming from Never's right ear.

He readied for another pull, but he found he didn't have the strength to do it. His tears were flowing, blurring his vision.

Then Never spoke, looking right at Jonah. His voice was impossibly weak. 'It's holding on,' he said, gritting his teeth. 'Pull the fucker out. *Pull it out.*'

Jonah looked at the blood flowing from Never's ear. 'I can't,' he said. 'Oh Jesus, I can't.'

'*Do it!*'

Jonah pulled.

19

The screaming started as soon as Jonah began to pull, but this time he didn't stop. He strained and gave it all he could, and suddenly the tether came free; Never went silent and slumped in the chair.

Jonah almost toppled back. The creature snapped out of its lethargy, squirming violently in his hands, but it was shrivelling in the lamp's light. The flesh became like mist, boiling off the surface of the rancid skin. It had more fight left in it than he'd expected, and he had to use both hands to hold it firmly in the intense brightness. Within its flesh, harder masses midway between bone and gristle protruded. A thick ichor flowed from the places where the skin tore; it, too, turned to intangible mist within moments.

He felt its life go, and within seconds he was holding nothing.

He stood there for a moment, out of breath. He didn't dare look at Never.

'Is it gone?' said Annabel, staring at where it had been.

'Yes,' said Jonah.

She set the sunlamp down and rushed to Never. 'He's

breathing,' she said. 'But it's very shallow and he's unconscious. Get Philip in here.'

He went to the door and nodded to Petro.

'We need Philip,' said Jonah.

Petro looked at him. 'Is the thing dead?'

'Yes,' said Jonah. Petro unlocked the door and opened it;
he stared at Jonah's hands, so Jonah looked too. The skin
was pockmarked with fine lacerations. The bleeding had
already stopped, though. Blood aside, his skin seemed clean
of the remnants of the creature, but it felt tainted to him. He
would wash and wash for days, he thought, however much it
hurt.

Petro gestured for Philip to go in. Cathy was there too,
looking anxious.

'Get something for the floor,' called Annabel. 'Mats, pil-
lows, whatever he can lie on.'

Jonah nodded and went with Petro to fetch some bed-
ding. When they came back, Philip was still checking Never
over.

Soon enough, they had Never untied and out of the
chair. With a mat on the floor, they laid him down with a
blanket over him, and a saline drip getting some fluid into
his system to counter shock. He was in good hands.

Jonah felt a sudden need to get out of there, to wash the
blood and the *darkness* from his skin. He made his way up
to the house. In the upper basement, he looked in briefly on
Sly, who still seemed asleep on the couch – Sara was keeping an eye on her.

He went to the upstairs bathroom and ran a basin of
cold water. He lathered up and started to scrub his hands,
ignoring the sharp pain of it, ignoring the fact that he was

making it bleed afresh. He was used to this kind of response. There was a tendency among revivers to develop a near obsession with cleanliness after revivals, especially the messier ones, or those dealing with corpses on the more decayed end of the spectrum. Bare hands had to be used for revival, and the corpse's hand was often held for an hour or so.

He realized he could *smell* the dying shadow on his flesh, a rancid and vinegary scent that seemed to have soaked into his skin. He emptied and refilled the basin, and began the process of scrubbing all over again.

There was a knock on the bathroom door. It was Sly.

She entered, looking drained. 'Sara told me some of it,' she said, staring at his injured hands. 'She said that Never had something on him. Something from the trip to DC. She said he'd been taken down to the shelter, and you were going to deal with it. Is he . . . ?'

'He's alive,' said Jonah. She was visibly relieved. 'I got it off him, and he's alive.'

Sly nodded. She rubbed at her arm, where she'd been injected with the sedative. 'Who jabbed me, by the way? I could've broken their neck, if I'd been compos mentis.'

'It was Philip,' said Jonah. 'We had a crowd holding you down, and you hardly stirred anyway. In hindsight a sedative might have been overkill. You were so exhausted.'

'Getting the thing off Never . . . was it the same as it was with Kendrick?'

'Harder,' said Jonah. 'It was small, but it had forged a strong connection to Never. It was sucking the life out of him. We got the fucker, though.' His tears started to pour. He dried his hands and brought a towel up to his face, wiping the tears away. 'I need a rest,' he said, and left. He went to his and Annabel's bedroom and lay down. The room was spinning a little, but it subsided. He stared at the ceiling, remembering the feel of the creature in his hands, and he had to resist the urge to go back and wash again.

After a while, Annabel found him.

'Philip's happy with his condition,' she said. 'His vitals are reasonable, but he's still out cold.'

'When I saw the blood coming from his ear . . .'

'I know. There's no clear sign of any brain injury, but all we can do is wait for him to regain consciousness.' She lay next to him on the bed. 'How are *you*? That was an experience I'd rather not repeat.'

'Me too,' he said. He held up his hands, which were still wet with the freshly drawn blood. He looked at the bed cover and saw that he'd left red handprints on it. 'Shit.'

'Yes,' said Annabel, deadpan. 'That's our most pressing problem. By the way, nobody wants to leave now. Petro's basically turned us into legends.'

'Really?'

'Yeah,' she said. 'He watched the whole thing. We kicked ass.'

'For all the good it'll do.'

She snuggled up to him. 'Don't worry about your hands,' she said. 'Just hold me.' She looked at the clock by the bed. 'Not even midday, and we have ourselves a little victory.'

Jonah stayed quiet.

'Never's going to be fine,' she said.

For how long, he wanted to say. In the daylight, it seemed easy for everyone to forget how dire the situation truly was. For them. For *everyone*.

'Talk to me,' said Annabel. 'I can hear your mind working overtime. What are you thinking about?'

'Pandora,' he said.

'What?'

'I had an image of Tess,' said Jonah. 'A vision, something. At the end of Grady's revival. She was saying Pandora, over and over.'

'A vision?' said Annabel.

'It was more than that. I think it means something, but I can't figure it out.'

'Pandora's box,' she said. 'Yeah, I see how that fits.'

'Andreas and his big dreams,' said Jonah. 'He certainly opened Pandora's box with that.'

'Andreas?' said Annabel. 'I was thinking more that *Kendrick* was Pandora.'

Jonah sighed. Maybe that *was* more accurate. Kendrick had been the one who'd seen the possibility. He'd been the one who set the dominoes tumbling, all because he'd had one simple *idea*.

In a revival, truth was guaranteed. Whatever branch of national security Kendrick worked for, the use of revival as a means to extract valuable information certainly hadn't been overlooked, whatever the ethics. Killing those you wanted the truth from, just so you could have them interrogated by a specially trained reviver, had quickly become an option for the unscrupulous.

It had taken Kendrick to go that step further: to ask the question, how dead was dead? Someone pulled from a frozen river could have been clinically dead for *hours* and still be resuscitated. Medically induced hypothermia had become a common tool for some forms of surgery. All brain activity could cease for an hour or longer, and still the person could be brought back to life.

Could a person actually be *revived* in that time? Could they be questioned, with the truth absolutely guaranteed, and then resuscitated as if nothing had happened? The ethical issues would no longer apply. They wouldn't have to *kill* someone to interrogate them.

Kendrick had spent a year trying to test that out, to push revival to the limit, but it had only been when Jonah was brought into the project that any success had been achieved. Jonah's involvement, indeed, had been the last throw of the dice for Kendrick's experiment.

It had been part of the Baseline research effort, the year before the FRS was brought into existence, and Jonah had been eighteen. As far as he'd been aware, the subject that he had been tasked with reviving was part of research into body-storage techniques, and was just like all the other subjects that Baseline had access to – a volunteer who'd been terminally ill, and who had given permission for their body to be used to further the understanding of revival.

Jonah had succeeded where all of Kendrick's usual stable of revivers had failed. Unknowing, he'd revived a subject who hadn't died, as such – instead, she'd been put in a state of extreme hypothermia, and had had her heart stopped artificially.

She'd been *alive* when he performed the revival.

Jonah hadn't known it at the time, but the experiment had been deemed a failure. The subject he'd revived had given bizarre answers, *meaningless* answers, which were thus useless for Kendrick's purposes.

In truth, it hadn't been the subject of that experiment who had spoken to Jonah.

Revival opened a door, and on the other side of that door was the soul of the person you had revived. If you opened it when the soul was still in the body, what would happen? The open door was an invitation, and something had answered it.

Something long dead.

When Kendrick's work was canned by his superiors, Michael Andreas took over. It was through revivals of the *living* that the lost souls, the thirteen creators of the Beast's prison, had been found and freed. It was through live revivals that, ultimately, the prison was dismantled and the Beast was unleashed.

Now, holding Annabel, Jonah realized that Kendrick wasn't really in the role of Pandora either.

'It was *me*,' he said. 'I'm Pandora.' He sat up, and so did Annabel. 'I did the first live revival. I opened the box. You know the story, right?'

'I guess,' she said. 'Pandora opened the box and all the evils in the world poured out, but hope was still there. She opened the box again and let hope out.'

'Not in the original myths, but yeah. That was how I'd always heard it. Once the evils had been released, she opened it again and let hope out into the world.'

He felt the blood drain from him. All the hours he'd agonized over what Tess's message could mean, and he'd had no idea where to even begin.

Now he thought he *did* know.

And he didn't like it at all.

20

Philip was shaking.

Jonah had shown him the footage the camera had recorded of Never in the shelter, as the darkness dripped from him, becoming visible, a hideous leech-like monstrosity writhing on the floor, then growing, solidifying. Its inexorable movement towards Annabel. Its defeat.

He'd had to show him. Even though Philip had seen the aftermath, even though he'd treated Never, he'd still been reluctant when Jonah had told him what needed to be done.

Being *told* what they were up against was one thing. Seeing it was very different.

'What you're asking,' said Philip, trying to regain his composure. 'It's too dangerous. If it was done in a hospital, with all the right equipment . . .'

'We can't go to a hospital,' said Jonah. 'There are others like Never, unknowingly infected. And there are others who are utterly lost to the Beast. We need to keep the lowest profile possible. It would just take one of those to see us, to know what we're doing . . .'

'It's just too dangerous,' said Philip. 'I can't condone something like that, let alone *do* it.'

'Every time the Beast attacks it will grow stronger,' said Jonah. 'We have to do this, with or without your help. And you have experience.'

'I have experience of DHCA,' said Philip. 'You're asking for something very different.'

DHCA. Deep Hypothermic Circulatory Arrest. It was a clinical method of lowering a patient's core body temperature, to allow blood flow to be halted without causing brain damage.

'People survive even when it happens accidentally,' said Jonah. 'They drown in a frozen lake, and they *survive*. This would be controlled.'

'We don't have the equipment.' The reluctance was still there, even after what he'd seen on the video footage.

'We have sedatives. We have a defibrillator. Whatever else we need, we can find a way to get it.'

Philip closed his eyes. It was almost a full minute before he said anything else. 'Putting somebody's life at risk . . . It goes against everything I've spent my life doing, Jonah.' He took a deep breath. 'But what choice do we have?'

*

They'd left Never in the shelter rather than move him again, taking shifts to sit with him and monitor his condition. Jonah knocked before he opened the shelter door. Cathy was there now, and Never was awake. He'd been cleaned up, of course, but his face looked puffy and his eyes were bloodshot. Mercifully, there had been no indication that he'd suffered any kind of permanent damage.

He gave Jonah a weak smile when he saw him.

'Hey,' said Never.

'I'll leave you to it,' said Cathy. 'Make sure he sips water regularly; Philip was insistent.'

'I will,' said Jonah. He took her vacated seat and waited for the door to shut again. 'Do you feel as shit as you look?'

'Do I look like I was hit by a train? If I do, then yes.'

'Do you remember much?'

The answer didn't come right away; Never looked straight ahead for a while. '*Too* much,' he said. 'I remember seeing through its eyes. If it even *had* eyes. I remember realizing just how easily it had taken me, to make me do what it wanted, and then to forget I'd done it. We're pretty fucking shallow animals, humans. A little threat, a little reward, and we'll do whatever the fuck we're told.'

Jonah tried hard to smile. 'You already knew *that*.'

He smiled. 'Thanks, man. You saved my life.'

'You'd do the same for me, if you could.' Jonah frowned. 'What is it?' said Never.

'I worked out what Pandora means,' said Jonah. 'It wasn't hard, really. Pandora is me. Opening the box was when I did the first live revival, and kicked the whole thing off.'

'Uh, OK,' said Never. He shook his head. 'You'll have to fill in the blanks for me. Intelligent thought is beyond me right now.'

Jonah nodded. 'After evil escaped from Pandora's box, she found a way to release hope into the world. She opened the box again.'

The penny took a while to drop, but when it did Never seemed to deflate. 'Ah. You think Tess was telling us there's something *else* out there. Something that can help us. And all it'll take is another live revival . . .'

'Exactly.'

There was a moment of quiet, before Never sat up a little, jaw set. 'Then I volunteer,' he said. 'I'd do the same for you, remember?'

'No can do,' said Jonah. 'You're a little bit fucked up right now. Besides, we have a volunteer already.'

'Sly,' said Never, nodding. 'She'd always be the first with her hand up.'

'Sly's out on a quick road trip with Philip at the moment,' said Jonah. 'There are a few things we need before we can do it, and we didn't want to risk stealing from a hospital. They headed to a veterinarian clinic they hope will be empty. Philip thinks it will have what's required. As for volunteering . . .' He shook his head. 'Sly's feeling a lot better, that's true, and like you said she had her hand up in a flash. But she's still recovering. She's not ready for something like this.'

'Not Sly?' said Never. Then he saw the look on Jonah's face. 'Hold on.' He stared at Jonah, then shook his head. 'You can't mean Annabel. Petro, right? Mark or Armel?'

'Annabel,' said Jonah. 'She's young, strong. How could we ask Mark or Armel, or *any* of the parents?' There was no answer. 'Come on,' he said, offering the glass of water. 'Do as Cathy told you, or I'll look like a terrible nurse.'

'Fine,' said Never. He took a drink. 'Pandora's fucking box,' he muttered. 'You realize that "hope" is a very vague word, right? You plan on reopening the door that started this whole thing off, and you have no idea what will be waiting for you. And for Annabel.'

'I know,' Jonah said. 'There is one thing I need from you, though.'

'Name it,' said Never.

'We have to know when the Beast will come back to DC. When you . . . when you got an insight into how it was operating, did you learn anything about its return?'

'I think it'll be obvious,' said Never. 'Watch the roads.'

'The roads?'

'What do you think the others like me would have done? People with friends and family elsewhere, out of the city? You're right that it will come back, because it wants to indulge itself. It controls the city, but it wants as many *cattle* as it can herd. Many of its puppets will have left the city, and found family, friends, whatever. And it'll bring them all back, just in time for the show. Make any old shit up to get them to come. Lambs to the slaughter.'

Slaughter.

Jonah felt his gut twist at the word. 'Watch the roads,' he said. 'Got it.'

*

Armel and Petro volunteered to take Armel's car on the ninety-minute drive to Hagerstown, to monitor activity on the I-70. What little radio they'd caught that day painted a picture of the country as *frozen*, waiting for something without any idea what to expect. The attacks were still broadly spoken of as rumours, and wild ones at that. It was forty-eight hours since the power had gone off, but there was no sign of the civil unrest that would surely come soon enough. People were digging in and hiding, rather than lashing out.

By 4 p.m., Sly and Philip had returned.

'No problems,' Sly said. 'There was nobody near the

clinic, and we were in and out in fifteen minutes. The roads are all but empty. It's dead out there.'

'We saw one police cruiser,' said Philip. 'Pulled us over and asked a few questions.'

Jonah was immediately wary. 'Anything suspicious about them?'

Sly shook her head. 'No. They were scared. Didn't know what the hell was going on. One thing they did say, though – a couple of their colleagues had left to see if they could help with whatever had happened in DC, and they hadn't returned. They looked us in the eye and told us to stay in our homes until this all blows over. They didn't for one second look like they believed it *would* just blow over, mind.'

Annabel was lurking in the background, arms folded and anxious. She'd stopped saying much when she volunteered, and Jonah couldn't blame her. Almost everything he said to her was a prelude to trying to talk her out of it – or at least to draw lots. That wasn't a conversation she wanted to have.

So, yes . . . he wasn't surprised Annabel had stopped talking. The decision was made, and Jonah's attempts to give her an out just weren't helping anyone.

The equipment Sly and Philip had brought back was laid out. They hadn't needed much, really – a nasopharyngeal thermometer was probably the most important, allowing Philip to monitor core body temperature, and the veterinary clinic had carried essentially the same models of temperature probes used in hospitals. They'd managed to find a small EEG unit, too, used for diagnosing seizure disorders in dogs, but more than sufficient for their needs.

'That'll let us see when cerebral activity ceases,' said Philip. 'The point of clinical death. We also found a cooling unit with a mat. This is fully waterproof, hence submersible. The normal clinical process for surgery is to use a bypass machine and cool the blood directly, as well as cool the body externally. It's more controlled, and makes sure the cooling is even. But direct immersion is effective. A healthy person immersed in cold water at ten degrees Celsius will reach hypothermic temperatures and die within an hour if they remain inactive. Water near freezing can kill in fifteen minutes.'

Jonah realized that Philip was now addressing Annabel directly. She was looking back at him, impassive.

'My plan,' Philip continued, 'is to fill the bathtub with water, chill it with ice to about five Celsius, and maintain that temperature with the cooling mat. We'll sedate you first. You'll be intubated, and have the thermometer put in place. I'll monitor breathing. We'll have two other people in the room, to take turns and keep the water moving to even out temperature differences. When your core temperature is low enough, I'll administer something to stop your heart, and then we'll monitor cerebral activity. Then it'll be over to Jonah.'

Jonah had been watching Annabel the whole time, and when his name was mentioned she looked at him. The moment she did, he looked away. 'Uh, right,' he said, turning to Philip. 'Once cerebral activity halts, it'll be at least five to ten minutes, I think, before I attempt revival. I can only guess at timing, but I know that the previous times this was attempted it didn't take long to perform the revival and establish contact. After that, resuscitation can begin.'

Philip nodded and took over. 'Resuscitation is hopefully just a matter of gradual warming. We'll relocate Annabel to the bedroom and monitor the rate of temperature rise, adjusting the room temperature accordingly. When her core temperature is high enough, her heart will start spontaneously, but until then we'll perform CPR. That will ensure the warming of the blood is transferred around the body, and make the temperature rise more even. We need to watch for fibrillation, and also for hypoglycaemia. I'll have thiamine and glucose ready if it's needed. Any questions?'

Annabel walked to the door and kept going, silent. Nobody spoke; they just watched her, and Jonah couldn't bear the sense of fatalism in the room.

He went after her and caught her in the garden, among the smashed solar panels and the incinerated batteries.

'Don't start,' she said.

'I'm not going to,' said Jonah. 'I'm sorry. I've not been what you need me to be. I know this is the only way, but I'm struggling to deal with it.'

'You have to be strong,' she said. She moved towards him, and embraced him with a fierce grip. 'I'm scared. I don't know what this *is*, Jonah. None of us do. Something sent you a message, maybe it was Tess, maybe not. It's the only hope we have to defeat what's coming, but think about it. This *hope* is coming from the same place that the Beast did.'

'Annabel, if it was a ploy, we wouldn't be needed. Once I'd demonstrated that it was possible, plenty of revivers could perform live revival, remember? The Beast's agents could have organized it themselves without this rigmarole, or the risk.'

'I didn't mean it was a *ploy*.' She paused for a moment. 'I always wondered how the jailers had done what they did

– the entities that Tess and the rest were host to. They fought the darkness, and trapped it. Did they work that out themselves? They would have been in the same position we are now, backs against the wall and facing extinction. Maybe something helped them. Maybe something *showed* them. They built a prison out of their own souls, to lock the Beast away for Christ-knows how long. What if that's what our last hope turns out to be? What if I'm going to end up as the first wall of a new prison?'

It was something that hadn't occurred to him, and it shook him badly. He held her as tightly as she held him. He could lie to her now, just dismiss what she was saying as if it were merely nonsense; but she needed him to be strong, and she needed him to be honest.

'Then I'll be the second,' he said. 'And I'll stay with you. Always.'

21

Armel and Petro brought back the news Jonah had feared. Something big was happening.

He'd suspected it already. About a half-hour before their return, the deep thump of a couple of Chinooks filled the air.

'That's out of Davison Airfield, I'd bet,' said Sly, as she came outside. Jonah came with her to see. 'I don't want to think about what their plan is.'

'Maybe they're friendly,' said Jonah, and Sly looked at him as if he was five years old.

'There are around ten thousand military personnel in and around DC,' she said. 'What percentage do you think are still friendly? I'd imagine most are dead by now, but those that aren't . . .' She shook her head. '*Friendly* is probably not the right word.'

By the time Armel and Petro showed up, preparations were well underway.

'There's plenty of movement on the roads now,' said Armel. 'All of it is towards DC. We even saw a gas station being pumped by hand, being given out for free.'

Petro nodded with a frown. 'Army men in charge there,' he said. Sly and Jonah shared a look. 'I said we go on by, not worth a risk. Same for talking to anyone about where they were going or why. I look in the cars, I see families, kids. You see the helicopters?'

'We did,' said Sly.

Jonah went inside. Annabel was in their bedroom, lying down. 'God I'm hungry,' she said when Jonah came in. 'I'd not eaten when you came up with your *idea*, and Philip told me I should really have an empty stomach for the procedure. Fate, huh?'

He lay down beside her. 'Armel and Petro came back,' he said. She saw the look in his eyes and nodded.

'How long before we start?' she said.

'Any minute. Philip's about to get the bath run.' Hours before, they'd filled the freezer with every plastic container they'd been able to find, trying to freeze as much water as possible. Now, the others were breaking it all up into smaller chunks. The sound of dull thuds from below was just about audible.

She took a sharp breath. 'Holy fuck, Jonah. We've been on point too long. I want a break from this. Promise me we'll have a holiday when it's all over?'

'I promise. Where do you have in mind?'

She smiled. She was crying, too. 'Right here would suit me fine,' she said, nodding to the bed. 'A mountain of chocolate, plenty of sleep, and plenty of the other.'

'Sounds perfect.'

There was too much to say, and neither of them wanted to say it. They held each other in silence. Eight minutes later, Philip knocked on the door.

*

Annabel put on her gym gear. She looked at herself in the mirror. 'I'm gonna look *good* as a corpse,' she said.

It was too much. Jonah looked away, close to tears. He was shaking a little.

'Shit, I'm sorry, I'm sorry,' said Annabel.

They went through to the bathroom. Philip was there, with Jansin and Mark as his assistants. The equipment was ready. Jonah found he couldn't look at the thermometer probe, or the breathing tube – the *invasive* parts. Philip clipped a little heart monitor onto Annabel's finger, and peeled the backing off two electrodes, sticking them to her temples.

'We only need the most basic reading from the EEG,' he said. 'Two of these will do just fine. OK. I want to get a line into your arm, ready for the propofol. That's what'll knock you out.'

She nodded. Philip's dexterity seemed to defy his age-swollen joints, and she didn't even wince as the needle went in.

'Lie down,' he told her.

Jonah squeezed Annabel's hand and backed out of the room. He watched as the anaesthetic was administered, Philip telling Annabel to count back from ten. At six, she fell silent.

Philip worked quickly, intubating her, attaching the breathing bag then carefully feeding the nasopharyngeal thermometer probe into her nostril. Slowly, he pushed it further and further in, and Jonah had to look away.

'OK,' said Philip, and when Jonah turned back, the three of them had lifted her and were starting to lower her into the icy water. 'Be ready in case we get a reflex spasm,' said Philip. 'If we do, just keep going slowly. Don't panic.'

In a few seconds, she was in the bath, the water coming up to her neck.

Jansin positioned herself at Annabel's head, holding her steady and taking charge of the bag. Annabel was breathing on her own right now, but as her temperature dropped that could quickly change. They needed to be prepared.

Mark was watching her heart rate and the reading from the cold-mat that was submerged in the water. 'It's staying stable at five C,' he said. 'Heart rate slowing.'

'Here we go, then,' said Philip. He was holding a small unit that was wired to the thermometer probe. 'It'll be a few minutes before we see much of a drop. We monitor breathing and heart-rate.' He looked at Jonah. 'You can wait in the hall, if it's easier.'

'I'm not going anywhere,' said Jonah.

Philip nodded. 'When she reaches a hypothermic core reading, thirty or so, there's a risk of arrest. If that happens, we'll have to bring her out, OK? It'd be too high a temperature for us to stop her heart. Hypoxia would be far too likely.'

Jonah nodded. He was looking only at Annabel's face, certain that her lips were becoming more and more *blue* by the second, but this process would take quite some time yet.

Philip and his newly formed team worked in silence, only speaking when Philip called out for readings. Annabel's temperature fell, slowly reaching the critical thirty-degree mark. Her heart rate was very low, but steady.

'Good,' said Philip. 'This is the most dangerous phase,

people. Her core will decrease more quickly now. Ten more minutes, at most. If she spontaneously arrests in the meantime, we're committed. If not, when she reaches twenty degrees she gets the potassium solution.'

That was what would stop her heart. That was what would *kill* her.

Philip reported each tenth-of-a-degree drop in her temperature. He ordered Jansin to begin to assist with her breathing.

Twenty-two degrees.

Twenty-one.

Annabel's hand gave a sudden spasm, almost dislodging the heart-rate monitor, but it was brief. Jonah stared at her hand, thinking back to revivals when that kind of spasm had indicated that the revival success was close at hand. He realized that he wasn't far off panicking, and he felt a moment of shame, watching Jansin and Mark play their parts without betraying any such weakness.

Twenty point nine.

Twenty point eight.

They watched. They waited.

Twenty.

Philip took the prepared syringe and attached it to the line in Annabel's arm. 'This is it,' he said. He pushed the solution into her bloodstream. There was no tremor, no drama. After fifteen seconds, the regular blip from the heart-rate monitor simply stopped.

'You can stop now too, Jansin,' said Philip. Jansin ceased squeezing the breathing bag.

The EEG monitor unit was sitting idle on a shelf at the

far wall. From it ran a bundle of cables, and Philip attached two of them to the electrodes on Annabel's forehead. He looked intently at the device, and Jonah stepped into the bathroom so that he could see the display.

A single trace-line ran across the screen, showing activity. Gradually, the peaks and troughs flattened out. As they did, Philip adjusted the display's sensitivity until it was at its maximum.

They watched for a full six minutes, and at last the EEG reading flatlined.

Annabel was dead.

*

They took her out of the bath and laid her on the floor. Mark removed the cold-mat from the water and placed it on top of her.

'It's set to ten degrees,' he said. 'I'll adjust it if you want, Philip.'

'That should be fine as it is,' said Philip. 'Do you need these out, Jonah?' He indicated the thermometer and breathing tube.

'Yes,' said Jonah. There would be no talking involved – when live revivals had been done before, it was simply a case of summoning the entity, at which point the reviver just released the subject's hand. However, he couldn't rule out the possibility of muscle movement; removing the probe and tube was precautionary. He planned to perform it as a typical non-vocal procedure, hoping to reduce the risk of damage to Annabel's muscles. Non-vocal meant that no initial breath would be taken when the entity came through.

Once he'd removed the thermometer and tube, Philip looked to Jonah; so did Jansin and Mark.

Jonah realized he was trembling. 'OK. How long since EEG flatline?'

'Three minutes,' said Mark, who'd been monitoring the time.

Jonah tried to calm his breathing. He realized he'd not taken any revival medication, but he didn't think that would be an issue. None of the meds dealt with *panic*, not the way it was bubbling up inside him now. He knelt by Annabel's lifeless body and took her hand.

He could only guess at how long it would be before he sensed a change, and felt that he could make his attempt. He'd already decided that, whatever happened, he wouldn't wait more than fifteen minutes.

After ten, however, he *did* sense something. *What*, he couldn't say, but after so many years as a reviver, his instinct was finely tuned. He trusted it.

'OK,' he said. 'I'm going to start.'

He closed his eyes.

The first stage of a revival, the *reversal* . . . He thought back to the live-revival he'd been tricked into doing, and used that as his guide. The reversal was about the illusion of being within the subject's undamaged body. That was the key, but it was difficult to get himself into that frame of mind given that the normal process involved addressing the various injuries that had been suffered. He imagined himself simply lying down, in the space where Annabel was.

It wasn't working. The panic threatened to rise again, but he forced it back. He tried another approach, and pictured her in his mind, seeking any injury that might help him. He breathed more slowly, and then he noticed a discomfort in his throat, and a pinprick hole in his arm.

Her throat.

Her arm.

In his mind, the pinprick vanished, and he knew he was making progress. Suddenly he had a clear sense of something he'd never directly observed before in a revival, even though it was surely the most important aspect of the procedure.

The *door*.

With a truly dead subject, the door opened in the background, the reviver too focused on the job in hand to really feel it. Here, it was an intense sensation of opening out into some kind of *space*.

He wasn't sure what to do. There would be no surge, he knew – no sudden rush of Annabel's thoughts and memories. In a way, he regretted that; but, of course, Annabel was not the one being brought *back*.

Tentatively, he reached out, in the way he always did in a revival, only now he had an unnervingly vivid feeling of reaching his arm out through a doorway. The space beyond was intensely cold, but still he reached, stretching further than he'd ever had to.

And then he touched something, and recoiled.

Or *tried* to recoil. But he was stuck, and as he pulled, he, in turn, was pulled, and *hard*.

He opened his eyes and felt a deep fear.

He was *nowhere*, again. The place with no colour, and *all* colours. Tess was there, sitting cross-legged, looking to the sky as she had before.

'Was this just a trick, Tess?' he said. 'Was it to lure me here?'

This time, she looked at him. She opened her mouth, and from it flew darkness so total that even the mottled grey of a shadow-creature's skin was as brilliant as the sun in comparison. It poured from her like thick vomit, and that black mass began to twist and stretch, writhing on what passed for a floor in this bizarre place.

Jonah stared at it, and he thought back to the shadow-creature as it had detached from Never, attempting to form into a body it could attack with.

Yet this was different. The squirming substance that streamed from Tess's mouth had no feel of desperation to it, the slow movement almost languorous. Part of the black seemed to form some kind of thick tendril, which twitched upwards and began to move back and forth as if smelling the air.

It froze, pointing at Jonah. Without warning it shot for-wards, directly at him, too fast to avoid. He cried out as it hit him, engulfing him in nothingness.

He opened his eyes with a gasp. He was sitting in the bathroom again, Annabel's cold body lying beside him.

'It is done?' asked Philip.

Jonah's eyes widened. He looked to his own hand, and saw that he'd let go of Annabel's.

Was it done? Had he let go in panic, and ruined the entire exercise?

No.

He looked at Annabel's body and knew that, whatever it was that had wanted his help to come into this world, it had achieved its goal.

'Yes,' he said. 'It's done.' He managed to hide the terrible fear he felt.

Oh dear God, he thought. *Oh dear God, what have I brought back with me?*

22

Philip replaced the thermometer probe and intubated Annabel again. They dried her and brought her through to the bedroom and laid her on fresh towels, then covered her body. The rewarming process had to be gradual, but without blood flow the temperature rise would be uneven. CPR, Philip hoped, would counter that, and also reduce the risk of hypoxia as Annabel's temperature lifted.

As before, Jansin would handle breathing, while Mark, Jonah and Philip took turns with chest compressions.

'This will be a marathon,' said Philip. 'We'll begin with a slow compression rate, one and a half seconds per compression. When she reaches the mid-twenty degrees, we'll up it to the standard hundred compressions a minute. Jansin, we'll pause after thirty compressions, and you breathe five times as before. Squeeze the bag, watch the chest, let it fall. Are we good to begin?'

His three assistants nodded.

Jonah was glad to be involved. Had he merely stood back and watched, he knew he would be screaming silently: here was the woman he loved, clinically dead as a result of *his* idea. He'd exposed her to a terrible risk, and a terrible *presence*.

As he took his first turn, his mind projected that black living *effluent* oozing from her mouth. He pushed the thoughts away and focused on his timing.

Philip called out the numbers, Annabel's core temperature remaining alarmingly flat. They had an electric fan heater in the room, keeping the air a steady thirty-five Celsius, and the oppressive warmth took its toll on them all. Jonah kept a wary eye on Philip. While the man seemed to have strength that defied his years, Jonah was certain this process was pushing him to his limit.

After ten minutes, Annabel's core temperature was making solid gains.

'We can let the room get a little cooler,' said Philip. He smiled. 'We'll all be grateful for that, I think.' He switched off the heater and opened the door a crack. The slight influx of colder air across Jonah's face was hugely welcome. Philip took over compressions from Mark.

A few seconds later, the tiny heart monitor clipped to Annabel's finger began to chirp rapidly.

'Fibrillation,' said Philip, stopping compressions immediately. He moved to the side and looked at the prepared syringes he'd placed there.

'Do I keep going?' said Jansin.

Philip shook his head. 'Hold off for now. Jonah, get the defibrillator.'

Jonah ran to the bathroom and fetched it. 'Here . . .' he started to say as he came back into the room, but the others had all backed away from the bed and were staring at Annabel.

She was sitting upright, eyes open.

Annabel's head turned towards Jonah. He felt horribly weak, as he saw nothing in those eyes he recognized.

Philip was frozen, too, a syringe in his hand.

The monitor's rapid chirping continued, her heart still fibrillating. Jonah stepped forwards. 'She's not ready yet,' he said, hoping the entity within her understood. '*She's not ready.*' Those eyes remained impassive. 'You'll kill her,' said Jonah. 'Lie down, or you'll *kill* her.'

The eyes closed. Slowly, she lay back down. Philip had a look of sheer terror on his face, but he snapped out of it. 'Quickly, Jonah,' he said, nodding to the defibrillator he was carrying.

Jonah placed it on the bed. It was fully automatic, but even though Philip was quick to configure the pads, it felt like eternity. 'Keep back, everyone,' said Philip. He pressed the activation button, and a calm voice played, giving instructions for use. 'Come on, come on,' he muttered. 'I've done everything already, just fucking *do it.*'

At last the machine fired, a deep thump followed by a high-pitched whine as the system recharged in case another use was necessary.

The chirping monitor settled into a rhythm.

Jonah looked to Philip and saw relief on his face.

'OK,' said Philip. He let out a long breath and stepped forwards, removing the defibrillator pads. He put the syringe he had in his hand back on the bedside table. 'Let's see how she's doing before we give her anything else.' He took her wrist to get her pulse. It struck Jonah as odd for a moment, given that the heart monitor was steadily ticking out the beats, but after a few seconds Philip nodded. 'Seems good

and strong,' he said. 'Mark, what's the temperature reading?'

'Twenty-nine point nine,' said Mark.

Philip closed his eyes for a moment, and rubbed at the
bridge of his nose. 'I think we should let her breathe un-
assisted soon, and remove the temperature probe.' He looked
at Jonah. 'Uh, could we have a quick word in the hallway?'

Jonah nodded and followed Philip through the door.

'She's doing well,' said Philip.

'Thanks to you,' said Jonah. 'I know that this whole . . .'

'Cut the small talk, Jonah,' said Philip. 'She's doing
better than she *should*, do you get me? Her body temperature is still deeply hypothermic, but I'll bet her heartbeat is
healthier than anyone else's in the room.' He shook his
head. 'I need you to tell me. What do we *have* in there?'

'I honestly don't know,' said Jonah.

'Can we *trust* it?' said Philip, looking at him with a mixture of fear and desperation that Jonah could entirely
sympathize with. Whatever Annabel had within her, it was
their single hope against the darkness that was coming.

Jonah wanted to say yes, but that was so far from the
way he *felt*, the word died on his lips. 'I hope so,' he said at
last.

It was the best he could do.

*

Jonah went down to see Never, who was still in the shelter,
lying on his makeshift bed with a drip in his arm. Armel was
with him when Jonah entered, and Never looked asleep.

'How's he doing?' asked Jonah.

'He's been quiet,' said Armel. 'Slept, mostly. Sometimes

he's . . . restless. Wakes up calling for you.' Armel looked squarely at Jonah. 'How did it go?'

Jonah gave a nod. 'Well,' he said. 'I think. I really wanted to talk to Never before we left.' In truth, he'd wanted to say goodbye. Whatever the outcome, he thought there was a very good chance that he wasn't coming back. He watched his friend for a minute or so, then decided that not waking him saved them both from a difficult parting.

He wished Armel luck and returned upstairs. Philip stood in the corridor.

'How was he?' asked Philip of his other patient.

'Sleeping,' said Jonah. 'I didn't wake him. Annabel?'

Philip raised his arm, pointing to the door. 'She's ready for you,' he said. Jonah moved to enter the room, and Philip suddenly grabbed his arm. 'Good luck, Jonah,' he said.

Jonah nodded, and entered the bedroom. He closed the door as he came in.

Annabel was standing by the window, looking outside. She was dressed, wearing jeans and a shirt.

'Annabel?' he said. She didn't turn. He walked up to her side. Her expression was blank. 'Annabel?' he said again. Her eyes turned to him, cold and distant. She raised her hands up and placed her palms on Jonah's cheeks.

Suddenly he *saw*.

Below him lay a city in ruins, wreathed in the smoke of a thousand fires, too thick to see much except rubble.

He heard Annabel's voice: 'Lisbon.'

His viewpoint changed. Below now lay an island, half covered by an airport. The vast expanse of concrete and runways was devoid of planes, covered instead by what seemed like a patchwork of some kind. His viewpoint moved closer, and he saw the patchwork was delineated by high wire fences crisscrossing the airport.

And within the fenced-off squares lay the bodies of tens of thousands. His viewpoint moved even closer, until he could see the terror etched on the dead faces. Terror, and mutilation – limbs torn from bodies, unrecognizable *pieces* strewn over tarmac.

Annabel's voice came again: 'Rio.'

She took her hands off his cheeks, and the vision ceased.

'St Petersburg was destroyed before the visitation could occur,' she said. 'They were the lucky ones.' She was speaking slowly, as if the words took great effort to form, and he knew it was the entity he was hearing. 'It must end.'

Jonah nodded. 'Yes.'

'Whatever it takes?' she said.

He looked at her, and saw emotion in her eyes at last: a deep sorrow, and a determination. He thought of Annabel's fear, that they would build a new prison. That they would be trapped in the darkness, for eternity. For a long moment, he couldn't speak. 'Whatever it takes,' he said at last.

'Annabel is safe,' she said. 'We must go. You and I. To the city.'

*

They left without fanfare. Sly hurried out as he and Annabel got into Annabel's car; she held up one hand in farewell, and Jonah held his up in reply. Annabel, or whatever resided within her now, ignored the gesture.

To the city.

Simple words, but so much was locked up within them. Jonah thought of the footage Never had captured, and the aftermath of the attack – bodies and cars abandoned on the roads. He thought of the images he'd had, of burning buildings, of bodies on concrete.

He drove through the tree-lined countryside route along Wardensville Pike. The day was disconcertingly pleasant. He wound the window down, and slowed for a moment. There were no other vehicles on the road, and the beauty around him almost seemed cruel. Forty minutes on, they reached I-66, but it wasn't until past Gainesville that traffic started to pick up.

He wondered who these people were; Never had spoken of the infected venturing out of the city to bring people back, but was that all this was?

'No,' said Annabel, even though he'd not spoken aloud. 'You'll see.'

His nerves were jangled; he tried to keep his mind blank as they drove. Then, approaching Centreville in the outskirts of the city, things changed. Military vehicles were stationary on the road ahead, and traffic was queuing. Jonah looked into other cars, at the faces of his fellow travellers. Children were common, he saw with dismay, but people didn't have the oddly blank faces he'd been expecting. They looked variously excited, bored, indifferent: the usual faces in a highway jam. Ahead, the traffic was being reduced to two lanes, and soldiers were in the road speaking to each driver.

Jonah tensed up. 'Can they tell?' he said. 'Can they tell you're different?'

Annabel shook her head. 'No.'

'But shouldn't we be infected? Shouldn't we have a shadow? At least *one* of us, anyway?'

'Not everyone coming back is being betrayed directly, Jonah. Be patient. And relax.'

As if.

The queue of cars made its slow way along, and eventually Jonah was looking into the face of a slightly nervous private.

'Welcome,' said the private, smiling. 'You're allocated to Fair Lakes Center, buses will transport everyone in for the festivities. Do you have a leaflet?' Jonah shook his head and the private handed him a sheet of paper, then waved him on; up ahead, cars were being directed off the interstate, and he went with the flow.

Jonah glanced at the private in his wing mirror as he drove on, wondering if the young man had a shadow latched to his back somewhere. 'Festivities?' he said. Annabel was reading the leaflet that Jonah had been handed.

'Their ploy,' she said. She read aloud: '"American Freedom and Victory Celebration: Today we celebrate the final defeat of the enemy who has attacked our Nation in an unprovoked outrage. The world has seen many such attacks, but under the leadership of this Great Country, Freedom has been re-established throughout the globe! Where attacks have been suffered, rebuilding will begin tomorrow! Now, it is your duty as a patriot to take the greatest pride imaginable and join with us all, as we rejoice and revel in the true victory of our Great Leader! Food and refreshments will be provided free of charge!"' She paused. 'The rest is instructions, all the places they'll be running a bus service from. You see? *This* has been distributed widely. People have been led to believe that the attacks they have heard rumours of are now defeated.'

'It sounded ludicrous,' said Jonah. 'And, *Jesus*, "join with us all"? They're being a little too honest with *that* one. "Our Great Leader" will be having food and refreshments later too.' He grimaced and swore, then looked at her with a raised eyebrow. 'What *are* you?'

She said nothing.

'I want to talk to Annabel,' he said.

'The process was difficult for her. She is barely aware. She needs rest.'

'You're saying she's asleep?' he said.

'Would you rather she was awake for this?'

It was his turn to stay quiet.

In the vast parking lot of Fair Lakes Shopping Center, they were guided to the next available space. The lot was almost full already, he saw. Jonah turned off the engine. He took a moment to look at the people waiting to get onto buses. There was an air of celebration now, he could see. Happy children taking the hands of their parents, smiles all round. 'Are many of these folk infected the way Never was?' he said.

'Some,' she said. She held up the leaflet. 'But it's easier to give people a lie they want, and let them condemn themselves.'

'They trust this?' He looked around again. It all felt so *wrong* to him, so artificial. But of course it did: he knew what was happening.

'Of course they trust it,' she said. 'For now.'

He looked again at the smiling children, and thought back to the words Never had used: lambs to the slaughter.

They got out of the car, and Jonah locked it. He almost laughed out loud, realizing what he'd done so automatically, but he suppressed it. It would have been the laughter of desperation, of hopelessness. The buses wouldn't be bringing him back here, to his car; the buses wouldn't be bringing *anyone* back here, and this parking lot would simply be a graveyard, the vehicles a short-lived memorial to those the Beast had taken.

They queued, but didn't have to wait long. Most of the buses had the Metro logo on the side, although some were tour coaches. Annabel took his hand, and he almost jumped. There was a sensation, close to *chill*, when her skin touched his. The presence of whatever was within her.

She smiled. 'Look casual,' she said.

He gave her a half-hearted nod, but let go of her hand. That was one piece of play-acting that was beyond him.

On the bus, he sat by the window, looking out at the streets of the city as they drove. The only vehicles on the road were buses and military transports. Occasionally, there were pockets of people at the roadside, waving banners that read WELCOME, and VICTORY. The banners seemed far too well made for supposedly spontaneous outpourings of support. He couldn't help but look at the windows of the houses and apartment blocks they passed, wondering what had happened to the people of the city.

Jonah also thought of the people Never had described moving bodies from the road as dawn broke. They'd been cleaning up the *mess*. The city had been sanitized, and it must have been done quickly, precisely to prepare for this mass influx of unknowing victims.

He wondered where the bodies had gone.

'There are carrion birds in Nationals Park,' said Annabel. She said it in a calm voice, but Jonah immediately knew what she meant. The baseball stadium had a forty-thousand capacity, but it wasn't as if anyone would be *seated*. Annabel took his hand again, and he could *see* it: the vast pile, still growing. How many, he could only guess. A hundred thousand, maybe? Three times that? The birds feasted; most of the eyes were long gone, yet there was plenty left for them to relish. Already the smell would be appalling nearby, and within another day or two it would taint the whole city. But what would it matter, by then?

And there were other piles, in other hidden places.

The bus rolled on, staying on the I-66 and taking the Theodore Roosevelt Bridge across the Potomac, then along Constitution Avenue, with the Washington Monument right ahead.

Jonah felt a shiver as he saw what was in the green spaces in the Constitution Gardens, running alongside the vast reflecting pool that faced the Lincoln Memorial. Twelve-feet-high steel fencing, newly erected, ran the length of the road, and on the other side were throngs of people. To everyone else, it would just look like a massive carnival was underway. To Jonah, it was cattle being herded into their pens, just as he'd seen in his vision of the airport in Rio.

Every green space was the same – the area around the Washington Monument was similarly fenced off, and filling with people. Further on, the National Mall was the same, presumably all the way to Capitol Hill. He could see plenty of food trucks within the enclosures, rows of portable restrooms, inflatable bouncers for the kids. The bus pulled up beside the Ellipse, the entirety of which had been similarly fenced off and supplied with the same amenities. He could see the entry gate, and the people in a steadily moving queue to get inside. The solidity of the barriers was ominous.

'Here we are, folks!' said the driver. 'Have a great day!'

Jonah was in a daze as they walked through the gateway. He didn't imagine it would be long before the gates were sealed off.

The Ellipse was still sparsely filled, but more and more buses were pulling up and unloading their livestock. Large VICTORY signs were dotted around the fencing, too. He looked to the sky. The cloud cover was significant, but he didn't need to see the aurora to know it was there. He wondered if those black veins were already starting to pulsate high above them.

Dark would start to fall in the next hour. It wouldn't be long now.

The Beast was coming, and Jonah was as ready as he would ever be.

23

They stood near the security fencing at the north side of the enclosure as twilight fell. The Ellipse was almost full, now; most buses drove past on the road, heading for the other enclosures. The crowd wasn't too densely packed any more, which Jonah was glad of; otherwise he would have had to avoid being jostled or risk people noticing the effect of *chill*.

There were speakers positioned at regular intervals, he could see, and patriotic music was playing just below the noise level of the crowd. He looked to where the cables led, and saw a large van two hundred feet from where he stood, on the outside of the fencing. They had generators on the go, yes, but one thing was missing, the absence of which was only occurring to him now that night was actually falling – there was no lighting anywhere.

He listened to what people around him were saying, and was astonished at how mundane most of it was. Comparisons of experiences over the last few days were the norm, and very little unease was expressed. These people, it seemed, had suffered from little more than an extended power cut. The rumours that had spread had scared them, yes, but they'd not been confronted with anything traumatic.

Various other leaflets had been handed out at the site, 'explaining' that power would be restored to most areas within days, and that seemed to be the only news that mattered to some.

There was utter ignorance about the real nature of the attacks. Biochemical warfare was mentioned more than once, in hushed tones. It baffled Jonah that people could accept that kind of explanation, while standing in the open air in a supposed attack site.

He watched the soldiers who were corralling the new arrivals, and as he did, he saw the first shadow of the day – a relatively large one clinging to the shoulder of a higher-ranking officer. He wondered if any of the soldiers were uninfected.

He turned away and caught Annabel looking at her skin, flexing her hands and turning them over.

'What are you?' he asked again. 'You ignored me when I asked before.'

She looked to the distance. 'What am I? I don't think I could explain it in a way you would understand. Not without you getting entirely the wrong impression.'

'Yet you've come here to help us. Why?'

'I was invited.'

'By Tess?'

She shook her head. 'By *you*.'

'That doesn't answer my question. Why are you willing to help?'

'Perhaps I'm *not*. Perhaps I'm here to take over, once the Beast has been defeated.' She smiled, as Jonah's face fell. The smile turned into a laugh. 'I know what thoughts

Annabel has had, Jonah,' she said. 'I was joking. Humour in darkness, isn't that a common trait?'

Jonah said nothing. There was a squeal from close by, and Jonah turned urgently to look. It was only a small boy, perhaps seven years old, being tickled by his mother.

Annabel looked at the child, and Jonah could see genuine sorrow in her eyes. He wondered if the real Annabel was starting to wake, or if the creature within her was truly capable of caring. 'You look at a child and see innocence,' she said. 'Look again, and you'll see an *adult* in the making. You tell yourselves that children are pure, only tainted by what happens to them as they grow, but this is wishful thinking. Your people are *formed* of hatred and jealousy. There are counters to that, yes, beneficence in all forms, but life gets by perfectly well without those. Tell me what you know of the Beast.'

'It spoke to me once,' he said. 'Through Michael Andreas. It told me that it thinks life, in its purest form, is pain. The Beast is made of souls, corrupted and lost, existing in torment. It seeks to corrupt all that it can. *Torment* all that it can.'

'You think that it touches a soul and fills it with the same taint it carries within itself?'

She was looking at him with something close to disdain. 'Yes,' he said.

'I just explained it to you, Jonah. Didn't you listen?' She shook her head. 'Billions of years of evolution, and intelligence has arisen. On what *scaffolding*? On death, Jonah. Your minds have risen from the dust on the backs of immeasurable deaths. Death is your past, and your future. Life is hatred, jealousy, fear. Life is violence and slaughter.

The darkness you think of as *taint*, external and thus some-how avoidable? That darkness is there, from the very beginning. Kendrick spoke of seeing the eyes of a child in the vessel they had chosen. A *child*. The dark was already there. Waiting.'

'You're wrong,' he said.

'Souls are dark to their very core,' said Annabel. 'The Beast is not really *corrupting*, Jonah. It calls you home.'

He stared at her. 'I *know* you're wrong,' he said. 'I've seen . . .'

She cut in. 'What have you seen? In your career, Jonah, cleaning up after atrocities? The worst of people, yes? Their petty vengeances, their stupidity, their *mercilessness*. You have come to know these things are not the exceptions.'

'But they *are* the exceptions,' he said. 'People don't give in to . . .' This time he stopped by himself, realizing what he was going to say. People don't give in to their nature. 'You're arguing that reason can't win against instinct, and that's just not true.'

Annabel put a hand on his shoulder. 'You *can* be light. You *can* be truly selfless. But that is not what lies at your core. The one thing that binds all life, intelligent or not, is malice to whatever threatens it. And with intelligence, the scope of threat widens ever more. Imagination turns in-animate rocks into devils. It transforms friends into con-spirators. Had the Beast not come, you would have found another way to destroy yourselves.' She sighed. 'Your world was always doomed. Most are.'

Jonah felt a deep cold. 'You're here to judge us? Is that it?'

She frowned. 'I told you, I'm here because I was called. Look inside yourself, Jonah. You fight for your friends. You fight for yourself. Tell me if you think you are immune to what I described? *Annabel* would die for you, and you would die for her. But would you die to save another, if you didn't know them?'

He hung his head. 'Don't take her,' he said.

She looked at him for a moment, appraising. Clearly she knew what he was referring to. 'A prison for the Beast requires sacrifice. Your myths tell you that, again and again. So tell me, would you really take your place by her side for an eternity, in the darkness?'

'I would.'

'And would you take *her* place, if you could spare her?'

'Of course.'

She stared into his eyes for long seconds, and at last she nodded. 'Good,' she said. 'For how can you call on another to sacrifice themselves, if you would not do it in their place?' She lowered her head, and remained silent for a while.

*

Above them, the clouds thinned as the sky grew dark. The aurora was by far the brightest yet, easily providing more light than a full moon, painting the world a sickening green, and Jonah was certain that the aurora was entirely an artefact of the Beast's power. He looked hard for signs of the black veins, hunting carefully for even the thinnest of threads, but he saw none. Yet.

And while the encroaching darkness was filling him with dread, those around him were creating an ever more carnival-like atmosphere. People were eating hot dogs and cotton candy, holding hands and laughing, releasing the tension that had built up since the power failures came.

It suddenly changed.

The music, which had been playing just under the chatter of the crowds, quickly grew in volume until it was distorted. People glared at the speakers, hands over ears, as feedback filled the air.

The sound died, leaving near-silence in its wake, and a panicked voice spoke.

'Everyone, please,' said the voice. 'You have to get away from here.'

There was a distant crack of gunfire.

The voice continued, breathless. 'This isn't our victory, do you understand? This isn't *our* victory. This is a—'

More gunfire came, but this time it came over the speakers. The voice was silenced. The crowd remained quiet and frightened. Parents were gathering up their kids to them, and Jonah could tell now who among them was infected – several in the crowd had an expression that was far too calculating.

A small military transport sped past them. There was a spray of gunfire, hitting several of the soldiers on the road; someone inside the fences cried out, and Jonah looked across to see a fallen man, blood on his face.

He looked at Annabel. She seemed utterly calm. Sounds of distant gunfire came from several directions, but it didn't last long.

Not all of the soldiers had been infected after all, he guessed, and some had even managed to organize themselves. It was an impressive achievement, extraordinary courage under the worst circumstances. And it was already over.

Jonah waited for the speakers to crackle into life again, for the music to start or a message of reassurance to play. Surely they would want to calm down the crowds? All thought of celebration was gone, now. The Ellipse was full of huddled groups, cowering on the grass; frightened children whimpered; adults stared out around them.

The speakers remained silent, and Jonah understood that this was the most frightening aspect of all. There was no need to calm the cattle any more.

He looked up. The black thread-veins were there, pulsating, thickening. Others around him noticed too, and pointed. Despair spread, and burst out in a vast cry of dismay when the thunder rumbled above them, and the great black column began to form, then reach down to the ground. It would have been the river it touched, Jonah thought, beyond the Washington Monument, presumably past the Jefferson Memorial. A mile away, and impossibly vast.

The continuous rumble was more like the deep growl of a rabid dog. Most of the crowd watched with a mixture of awe and terror, but some among them were attempting to climb the fences; at the gate, a few were trying to force their way out.

The soldiers there had no hesitation; small-arms fire popped every few seconds. People backed away.

The dark column widened. The sounds coming from it grew and grew, and Jonah thought he could feel his *organs* vibrate from the sheer volume. He turned to Annabel.

'Whatever you're going to do, surely now's the time to start.'

She was impassive, watching the column.

'Did you hear me?' he said, shaking her.

Her eyes turned to his. 'Protect Annabel,' she said. 'Protect yourself. At all costs. You'll be needed.'

Jonah looked around at the thousands of people, old and young. 'After what you said about selfishness? Can't we do *anything*?'

A sudden roar snapped their attention back to the column, which collapsed down and vanished. He was expecting the river to rise up now, as it had done before.

'*Hurry*,' he said. It was already too late, surely. They would be swamped by the shadows – consumed, or taken as Never had been.

A dark mass rose, accompanied by a wail of fear from the crowds. But the mass didn't form a wave to *engulf* them all. Instead, it kept growing taller. Like the shadow that had come from Never, it seemed to be forming itself, adopting a shape, extruding limbs.

People were crying now, but not all. Some were smiling, holding up their arms in supplication.

Their master had come. The *Beast* had come.

It rose up as it stepped from the water, five hundred feet high, a thousand . . . Jonah didn't know. All he could do was stare at the creature as black wings spread wide, and its near-featureless head opened in a gaping maw.

It reached down, and Jonah knew it was into one of the other enclosures nearer the river. The creature howled its pleasure as it picked up handfuls of living flesh and watched it *burn*, letting the dead and dying fall back through its new-formed fingers.

Jonah turned to Annabel. 'Are you just here to *watch*?'

She shook her head. 'No,' she said. 'Forgive me. Gods die too. And they fear it just as much.'

She seemed frightened. He stared at her, an idea forming in his mind that he almost didn't dare believe. She nodded, though, confirming it. She fell to her knees, her hands on the ground, and started to tremble.

In the distance, the Beast roared. Jonah looked up at it. The creature seemed to pause in its carnage, victims falling from one outstretched claw. It turned its head, and Jonah felt his stomach fall away.

It was looking towards *him*. It took a vast stride.

He looked at Annabel. She was shaking even more, and she heaved as if ready to vomit.

The people within the Ellipse enclosure were panicking as the Beast took another stride towards them, groups surging towards different parts of the fence, trying to climb the wire. Gunfire broke out again.

'*Do something,*' Jonah cried. Annabel's shaking grew more violent, and there was a scream from behind him. He turned in time to see soldiers firing into the crowd again, but suddenly the soldiers spasmed and fell; the metal clasps fastening the sections of fence exploded in sequence, and Jonah realized he could *see* something moving rapidly, from soldier to soldier, from fence to fence.

Countless thin tendrils, like the tentacles of jellyfish, flailed in the air. As sections of unsecured fence toppled, Jonah noticed that the people nearest him weren't looking at the fence, or at the fallen soldiers.

They were staring, horrified, at him. No: at something *behind* him. He heard it, before he turned – heard the gagging, choking sound, the wet *hissing*.

He looked.

A black living mass was streaming from Annabel's mouth, the way it had poured from Tess in the vision he had had during the revival. The writhing blackness was gathering itself on the grass, growing, and from it the thin tendrils streamed out, impossibly long, the source of what had killed the soldiers and destroyed the fencing.

Jonah backed off. The people near him watched in pure horror until they turned and ran from this abomination in their midst, to join the rest of the panicked crowd who were fleeing into the streets surrounding the Ellipse, all heading north away from the river and towards the White House.

Annabel continued to retch as the last of the black pulsing flesh emerged from her mouth. She fell to her side. Jonah edged forwards, and the black shape in front of him lurched suddenly. He shielded his face. When he looked again, it was gone.

He went to Annabel and took her pulse. It was weak, not the unnaturally strong beat that Philip had been so wary of.

The black creature was gone, but the slow strides of the Beast continued. Now, a vast dark foot stepped on the southernmost edge of the Ellipse, and with a sense of desolation Jonah looked up, *up,* at the Beast's head, which was lowering down to leer at him.

It knew what he was, he thought. It knew the history it shared with him.

Yet it seemed wary. Jonah presumed it had sensed the other creature, and still *could* sense it, even though it had fled. The fear that it had expressed before, in Annabel's voice, had clearly won out.

The Beast reached down, its claw coming ever closer. Jonah could feel a terrible heat emanate from the Beast's flesh, and he could see the writhing mass of shadows that it had constructed itself from.

In his arms, Annabel stirred, but she didn't wake. He was grateful that she would be spared seeing this, as the end came.

But just as the claw drew within feet of him, Jonah saw thin black tendrils begin to wind around it. The tendrils thickened, engulfing the claw, and then the arm, pulling it away. The Beast screeched and stood, and as it did so, the tendrils reached around from behind its back, joining at the front and holding fast. The Beast fought to free itself from its captor, screaming and shrieking with sheer outrage.

He had to move, *now*. Outside the fence, two soldiers lay dead beside their jeep. He lifted Annabel in his arms and carefully walked over the fallen section of fence, then across to the vehicle, lifting her inside. The only other military personnel nearby were at least two hundred yards away, and they seemed utterly bound up in the sight of the Beast's struggle.

The Ellipse itself was virtually empty now, the dead and dying all that remained. He thought of them, and of the people in the other enclosures, but he knew he could do nothing. Indeed, the entity that had been in Annabel had told him as much: protect Annabel and yourself, at all costs.

He got behind the wheel and started the engine, taking one last look at the screaming Beast above. It was bound from shoulder to knee in thick black living rope; its wings, too, were trapped. Behind it, a black outline was rising up, more vast tentacles spreading in the air as if underwater. *This* was what Annabel had carried here, a pure blackness that looked like it had come straight from a nightmare even more primal than the Beast, a nightmare of ancient evils dredged up from the deepest ocean.

Yet this was their *champion*.

He could see the difference in colouration more clearly than ever. The Beast had always seemed black to him, but he knew it was formed of the same shadow-flesh that the smaller creatures had, grey and diseased and glistening; the other entity was pure black. It was void, and nothing *but*.

He drove north past the White House, slowly through the running throngs still fleeing the Ellipse. There was no military presence here, but perhaps that wasn't surprising. They'd had their perimeter, and none of the Beast's acolytes would have wanted to miss their Lord blessing his flock. Now, they were getting an altogether different spectacle.

He reached Logan Circle, maybe a mile from the river. Jonah looked in his rear-view mirror and slammed on his brakes.

The Beast was engulfed; silenced, the dark mass began to sink lower. As it sank, a bright pinprick lit up within it. The pinprick grew in size and intensity, until he had to look away – a ball of white fire consuming everything, the heat from it overwhelming, even at this distance.

A new Sun, its life brief. The light faded. The Beast was gone.

He glanced at Annabel, and felt a lurching within him.

She wasn't breathing. He felt for a pulse.

'Oh God,' he said. 'Oh God.'

Her heart had stopped.

24

He jumped from the vehicle and pulled Annabel out onto the road, ready to start CPR, the way Philip had shown him: one hundred compressions a minute, each compression going down two inches. He focused and began. Breathing for her wasn't important now – the flow of blood was the critical factor, and pausing that flow could do more harm than good, at least to begin with.

'Annabel,' he said. 'Come on.'

He tried to keep count, but he was in pieces now. They'd come through all this, they'd reopened Pandora's box and brought hope . . .

'Come on,' he said. 'Please. *Please.*'

Hope.

He continued the compressions, hardly noticing his own tears as they fell. He looked at Annabel's face, cursing himself. This was all *his* doing. If she'd never met him, she wouldn't be here now; if he'd never performed that first ill-fated live revival, the events that had led to her father's death would not have started. The Beast would not have returned.

Annabel would not be *dead.*

He tried to keep count as he kept up the compressions, and as he counted he couldn't stop himself thinking back to his mother's death. They'd been on the way to the airport, he and his mother, with his hated stepfather driving, overtaking where it wasn't safe, careering off the road to avoid an oncoming bus.

And hadn't it been Jonah who had caused that? Hadn't he been *needling* his stepfather on purpose, looking forward to the time he and his mom would share, once the man had left on his business trip? He'd been unable to resist, and in doing so he'd wound the man up into a tight ball of irritability. The crash was his own fault. *Jonah* had killed his mother.

Then he'd taken her dead hand, unwilling to admit that she was gone, unwilling to even *think* it, and he'd pleaded with her to come back to him. *Please don't leave me. Please don't leave me.*

And she *had* come back, but in a terrible way, a way that revealed what Jonah really was, and how Jonah would spend the rest of his life.

She'd taken that deep, howling breath, her dead eyes still blank, and she had spoken: *Jonah, please. Please let me go.*

His first revival. An accident. And by then, people had come to help. His stepfather, injured in the crash but able to walk, had appeared beside him, staring. Appalled, he'd torn Jonah away from his mother: ripping them apart, just as he'd been doing since the moment he met her. Jonah had been left lying in the mud, alone in the world and despairing.

And now he looked at Annabel, and all he could think was: *Please don't leave me.*

Her mouth opened suddenly. She drew in a lungful of air and Jonah stared, horrified. *Not again. Not again.*

She breathed out.

And then she started to cough.

She opened her eyes, unable to focus on him. 'Jonah . . . ?' she said.

He felt her wrist. Her pulse, weak as it was, had returned.

'I'm here,' he said, smiling through his tears. 'I'm with you. I'll always be with you.'

She managed to smile, but the smile turned to fear: 'Is it time . . . ?' she said. 'Is it *time*?'

He knew why she was so frightened – terrified that she would become that first wall in the new prison, and spend an eternity in the darkness keeping the nightmares at bay.

'It's over,' he said. 'The Beast is gone.'

Protect Annabel, the entity had said to him. *Protect yourself. At all costs. You'll be needed.*

When he'd heard those words, he had assumed the worst: after the entity's talk of sacrifice, and the questions of his willingness to take his part in the *prison*, he'd known very well what he and Annabel were needed for. Or he'd *thought* he knew.

But then there had been that *other* statement: *For how can you call on another to sacrifice themselves, if you would not do it in their place?*

Just before the entity emerged from its human host, he had seen something in Annabel's eyes, and an idea had formed. Perhaps it was similar to the way she had been able to tell what he was thinking, on the way to the city. Perhaps that ability had gone both ways, in part.

He had seen deep within her, and had seen her reluctance. Her *dread* of what she was about to do.

Gods die too, she had said. *And they fear it just as much.*

He had dared to hope, and she had nodded to confirm it.

He and Annabel would be needed, but not to build the prison for the Beast. The entity, whatever it truly was, had decided to sacrifice *itself* instead, and spare them both. Spare them *all*.

'We're safe, Annabel,' he said. 'We've played our part. There's no need to be scared any more.'

*

He helped her back into the jeep and they drove. Above, the black veins in the sky had grown thin and unstable. The aurora itself was beginning to fail, dimming gradually.

He looked at Annabel.

'It's time to go home,' he said.

They had done so much; they had been through so *much*. Surely they deserved to rest at last. He would get them to safety.

After all, they would be *needed*. Although that was something he didn't yet understand.

What would they be needed *for*?

EPILOGUE

Jake had been busy that morning.

He'd set his alarm early, and it hadn't been easy to focus, because he'd been tired. He still didn't sleep much, but that wasn't exactly a rare problem these days. It had been seven months since his dad had driven them to DC for the supposed victory celebration, and Jake had stood with his parents outside the Capitol building while the world seemed to be ending.

At least the bed wetting had stopped, for now. Eleven years old, and wetting the bed. He remembered his gramma talking to his mom, way back when he was, what? Six? Must have been about then, since his gramma died when he was seven.

'You should shame him,' he'd overheard her say. 'Talk about it in front of his friends at school. Make him damn well grow up!'

And his mom, timid with Gramma as always but on his side all the same: 'He'll grow out of it.'

'Bullshit he will.'

Gramma was his dad's mom, and Jake didn't think even his *dad* liked her much.

He wondered what Gramma would have said about it now.

His dad had gone to DC the day after the power failed, because he worked for the power company and wanted to know what the hell they were supposed to *do*. He'd come back the next day with what his mom had called a *bee up his ass*. And he'd hit her. Just like that.

And then – just like that – he'd told them the problems were over, and they had to go into the city to celebrate. Jake's mom had talked to their neighbours, but nobody had heard anything. Everyone was staying put, scared of the rumours that had been popping up, but it turned out his dad was right. There were leaflets and everything.

The party had been huge. They'd said there would be fireworks. Jake supposed that was true, in a way. When the thing that still haunted his nightmares appeared, he'd been pushed over in the panic and got knocked out cold. He'd missed some of what happened next, which was a blessing. But not all.

And right now he was sitting in a seat in the kitchen, and a stranger was looking at him while his mom sat in the corner, and his dad loomed above him. Behind the stranger stood a young woman. She looked wary, he thought.

'When will the priest come?' said his dad.

'The priest?' said the stranger.

'The fella who does this. The exorcist.'

'I can't be sure,' said the stranger. 'Soon enough. Then he'll be able to tell us if that's what your kid's problem is.'

'Oh it's his problem, I guarantee it,' said Jake's dad. 'He ain't been right, not since it happened. The things he saw would change any kid, I know, but he ain't been right. Shelly? Tell him, Shelly.'

Jake's mother, over in the corner, nodded her head. 'It affected us all, Nate. I don't know if . . .' She fell silent, and Jake knew his dad was giving her a look. He'd had that look often enough lately. To a stranger it'd seem like a smile, but there was no smile in the eyes. His mom had been hit more than once when that look was on his dad's face.

There was a knock at the door, and another man came in. He was a little older than the first stranger.

'Hello,' he said. He sounded Irish. He smiled at Jake, and he certainly didn't have the problem with the smile not reaching his eyes. Jake smiled back, even though he felt real uneasy. 'Uh, things are progressing. We can get started.'

'Do you have it?' asked the first man, and the Irish guy nodded. 'Good. I think you get the honours, OK?'

'OK.' He pulled a syringe from his pocket and knelt beside Jake. 'Right then.'

'I don't like this,' said Jake. He wriggled his arm out of the grip of the first stranger, who turned to his father.

'Could you hold his arm for me?' said the first stranger. 'Hold it securely.'

Jake's dad was more than happy to do it, but as he held Jake's arm, the Irishman plunged the needle into *him*. 'What the fuck are you doing?' said his dad, standing up and backing away. Jake felt himself flinch, as he tended to do now when he heard his dad swear. 'What the fuck are you people *doing*?'

Jake's dad was a stubborn man, though. Always had been, even before he changed. He stumbled across the room and reached down in the corner, into a cupboard. The shotgun came up surprisingly fast, but the woman was even faster. She had the gun out of his hands before Jake's dad had even noticed her move, and then she had his arm up behind his back and threw him to the floor.

'Don't hurt him!' cried Jake. 'The gun's not loaded!'

'It *feels* loaded,' she said. She cracked it open and took out the two shell casings Jake had doctored. He'd emptied them, and filled them with sticky tack for the weight.

'Was that you?' said the woman.

He nodded. 'Uh huh,' he said. 'He could've noticed if it was light.'

That's what had kept Jake busy that morning. He'd seen his dad the night before, stashing the gun in the cupboard.

'Smart kid,' said the woman.

Jake looked at his father, lying unconscious on the floor. He went to his mom and hugged her, proud that he'd done what he needed to do.

'You did good,' said his mom. And for the first time in months, Jake felt safe.

*

Jonah nodded to Sly. 'Much appreciated,' he said. 'That could have turned nasty.'

'We need to be even more careful than we have been,' said Sly. 'They're getting more astute.'

She was right. In the months following the Beast's defeat, people had sought him out for help. Cathy had been the one to bring them to him, and he'd known he needed to be cautious. Sly, naturally, had been best placed to organize how they did things.

Jake's mother had come to them the usual way – a

friend of a friend of a friend. Her husband had let her seek help and bring them to the house, thinking she trusted him, thinking she believed *Jake* needed the help. Thinking he could do his duty to the shadow he carried, and kill Jonah.

For most of the world, things were getting back to normal. Some of the sabotage that the Beast's followers had managed to achieve turned out to be breathtaking in its audacity, but the level of damage to electricity grids across the globe had been particularly effective. Critical elements in the supply chain had been destroyed, knowing that the numbers of replacement parts, and the capacity to manufacture more, was severely limited. The full restoration of power supplies had taken months, and chaos had threatened to overwhelm all attempts at recovery.

Yet the old theory proved true: give people a shared enemy, and they will come together. The deaths of an estimated thirty-eight million had focused the minds of all who heard it on the re-established radio broadcasts.

For Jonah and his friends, *normal* hadn't been a meaningful idea for years.

All the cities that had been *prepared* for the Beast's revelry fell soon after the Beast vanished. Just as in DC, military groups had contained some who were uninfected, uneasily following dubious orders; they had borne witness as most of their infected colleagues either fell dead or became themselves once more.

There were stragglers, though. The shadows didn't all perish. Weakened, barely able to survive, yet somehow hanging on. It took some time to confirm, but Jonah soon saw the harm they did, to those around them – those they loved, those who loved them back. The shadows changed a person, weighed them down and made it impossible for them to choose to deny the dark. Freeing them was a *triumph*. To see their lives transformed for the better was worth the risk.

And here was their latest example.

Jonah and Never carried Jake's father out to the front of the property, where their modified van waited. Annabel and Sly stood by the rear doors and opened them as they approached.

They laid the man down on the van floor. Annabel and Jonah went in with him, leaving Sly and Never outside.

Jonah took off the man's shirt.

'How does it look?' asked Annabel.

Jonah appraised what they were dealing with.

The shadow was – like most of them now – a withered, pitiful thing. This one sat on the man's chest, above his heart. It looked almost desiccated, the grey-black flesh pocked with white in places, like ulcers.

Sick as it was, it was holding on. The creatures had been defiant at first, difficult to remove. The ploy he had used with Never and Annabel to tempt the creature off its host had been required, dangerous as it was. Soon, though, they had shown further signs of weakening, so much so that after the first four months, Jonah had felt a degree of confidence that they would all simply *die*, in time. Sadly, this weakening seemed to stop, but Jonah had found a way to work loose the tether between parasite and host. With the tether threatened, the creatures were forced to attack.

That's what he did now: he placed his fingers on the man's chest, where he could see the shadow. It was hard, of course – to him it looked like his fingers were disappearing into the dark mass, and within moments he could feel it attempt to take on solidity, the thing nipping at his skin. Since gloves stopped Jonah's fingers from grasping the tether, he just had to suffer. He suspected his hands would be bandaged, to some degree or other, for the rest of his life.

He usually located the tether quickly, but this time he struggled a little. He pulled back and waited for the shadow to fade again, as he knew it would. When he made another attempt, it was quicker off the mark and drew blood almost at once, but this time he had it.

'There,' he said. He tugged, drawing the tether out until it caught. Blood was dripping from his index finger, the gouge deeper than normal because it had torn a scab from an injury he'd got at his last outing.

The creature started to detach, because it had no alternative. Jonah watched it, and readied himself to grab it once it was loose enough. It was almost routine, now. As the last of its corpse-fingers came free, he snatched the creature up before it even had a chance to throw itself at him. It was a sorry thing, really – it tried to squirm in his grip, but it didn't stand a chance.

'OK,' said Jonah, and Annabel banged at the side of the van; outside, Sly and Never were waiting. They pulled the tarp from the roof, and sunlight poured through the transparent plastic they'd used to replace most of the roof's metal.

It only took a few seconds for the creature to boil away in the glare. The tether shrivelled to nothing, but the unconscious man barely moved.

It was done. Some cases were still difficult, of course, but once the subject was unconscious most of them were straightforward.

'All clear,' said Jonah.

Annabel reached for the first aid kit and set to work cleaning up his hands, then bandaging them. She gave him a gentle kiss on the cheek when she finished. 'Good work, kid,' she said. 'When we're finished here, I vote we get home and have some more of that holiday we agreed to.'

Jonah smiled. 'I was thinking the same thing.'

She took out the little heart-rate monitor she'd worn that fateful day, and put it on the man's finger. They sat together and watched him until he started to stir.

'Nate?' said Jonah. 'How do you feel?'

Nate was looking around him as if stalked by something. It was a familiar look – someone waking from a nightmare. How a person reacted now was extremely telling. Some didn't really get over what they'd had nestled into their *being* for so long, and they would wake with surly glances and suspicion. Those were the ones you still had to watch out for. Sometimes the darkness had become a habit.

Nate seemed scared, and that was a good sign. 'God, I'm *cold*,' he said.

'Let's get you back inside,' said Annabel.

She and Jonah led him indoors to his wife and son; Jake's mother took him upstairs, and came down a few minutes later.

'He's asleep,' she said. 'Out like a light.' She was dazed, Jonah saw. 'Did it . . . did it *make* him do those things? Now it's gone, is he Nate again?'

'It pulled him down, somewhere dark,' said Annabel. 'That was him at his worst. Just take care of yourself, OK? It won't be easy for him, which means it may not be easy for *you*. If you need help, get in touch.'

Annabel bade them farewell and left. Jonah went to take his jacket from the chair, where he'd put it as he'd first come into the house.

'Will my dad be OK?' said Jake.

'He'll be more like he was,' said Jonah. 'Before it happened. Is that good enough?'

Jake thought about it, and then he nodded. 'I guess it is,' he said. 'Do you think those things will all be gone, one day?'

Jonah looked at the boy, wondering how to answer. He didn't know how many there were. Too many for him to deal with, most likely. In the end, though, he did what he did to help the people affected, not to rid the world of the creatures. For every human he freed, there were thousands more who were just as darkly motivated, yet who were *not* infected by shadow. People for whom hatred and resentment were the only things they knew; the only things they cherished.

The soul was dark, by its nature. The human mind had been born from death and rage and suffering, and perhaps that was how it would always be, shadows or not.

But perhaps the day would come that it wasn't.

'I hope so,' said Jonah.

Hope.

There was *always* that.

He picked up his jacket and went to join the others.